THE PRAGUE SPRING

COLD WAR SPY THRILLER #7

BY BILL RAPP

Kenmore, WA

A Coffeetown Press book published by Epicenter Press

Epicenter Press
6524 NE 181st St. Suite 2
Kenmore, WA 98028.
www.Epicenterpress.com
www.Coffeetownpress.com
www.Camelpress.com

For more information go to: www.coffeetownpress.com

www.billrappsbooks.com

All rights reserved. No part of this book may be reproduced or transmitted in any form or by any means, electronic or mechanical, including photocopying, recording, or any information storage and retrieval system, without permission in writing from the publisher.

No generative AI was used in the conceptualization, planning, drafting, or creative writing of this work. No permission is given for the use of this material for AI training purposes.

This is a work of fiction. Names, characters, places, brands, media, and incidents are the product of the author's imagination or are used fictitiously.

The Prague Spring
Copyright © 2026 by Bill Rapp

ISBN: 9781684923328 (trade paper)
ISBN: 9781684923335 (ebook)

LCCN 2025946379

DEDICATION

To the women in my life—Didi, Eleanor, Julia, Moose, Mitzi, and Marguerite—who have provided inspiration and support, and who have taken me out of myself and given added meaning to my life.

ACKNOWLEDGMENTS

As with any novel, many people contributed to the final manuscript. That is certainly true for mine. I had visited Prague on numerous occasions in the past, but it had—unfortunately—been over two decades since my last trip there. I had the good fortune to return to the city in November of last year with my younger daughter Julia to reacquaint myself with that gem and all its history and beauty after I had completed an earlier version of this story. I also benefited from a long conversation with a friend and former academic colleague, Professor James McAdams at the University of Notre Dame, who pointed out several important points and references for the events of 1968 in Czechoslovakia, including the extremely helpful and informative memoir by Zdenek Mlynar, *Nightfrost in Prague. The End of Humane Socialism*. Several essays from *A History of the Czechoslovak Republic 1918 – 1948*, edited by Victor Mamatey and Radomir Luza, eds., proved to be valuable for the section of the novel covering the coup of 1948.

Additional help came from a former colleague at the CIA, David Bridges, who spent many years living and working in Eastern Europe, including under the *ancien regime* prior to the revolutions of 1989. His memories and insights allowed me to paint a much more accurate picture of Prague in 1968 than I could ever glean on my own. The senior editor at Coffeetown Press, Jennifer McCord, as usual, kept me on a more complete and readable narrative, especially when I assumed that all readers would know immediately what I meant to say. Finally, and certainly not least, my wife Didi continued to act as reader, editor, and fact-checker, without whom I would have had to face many embarrassing questions over the mistakes I insisted on including.

PART I
PRAGUE 1968

PROLOGUE

It was assignments like this that brought up those periodic doubts about his job. About the direction of his country as well.

"Why isn't his body sinking?"

"Because we didn't weigh it down, Pavel. You know, with rocks or something heavy." He paused to laugh. Not loud. It was little more than a chuckle. "What did you expect?"

The young Czechoslovak security officer studied the corpse floating about six feet from the banks of the Vltava River. Caught in the swirling eddies along the shore, it drifted and turned to no apparent purpose. Unfortunately, it was also not moving further out into the river, where the current could carry it away. Isolated lights from the city center sparkled against a sky of deep purple, and the night's silence was broken periodically by the occasional car leaving the Old Town on the Charles Bridge.

"Are you sure he's dead, Karol?"

"Well, if he isn't," the older officer said, "maybe his American friends can come rescue him." He laughed, louder this time. "I doubt even they can help him after the beating we gave the treasonous son of a bitch." A long, slow breath of stale air escaped with the next few words. "If he isn't dead, he will be soon. That makes one less problem for us these days."

The young Czech surveyed his older colleague's heavy face, the added weight of so many pilsners beginning to roll down from his cheeks and chin and settle along the lower ridge of his neck. Pavel could see thin rolls of fat disappear underneath the collar of a dark green shirt stained with sweat. His integrity must have gotten lost somewhere down there, too.

"And the schnapps you poured down his throat? Was that necessary if you were going to hit him so hard and so often? He could barely swallow that swill."

"It will give whoever finds him something to think about."

The older officer shook his head as he studied his young colleague, a Czech from a small village just outside Prague. Karol doubted this fellow Pavel had ever been outside the country. He had to wonder sometimes where the security service found these young idealists.

"Think about what?" Pavel asked.

Karol shrugged. "Whatever." So many damn questions. "We're not really trying to cover up anything. We were instructed to make an example of the prick. It doesn't hurt to dirty his reputation in the process."

"But no one will think he simply fell off the bridge. Not looking like he does," Pavel said.

Karol shrugged. "It doesn't really matter. Maybe it's even better this way. It will certainly give people good reason to think before doing more of the same."

"You mean reaching out to the Americans?"

Karol, a Slovak, nodded. God, but he was tired. Tired of this job, this city, these blasted reforms of the new government. More than anything, he wanted to go home to Bratislava. He had been in Prague long enough.

"That and whatever else he was up to with those imperialist bastards. We always had ways to deal with traitors during the war."

"But that was when you worked for the Slovak puppet government. The Nazis' allies."

"Same difference." He shrugged. "You adapt. Or you die." He motioned toward the corpse. "Like this dumb bastard."

The two men stood on the shore for about a minute. Then the older one bent low and picked up a long wooden oar lying near the bank and handed it to his young colleague.

"Here. Use this to push him further out into the current."

"Why me? That water looks pretty damn cold. Too cold for June anyway."

"Don't be such a baby. Just do it. We need to get it done. It will be light soon. That way, he'll drift south, further from the Old Town. That should be good enough."

"For what?"

"For some unlucky sucker to find him."

"Like who?"

Karol shrugged again and shook his head. "I don't really give a shit."

CHAPTER ONE

"I can't believe this place."

Karl Baier settled into the seat behind his desk and glanced at the rolling hills outside his office window. The view was an attractive one, spreading out over the American Embassy's tiered gardens. But he did wish it included something more famous, something that captured this city of spires, as some visitor or historian had named it years ago. He loved the fabled, ornate rooftops that gave Prague so much of its historical and architectural beauty. Baier admitted to himself that this was one European capital that would never cease to amaze him. Even if the Communist regime had shrouded the town in shades of gray and brown drabness. The sheen of a workers' paradise, he wondered.

"What is it that you can't believe? The politics? Or the beauty of it all?" Baier's arm swept toward the sky and history outside that beckoned just beyond the window's edge.

"Well, the politics for sure. One does have to wonder just what the hell Dubček is going to be able to get away with. I mean, he's already achieved what I would call miracles with the open press and vibrant artistic scene. And now they might even have free elections here."

"Not right away. More like a couple of years down the road. But you're right."

Baier smiled at the enthusiasm and awe of this new officer. Paul Krohn had joined the Agency just a little over two years ago, a bright-eyed college graduate from the University of Wisconsin. He had done well in his initial training program down at the newly minted 'Farm,' but he could have used some additional seasoning at Headquarters before being thrust into the maelstrom that was Eastern Europe in 1968. Czechoslovakia in particular. The uncertainty and significance of what was unfolding here would challenge even a more experienced case officer.

As the CIA's Chief of Station, Baier saw the first-tour officer's enthusiasm as an excellent opportunity to develop his tradecraft and his reporting skills. And the young man would probably have a lot of fun and maybe even have something to pass along to his children and grandchildren.

His potential and eagerness could even prove to be an advantage, especially when you considered how the Dubček Government was pressing forward with its program of 'Socialism with a human face.' There were so many opportunities it offered; not just to the United States, but all of the West as well. Where else at the moment were the lines between the good guys and the bad guys so clearly drawn? He thought back to his brief engagement in Vietnam four years ago. Those lines were certainly a helluva lot clearer now than they were in that mess back then.

"Is it just the politics that amaze you?"

The junior officer shook his head. "No, not really. Don't get me wrong. I'm really glad to be here in this city and at this time. It's like standing at the intersection of one of History's turning points. But at the same time, it's all so beautiful. You know, the way the fading sunlight skips across the Charles Bridge and its statues over the Vltava. Jesus! At night, it almost looks like they're only sleeping, outlined in the dark, just waiting to come alive and join the crowds."

"Yeah, it is impressive. Even if those are not the original statues. But they are pretty good replicas."

The young man halted his reverie. His right hand slid over his mouth, and his lips parted slightly, attempting to grin. "Sorry. I get carried away, I majored in art history, you know."

Baier smiled, if only to reassure him—but he was enjoying this discussion. "That's okay. I'm glad you're getting to put some of that liberal arts education to use."

"Yeah, but I expected more in the way of destruction from the war. What happened?"

Baier shifted in his seat and looked outside again. It was as though he was imagining the elaborate stone and mortar facades with their religious and historical figures that graced the portals and doorways of the city for the first time…or in an entirely new light.

"It's more like what didn't happen. There was some fighting in the last days of the war here. In fact, we even bombed Prague, although it was a mistake."

"You mean the Americans? A mistake?"

"Yeah, the pilots got lost and thought they were over Dresden."

"Well, that mistake didn't help that poor city later on."

"No, it didn't. But the locals broke out into a popular uprising that the Red Army finally supported once the Germans had surrendered. It was around May 4, I believe, that the fighting started, and it finally ended a day or so after the official German surrender on May 8. But the combat never got as intense as it did in Berlin and other cities. In fact, I think the German commander tried to limit the damage since it was obviously a lost cause. The two sides eventually agreed to make Prague an open city."

"But did all the Germans agree to that? Like the SS?"

Baier sighed. "There was always that uncertainty. But once Hitler was dead, there was no reason to continue the fighting, or to honor their oath to the Führer." He paused. "Fortunately."

Krohn shook his head. "Man, this place really is something." He looked up at his chief. "I understand you've been around quite a bit, seen a lot of things. Have you ever seen anything like this, experienced anything like what we're going through now?"

Baier smiled again, this time more broadly. He studied the face of his new officer, wondering what sort of adventures were waiting for the young man in his career—if he stuck with it, that is.

"Yes, I have. As a matter of fact, I've been here before. It was a while ago, a different time. Just twenty years, in fact, but it feels like it was centuries ago. At the same time, it's also kind of familiar."

PART II

PRAGUE 1948

CHAPTER 2

Karl Baier nursed his pilsner at the window of one of the many wonderful cafes that bordered Prague's Old Town Square. Not only was the beer good; the atmosphere was comfortable and pleasant. Of course, if the air outside carried some summer sunshine and warmth it would be nothing short of marvelous. This was especially true when you were stuck in the middle of a Central European winter. Baier could only hope he would get to experience the warmer summer climate at some point. Even so, the history and architecture, the late medieval and early baroque stone buildings with their elegant spires that pierced the sky, the juxtaposition of Gothic and baroque all provided more than enough pleasure and inspiration.

More importantly, this evening his seat provided a clear view of the Old Town Hall and its famous tower with the elaborate set of astronomical clocks. He could never tell if it kept the actual time, but the show was intriguing, even magnificent at times. The small crowds that gathered in front of the clock certainly enjoyed it. The tower displayed an hourly dance routine by a set of carved puppets that circled through the twin openings below the timepieces, consistently drawing crowds to enjoy the musical promenade. The figures represented Jesus and the Twelve Apostles, allegedly. Baier did not recognize the individual characters. Then again, how well could a set of carved wooden puppets resemble real-life models no one in the modern era or even the Middle Ages had ever seen? Nonetheless, the entire show—the clock, the dance, the whole damn square—was easily one of the city's main attractions. It had the requisite old-world charm, constructed in 1410 when the Old

Town Hall had been rebuilt after a fire destroyed its predecessor, and it all fitted perfectly with the magical atmosphere of Prague's medieval core.

He sipped his beer, keeping his eyes on the square and the town hall, glancing occasionally at the clock. But this was nothing more than a momentary diversion for Baier.

He was much more interested in the crowds that strolled past the building and its famous ornament. He fingered the slip of paper in his pants pocket. He had collected the piece from one of the stone arches fronting the cafes and restaurants opposite the town hall. The note had been placed inches above eye level in one of the narrow spaces where time and weather had worn the mortar away just enough to allow someone to cram a note deep enough to escape notice by a passerby. This was unless, of course, he or she knew what to look for. Otherwise, it was nearly impossible to find; he had chosen the last arch at the corner of one of the narrow lanes that meandered away from the town square, secure enough—he hoped—for someone to pause as he left a note behind. Now he wanted to make sure there was no follow-up by other, unwelcome parties.

Baier had been suspicious when the initial message had been delivered to his temporary office at the American Embassy. The author had given the time and place for this particular exchange, informing Baier that it had become too dangerous for him to visit such a conspicuous outpost as the U.S. Embassy more than once. Baier agreed. Instead, the messenger would establish a set of dead drops, with each message containing an important piece of information, as well as instructions for the next exchange.

He had not read this note yet, his first from this source. No, Baier was far too nervous. His first concern—just as the trainers instructing him at the Central Intelligence Agency's preliminary surveillance course had taught him—was to run a countersurveillance route to determine if he had indeed shaken whatever tail the local service had placed on him. Given the heavy infiltration by the Soviet secret police—the NKVD—and the local communists, who controlled the Ministry of the Interior, Baier was pretty certain that he was under observation. Nonetheless, after an hour of hiking through the winding alleys and cobbled pathways of Prague's city center, Baier was confident that he was free to retrieve the note.

The most difficult part of this whole operation, though, was that Baier knew next to nothing about this source. He had no name, no idea what he looked like, or what his background or motivation was.

Well, almost nothing. The consular officer at the Embassy who accepted the sealed envelope from the stranger did remember a middle-aged local, wearing a worn, almost threadbare overcoat and scuffed brown leather shoes. His glasses rested at a slant on his nose, and the gentleman repeatedly had to push them back against his face and up toward his forehead.

The British, actually, were more helpful…a little bit more helpful, anyway. Baier had first learned of the asset from his British colleagues shortly after his arrival in Prague in mid-January. They had recommended that the man contact the Americans, and Baier was the only real option.

Baier was acting as the sole representative of the newly established Central Intelligence Agency in a one-man operation that sought to establish some kind of presence along what was fast becoming a new line of confrontation with America's former ally, the Soviet Union. The Agency had almost no presence in Eastern Europe, and Baier's assignment to Prague was really an experiment of sorts. The evolving politics in the region certainly demanded some kind of participation by the CIA as it sought to find its place among the emerging national security organizations and the anxious, competitive environment in Washington, D.C. That anxiety and initial uncertainty had been reflected in the legislation that had created the CIA and the National Security Council just the year before.

Now, here it was, early February in Prague. Baier had been in place about a month, and he still knew only what the Brits decided to parcel out, bit by bit. The agent had reportedly been an asset of theirs just before the war, working in the

Protectorate, the Czech puppet government installed by the Germans after they broke the Czechoslovak state apart in 1939. He had reportedly provided invaluable intelligence not only to the Czechoslovak government-in-exile in London under the leadership of the exiled President Beneš, but directly to the British as well.

The only glitch in that impressive record was the fact that he had been arrested by the Gestapo in 1941. After a brief spell in prison, the Nazis had released him to return to his job at the Protectorate's Foreign Ministry.

• • •

"Kind of suspicious, wouldn't you say?" Baier objected. "I mean, that's not what I would call the typical m.o. for the Gestapo."

"M.O.?" his British interlocutor had asked. "Since when did you Americans start using that Latin abbreviation?"

Baier smiled. "You mean, *modus operandi*. We've used it for quite a while now. How about you Brits? I'm assuming you've heard of it. Unless, of course, you skipped your Latin classes at the precious boarding school I'm sure you attended."

"We were using it well before your country was even born. I wasn't aware that anyone in the colonies had Latin training."

"Come again. 'The colonies?' Not for a while, chum."

"Oh, that's right, you're a Catholic. Probably picked up some snatches of the language as an altar boy, I gather." The British colleague, Peter Jackson, smiled and poked Baier's shoulder. "No, all kidding aside, I've never heard an American employ that abbreviation before. But believe me, this fellow proved his *bona fides* on numerous occasions. And besides, if he was working for the Germans, it obviously didn't do them much good. As far as we can tell, they never got anything valuable out of the exchanges. We did, of course, provide our gent with the odd tidbit now and then to allay any suspicions the Huns might have had." Jackson shrugged. "But it was the sort of thing we believed they would have discovered in any case."

"But why aren't you still running this guy yourselves and then passing the information along?"

"Well, it seems he insisted on bringing you in." Jackson shook his head. "You know, you are the new global empire of sorts. It may not have been his ambition, but the one thing Herr Hitler succeeded in doing was to bankrupt ours. Not officially, of course. But practically."

"And he saw us as the only power capable of deterring the Soviets from advancing any further in Europe?"

Jackson nodded, a faraway look in his eyes, as though he were looking for past imperial glories. "Apparently."

Baier thought for a moment. He realized that in this case—and probably others—he and his organization would have to rely on a new relationship with the United Kingdom that was fast becoming special, at least for the immediate future. After all, Baier had been sent into the country alone, before the Agency had a chance to build a support network or assign other officers to the mission. Baier recognized that he and his countrymen were still novices to the business.

"So, how do you want to run this operation?" Baier asked.

"Oh, he insists on dealing directly with you. He will reach out in his own way."

"Just what does that mean?"

"I guess you'll just have to wait and see." Jackson stood to leave. "But do remember to share whatever he gives you with us. Please."

• • •

Baier stood from his seat by the window in the cafe, dropped some coins on the table, and then departed. He swung to his left as he stepped out of the café and headed for the Charles Bridge. He made sure to check if he was being followed, pausing periodically to study the scant offerings in the shop windows along the way. When he reached the Bridge, Baier paused midway across, just underneath the statue of St. John of Nepomuk, then leaned over the side far enough that his upper body stretched out over the water. Only then did he bring the paper out of his pants pocket and read the message.

"Soviet Ambassador Zorin and Czechoslovak communist party leader Gottwald and his delegation returned from Moscow last November with instructions to prepare a coup. Planning underway. Recent government purge in Slovakia seen as a dress rehearsal. Likely to happen within the next month to six weeks." The note also gave the date and location for the next drop.

Baier shook his head in disbelief—but then the more he thought about it, the more sense it made, especially given the behavior of the local communist party and their extra-parliamentary activities of late. He ripped the note into tiny shreds and watched them float to the river below, where they disappeared. Despite the winter weather, the river had not frozen completely. The thin slices of ice along the banks did nothing to keep the pieces of paper from sinking deep and out of sight.

Let the pricks the Communists have been shoving into the police and security service swim after the scraps, Baier mused. Despite the legend, he seriously doubted the spirit of S. John, who had been thrown into the river by some disgruntled king, could save the paper shreds from disappearing. He realized that there was little time left to prepare for a counterstroke to block the Communist plans. If one were even possible.

As he turned to go, Baier saw a familiar figure watching him from the middle of the bridge. Despite the late hour, the man stood out in a vague silhouette, his body shaded by the evening sky and the light snow that had begun to fall. But his face stood out clearly, and he was smiling. It was a look intended for Baier. The face was familiar because Baier had picked him out from the crowd twice while he enjoyed a local pilsner at the cafe just moments ago. The man's grin was interrupted momentarily when he pushed his glasses back along his nose. There was no threat in the smile. Baier was relieved to see that it was more a nod of acknowledgment.

CHAPTER THREE

"Say that again," the ambassador ordered.

Laurence Steinhardt, the American ambassador in Prague, sat behind his desk as unmoving as the stone buildings that lined Tržiště Street out front. He struck Baier as the quintessential senior diplomat, although he was what was known as a political appointee, not a career foreign service officer. Baier had been impressed when he read the man's biography shortly after Baier got the assignment to Prague. The ambassador had served in several tours as the chief of mission already, including one stint in the Soviet Union just before and during the German invasion. In fact, he witnessed the initial German bombing runs over Moscow in July of '41 and oversaw the transfer of the embassy to Samarra shortly thereafter. From what Baier had heard, his most successful assignment, however, had been in Turkey during the war, where he had to go head-to-head with the German diplomatic and espionage campaign to secure the support of the Turks for the German war effort. Steinhardt had excelled in getting bomber pilots who had to crash land in Turkey—especially after the raid on the Ploesti oil fields in Romania—back to safety in the West. Even his wife and daughter had helped, smuggling two pilots to freedom on a "shopping trip" to Beirut.

The Ambassador's perfectly pressed white dress shirt and broad striped tie, set against a backdrop of walnut cabinets that held an array of books on American and European history, as well as numerous legal volumes, made for an impressive display. These were accompanied by a range of photographs featuring him with the *Illuminati* of American foreign policy past and present. His years studying at Columbia University and its law school must have helped him establish his career. His deep blue, pin-striped, and double-breasted suit jacket rested comfortably on the back of his brown leather desk chair. He was also smart as hell.

"The source claims that the Communist Party of Czechoslovakia is following the order of Josef Stalin and his acolytes in the Kremlin to instigate a coup here in Prague. And that Klement Gottwald and his gang are following those orders wholeheartedly," Baier responded.

The Ambassador leaned forward, his elbows resting on the desk while he folded his hands together. "And when is this supposed to take place?"

Baier glanced at his wristwatch, an empty gesture since they were not speaking of hours but days or weeks. At least, not yet. Or so Baier hoped.

"Sometime in February. So, this month, I guess. Certainly, no later than March."

"You guess?" Ambassador Steinhardt's eyebrows arched. "It would help to be more precise, especially if we're going to send this information back to Washington."

"The source probably doesn't have that sort of access, Sir. I doubt he's part of the coup, at least not directly. This sounds more like information he's acquired from discussions in the government or parliament."

The ambassador leaned back. "You mean corridor gossip?"

"Well, I'd say it's a bit more authoritative than that, Sir."

"Tell me again about this man. Just what does he do? And how do you know he has the access he claims?"

"Well, Sir, it's not what he claims. It's what our British partners claim he has, and, more importantly, what he's done in the past."

"Such as?"

"They claim he provided invaluable information on developments in the Protectorate, the Czech rump state of Bohemia and Moravia after the German occupation. And that included occasional information on German military deployments. He continued to do so after the Gestapo released him from prison in 1941."

"Sounds suspicious," Steinhardt interjected.

Baier nodded, his first outright concession. "Yes, Sir. But apparently, he continued to pass the Brits valuable stuff that always checked out."

"And how did he get away with that?" The ambassador leaned forward again, as if to make sure Baier heard him and understood. "We need to know this. People in Washington will ask these same questions, Karl."

"Well, our good allies supplied him with what you might call 'throw-away' material. Things they did not consider all that dangerous and what the Germans would probably learn in any event."

"Okay. So, back to my original question. Just when is this supposed to happen? Any specifics on when in February?"

"No, Sir. But I doubt the KSC, or Communist Party, has a definite timeline. It probably depends on how things play out and the resistance they encounter. But I would say it's probably already underway."

"You mean the current demonstrations and strikes organized by the factory committees? I agree that does not look promising."

"Exactly." Baier almost jumped out of his seat in front of the ambassador's desk. As it was, his own charcoal gray suit jacket fell from the back of his chair to the floor. Baier left it there, not wanting to lose his moment.

"The Communists have also been placing their people in critical positions in the police and security services for a couple of years now. And the Minister of Defense, Svoboda, has been won over. He has packed the officer corps with communist sympathizers."

"Okay," the ambassador agreed. "But I want to be sure we've answered all the possible objections. I realize you just arrived here, what, four or five weeks ago?"

"A little longer, Sir. Just a few weeks after Christmas."

"So, you may not be aware of the political background here, and why the Communists have been able to maintain so much popularity. Such as it is."

"I do know," Baier reassured Steinhardt, "that the Communists cooperated closely with the other parties and resistance groups during the war and that afterward, they all continued that effort as part of the National Front."

Steinhardt nodded and sat back. "That's right. And there was a genuine feeling—broadly shared—that this country needed to institute a series of political and economic reforms after the war. And the Communists did win the largest share of the vote in 1946, even if it fell short of a majority."

"I get that, Sir. But their popularity has been waning over the last year, and it's doubtful they'd be able to repeat that success. The economy has slowed down, which has hurt their popularity. I'm also guessing that after the Communists suffered setbacks in elections in Italy and France, Moscow and its lackeys here decided to stop playing Mister Nice Guy."

"And that is why Washington decided to send you here? I have to be honest with you, Karl, I doubted that you'd be able to add that much since we already have a capable group of diplomatic observers in the Embassy. I mean, you guys are what, a year old now? And you are working here alone."

Baier leaned forward in turn. "I think my mission here arose out of the elevated concern over the future of Eastern Europe after the coup against King Carol in Romania last December. It seems Stalin and his boys are on a roll now, and we need all the help we can muster to determine—and possibly prevent—what they have in mind for Czechoslovakia."

"Well," the ambassador concluded, "we may soon find out." He fixed Baier with a hard stare. "And I hope you'll be able to help."

CHAPTER FOUR

He would remember the date until the day he died. Of that Baier was certain. February 20, 1948. It was the date of what proved to be the catalyst for the Communist coup in Prague.

He would remember shuddering when he learned the news. Baier had been walking the streets of Prague's city center, a new note gripped in the fist he had shoved deep into the pocket of his *Lodenmantel*, a souvenir from Berlin his fiancée had given him just a couple of weeks ago as a Christmas present. He hadn't had the time—or the cover—to read the note. Baier figured there was plenty of time for that. At the moment, he was watching yet another demonstration by one of the workers' committees that the Communists, known locally as the KSC by their Czech initials, had created to build alternative sources of power and authority to the institutions of government they were struggling to subvert or replace. The streets and pavements were filled with shouts and banners calling for unspecified reforms and workers' rights, as well as cries for a general strike.

Then he heard all about it, the main event. The catalyst. Baier's understanding was limited. But he had picked up enough Czech—along with the press coverage—to get a sense of what was being bandied about. People were speaking of the new development in words of praise, shock, or distaste. The news did not sound like a rumor, certainly not something included in the workers' demands floating above the ranks marching through Prague. Twelve non-Communist ministers had resigned from the government in protest against the actions of the Minister of the Interior to extend his purge of the National Police.

Not that this sort of thing was new. The purges and forced appointments had been a part of the KSC playbook for about a year now. But this time, the Minister—some clown named Nosek—had purged eight senior officers in an effort to complete the takeover of the police force. This had been a step too far. The non-Communist ministers were demanding the recall of the eight officers and an end to the purges.

Baier pulled the slip of paper from his pocket and hurriedly read the note. It claimed that Gottwald, the leader of the Communist Party, and Soviet Ambassador Zorin, believed they occupied the appropriate positions and had built enough popular support to push their plan to its logical conclusion. They were also convinced that the KSC had little hope of winning the majority they had originally hoped for in the election scheduled for May. So, in his mind, Gottwald needed to move now.

Baier jammed the slip of paper back into his pocket and ran to the British Embassy located in the Malá Strana, or Lesser Town. The receptionist called Peter Jackson's office, then simply nodded at Baier with a look towards the stairwell. Baier's mind was too overwhelmed by the rush of events to appreciate the centuries-old beauty the Thun Palace displayed as he rushed up the stairs, two steps at a time, and burst through the door, not bothering to knock or grab a seat. Baier brushed against the front of the desk and leaned halfway over.

"Just what the hell do they think they're doing? Don't those twelve morons realize it's not the same game they've been playing with a cooperating and contented National Front?"

Jackson stood, shaking his head. "I agree, Karl. They've clearly misread the current atmosphere here. The Communists no longer share their goals for a stable and democratic Czechoslovakia."

"What about President Beneš? What will he do?" Baier pressed.

Jackson nodded, then shrugged. "Excellent question. I no longer know myself. The man seems tired, almost broken by the trials and tribulations he and his country have endured over the last ten to fifteen years."

"I've got a very bad feeling about this, Peter."

"And I share your misgivings, my friend."

Baier pulled the note from his coat pocket, then threw his overcoat on top of one of the two chairs facing the desk. He fell into the other one, but not before passing the message to his British colleague.

"Here. You should read this. It's the latest message from your friend."

"How recent?"

"Today, as a matter of fact," Baier replied.

Jackson read the note, then looked across at Baier. "I see now why you're in such a state, why you're so worried. What do you propose we do?"

"I think it's time I met your source in person. I don't think we'll have time for dead drops and the waiting periods between them."

"Yes, I see," Jackson said.

"In fact, I'd like to meet the guy today, if possible."

The British officer pursed his lips and looked down at the note again. He even rubbed the paper between his fingers, as though testing its authenticity.

"I doubt that will be possible. We can't be sure he's available or that it will be safe." The Brit studied Baier. "And not just for him. If the Communists are pushing their plans forward, my guess is that we—both of us—will be under even greater surveillance now."

Baier was silent as he studied the looming outline of Hradčany Castle that overlooked the Embassy's gorgeous garden. Czechoslovakia's first president, Tomáš Masaryk, reputedly used to wander through that garden to visit his friends and allies in the British compound. Peter Jackson truly enjoyed an impressive and historic view.

Today, though, the age-old rooftops that spread at the foot of the Castle's hill looked to Baier just then as though they might finally collapse under the burden of history. That history had not been kind to this city of late—not for the last fifty years, or even longer if one considered the preceding centuries that stretched back as far as the Thirty Years' War. That conflict had begun here with a defenestration amidst the religious differences of the seventeenth century that would leave the entire continent a landscape pillaged and destroyed. Baier was beginning to understand why people here could become so fatalistic.

"And I suppose you'll need to clear a meeting with your superiors as well," Baier said.

Jackson let a grimace slide over his lips and eyes. He nodded. "Yes, of course. But I will push to have that done as quickly as possible. In fact, I'll see to it as soon as we're done here."

"Could I at least have the man's name? I realize that's a big request, but I promise not to act on it until I've heard from you."

Jackson looked down at his desk for what felt like a full minute. It was as though he was searching for the right document that would permit him to give the American a positive response. Finally, he glanced across at Baier with what appeared to be a look of resignation.

"Janos Hašek."

Baier thanked him, then walked through the office door and down the steps at a slower pace than when he arrived.

• • •

Baier spent the rest of that day and the morning of the 22nd as though in a fever. His pulse seemed to race with the crowds that marched through the streets, and he gasped for breath at times like some out-of-shape marathon runner. Baier expected to see hordes of police, even an army brigade or two, ready to push back against the waves of civilians that raced back and forth or marched behind banners proclaiming the need for social and economic justice, power for the workers' committees, independence and freedom from foreign interference, and an end to American imperialism. But there were no clouds of drifting tear gas, no bloodied foreheads, no screams for help. In fact, there was little or no violence at all. It was as though a mood had seized control of the city, not a mob. But the intent and purpose were clear.

Finally, drawing on his cover as an American diplomat Baier walked to the Foreign Ministry to see if he might learn more from inside the government. He guessed that his American diplomatic colleagues had been there already. Hell, they might even be there now. But he was still an outsider, an agent from a new organization still establishing its place and power within America's government bureaucracy.

Baier strolled across the courtyard that fronted what had been the Černín Palace, yet another one of the seemingly countless and beautiful baroque structures from centuries past. Climbing the small set of steps at the front entrance, Baier thought about how it was almost impossible to avoid these impressive landmarks of the city's past as an important outpost and sometimes capital of the Habsburg Empire. This one, too, sat in what was called the Castle district, as the overwhelming presence of the Hradčany complex bestowed its regal blessing on the buildings below.

Baier showed his diplomatic passport to the reception desk on the ground floor, set in an array of marble that glistened with light and history. As time moved on, however, this building and the entire district surrounding the Castle had come to represent a declaration of Czechoslovak independence after the breakup of the Habsburg Empire in 1918. Baier skirted past the main staircase that beckoned to visitors entering the foyer, figuring it served primarily as a diplomatic stage to impress any visitors to the seat of the new country's foreign policy—and it worked.

Instead, he headed for a staircase perhaps twenty yards down the first hallway on his left and climbed the stairs to the second floor, where he found the division responsible for the Western Hemisphere. Another receptionist, or secretary, accompanied him to an office down a narrow corridor where she spoke to a young gentleman seated behind a desk in a white windowless office. Baier assumed that this was probably a junior officer, guessing not only by the small and sparsely furnished office, but also by the young face that looked as though it had yet to meet a razor.

The young man stood and offered Baier a seat in the only other chair in the room. His blue sweater looked a bit frayed at the cuffs, as did the shirt that peeked under the woolen sleeves. The sweater was also tucked into a pair of gray woolen slacks, the entire ensemble hopefully acting against the chill that pervaded the room.

"Please, sit down. How can I help our American guest?"

Baier was struck by the excellent English, which sounded as though it had come straight from Oxford or Cambridge.

"Thank you for seeing me. First, though, I have to ask where you gained such a command of your English. It's almost as if I was back in London."

The young diplomat smiled. "I was with the government-in-exile there during the war."

"Impressive."

"Why, thank you. My parents fled there after the infamous Munich agreement in 1938. I was 20 at the time, and after I completed my university education at Kings College in Cambridge, I joined our government as an aide to President Beneš. Once we returned here, I joined the Foreign Ministry." The diplomat extended his hand. "My name, by the way, is Jaroslav Havlíček."

Baier rose, took the hand offered, and then both men sat.

"I assume you are here about the unrest and collapse of our government," Havlíček continued. "In fact, I am glad you dropped by. I would like to know where your own government stands on the developments here, and what it plans to do about them."

Baier nodded. "Well, I'm afraid I have not heard anything about what my government plans to do, or how it will react. I imagine they are still trying to digest what is happening here and what it means for Europe." Baier paused before continuing. "In the meantime, can you tell me how you think this will all play out?"

Havlíček threw his arms in the air and blew out his breath. "Unless someone like the United States does something, it will probably lead to a communist takeover."

"Why do you say that?"

"Because they control the streets and the army and the police. Not to mention significant departments like education and agriculture."

"But they have over a year now, haven't they? What is different now? Why push things forward now?"

"Because they have the opportunity now. Those twelve fools have resigned from the cabinet, and Gottwald is pressing to name a new cabinet fully under the control of his party. And that includes the Social Democrats, who are led by a man who has aligned his party with the KSC. Why, I do not know."

"You mean Fierlinger?"

"Yes, that's the one."

"What about the other parties?"

Havlíček threw his response out like a challenge—not so much at Baier as at his countrymen. "Those fools." He leaned forward. "They have become nothing more than fellow travelers, all packed with communist hangers-on."

"What about your President? Surely, he wants to preserve a free and democratic Czechoslovakia. It's what he's spent his life working for. You of all people should know that, having worked for him in London."

The young diplomat sat back against his chair and crossed his arms. "I'm afraid our President is a spent force. His health has been declining, and I believe he is more concerned with preventing the Red Army from marching in. After five years of war and six years of occupation, peace has become a more important objective than freedom or independence."

Now Baier felt really depressed. It seemed that every conversation he'd had since arriving in Prague only made him sadder and more frustrated. He tried to think of something to say, but soon gave that up. He stood to go.

"Well, Mr. Havlíček, thank you for your insights. If there is anything I can do, please do not hesitate to call me at the Embassy."

The Czech stood, then walked around his desk and embraced Baier. The American was too stunned to respond.

"Pray for us, please. I was raised a Catholic, but I no longer believe. Or let us just say that I am no longer practicing." He smiled. "Old beliefs like that seem to run deeper and linger longer than we may realize. Someone else has to pray for us, however. Perhaps you can inspire your government to find a way to prevent the worst from happening here."

"It's ironic, I guess, but I was also raised as a Catholic and seemed to have drifted away from my faith. But I will try to think of something."

It was little more than a polite response. Baier realized it was still better than saying nothing.

CHAPTER FIVE

Peter Jackson was true to his word. Within forty-eight hours, Baier was sitting across from Janos Hašek at a kitchen table in an apartment that served as a British safehouse on the outskirts of Prague. The building stood two blocks from the Vltava as it flowed past on its way to the countryside from the city center and the Charles Bridge, so named after Emperor Charles IV who ordered the bridge rebuilt back in the 15th century when the original was destroyed by one of the many floods that plagued Prague until the city's foundations were elevated. The flat was sparsely furnished. There was no need for anything elaborate, of course, since the space served primarily as a meeting point for gatherings of two to four people, rarely more than that. In fact, the table and four chairs were all Baier could find in the kitchen. The bedroom had a medium-sized bed and dark brown dresser, while the living room hosted a sofa and two chairs. Two end tables with a pair of lamps completed the furnishings. Some accommodations clearly had been made to create the appearance of an inhabited apartment.

"Ah, Mister Jones, we finally meet. I am so glad," Hašek said. "I would ask if your family is Welsh, or comes from Wales," he smiled, "but I realize that is probably not your true name."

"Thank you, Mister Hašek," Baier replied. He smiled, remembering the friendly face that had stared at him on the Charles Bridge just weeks ago. "It is good to meet you in person as well. Let me begin by thanking you for the information you have provided thus far. It has truly helped my superiors in the American government understand and appreciate what is going on here and what is at stake."

Hašek nodded and spread his arms. "I hope it will influence them to respond forcefully. My country has gone through too many trials over the last ten years."

"Well, I'm afraid the decision is not mine, but I will certainly do what I can. Tell me, though, how do you expect this crisis to play out? That could help them understand the challenge we face here."

Hašek stared at the American for perhaps half a minute before responding. "It will almost certainly end with a Communist seizure of power. That is their goal and their plan. There is no secret about that in the government and the parliament."

"Are they speaking openly about this?"

Hašek shook his head. "Not explicitly. Not in so many words. But believe me, it is no secret. Some of us wonder what has taken them so long."

"So, what has taken them so long?" Baier asked.

"I think it has only been a matter of time, one of waiting for the most propitious moment. And that has now arrived." Hašek said. "Too many of us were lulled into complacency by the cooperation the parties shared during the war and in the years immediately after. Too many of us assumed that we shared the same goals for our country. That assumption has proved to be fatal. Once the moment was right, the KSC moved." Hašek held up his right forefinger. "Along with the permission…no, the push from Moscow."

"You are certain of Moscow's role in promoting the coup?"

Hašek nodded vigorously. Yes, of that we are all—I mean all of us in the government— certain. People speak of it openly."

"But why now? Why not earlier, right after the war, for example, when the Red Army was already here?"

Hašek smiled. "The Red Army did not have to retreat very far, my friend. True, they did leave, and I believe that is one of President Beneš's objectives now: to try to keep the Red Army from marching in."

"I see. Tell me, though, what has changed in the Communists' calculus?"

"I believe it is the international scene. The French and Italians have successfully blocked the communists in their countries from gaining access to power." Here, Hašek smiled once more. "There are rumors, Mister Jones, that your government, and perhaps your agency, was instrumental in that success."

Baier ignored the reference and the belief that Hašek's words implied. Baier was certainly not going to respond to this man's obvious fishing as to whom Baier's true employer was.

"Anything else?"

"Yes, of course. There is also the domestic situation here in Czechoslovakia. Before this year, it looked as though the KSC had enough popular support to allow them to pursue a peaceful path to power. That support has evaporated, as the communists have spoken too often and too lovingly of farm collectivization, which has alienated many in the countryside. Workers have also disliked the emphasis on increasing production without an increase in wages. Meanwhile, our exports have suffered from the mismanagement of the economy. And then there has been the blatant stacking of the government—and the police in particular—with communists and their sympathizers."

"I've heard that they initially expected to win a majority of the seats in parliament in the elections scheduled for this spring. You say, they no longer have that option?"

"Not only do I say it, Mr. Jones. Nearly everyone says it. Knows it."

"What do you think my government can do?"

"Mister Jones, your government is the most powerful nation in the world. Surely it can muster the necessary military, political, and diplomatic force to block this move."

"What do you think Moscow's objectives are here? Is it worth starting another war?"

"No, it is not worth that. But is it worth it to watch my country once again fall under the control of another foreign power? To see our freedom and democracy crushed?"

"As I said earlier, I do not make or even recommend policies for my government. Nor do I have insight into the deliberations in Washington. I can only hope to provide the information that will help my government make the best possible policies." Baier thought for a moment. "Have you heard anything to suggest that Moscow will not be satisfied with a coup in Czechoslovakia alone? The Soviet Union does appear to be on a roll after the coup in Romania."

Hašek shook his head. "I can only speak for my country and what I have heard in government circles. And that focus is on this country alone. You recognize, of course, that the Soviet Union enjoys the advantage of geography here in central Europe. It would not take much for their army to return."

"Yes, that's why the challenge is especially difficult for us."

"And there is another thing," Hašek added.

"Yes?"

"In the past, we have often looked to Russia as a counterweight to the Germans, who have generally posed more of a threat. But the Bolshevik Revolution made that option less attractive."

"That would seem to make the Communists less attractive as well."

"Ah, but the memories of the last war are still very fresh here. The USSR still looks like the lesser evil." He paused and raised his finger again. "At least for some."

"Then whatever we do, we will face serious difficulties. Especially since your nation seems so divided and uncertain about its future."

Hašek smiled and stretched out his hand as he stood. "I disagree. But I also understand your concerns. I will continue my efforts to keep your people informed, Mister Jones. Shall we meet again in, say, two days?"

Baier stood and took the hand offered. "That sounds like a good idea. I hope your president will think of something by then to keep the Communists at bay. I understand Gottwald is demanding that President Beneš approve a new cabinet, handpicked by Gottwald alone, that will be controlled by the KSC."

"Yes, let us hope. And pray." Hašek's other hand folded Baier's between both of his.

"Is there anything I can do for you here in Prague?" Baier asked.

"Not today. But if things take a turn for the worse, I may need your help."

Baier looked puzzled, but he still held Hašek's hand. "My help? On a personal matter?"

"Yes. I may need your assistance if I have to flee my country. It will be a difficult decision, of course. But probably a necessary one."

"I understand," Baier reassured him. "I will be happy to work with my friend and colleague Peter," Baier nodded in the direction of his British counterpart, who had waited patiently throughout the discussion, standing silent by the sink.

"Thank you."

Hašek dropped Baier's hand, then walked without another word to the door. He did not look back.

• • •

"I hope I did not assume too much there by promising on your behalf to help with an escape?"

Peter Jackson shook his head and waved a free hand in the air. "No, Karl, that's quite all right. I hope it doesn't come to that, but we will do whatever we can to get that man out of here alive. He has been a valuable friend and ally for the West, and the United Kingdom in particular."

"You're not going to try to get him to stay on so you'll have a valuable asset in the new government?" Baier asked.

"There's no guarantee he'd keep his post. A purge is likely to follow if Beneš gives in. And the Communists would probably want someone more closely aligned with Moscow in such an important and influential position as a high-level foreign policy adviser in the prime minister's office."

Baier laughed. "So, that's his post." He pointed his finger at Jackson. "Careful. You let that one slip out. But thanks anyway."

"Oh, hell, Karl, I'd say we're well past that point, especially if we have to sneak the man over the border. Besides, an awareness of his position and role should help give his observations greater weight in Washington, don't you think?"

"Let's hope so. As for the exfiltration, I guess we'll see just how well this budding special relationship people are talking about functions in a crisis."

"I'd say it's gone pretty well so far. But this would certainly be a new challenge for me. It would be my first exfiltration."

Baier nodded and moved to the door. "Mine, too. Hopefully, we can learn from each other."

CHAPTER SIX

"Where have you been for the last few days?" Steinhardt asked.

Baier stood across from the ambassador, who was seated, as usual, behind his desk. The man looked as though he had had a rough night...more like a rough few days. His suit looked like he had been wearing it for that long, this one a dark gray number with a jacket that carried a row of wrinkles along the sleeve and front. The shirt was wrinkled as well, and when he looked close enough, Baier could swear that the collar had a ring of light brown around it, the cuffs, too.

"Walking the streets, trying to get a sense of how all this is going to play out," Baier answered.

"What about this British source you know? What does he have to say?"

Baier glanced out the window at the ambassador's back, as though the source himself might be standing there. The elaborate garden at the back of the embassy on Petřín Hill, brown and mostly bare in its winter slumber, stretched toward the low chain of mountains behind them and matched the mood in the room—weathered and somber. It was a marked contrast to the beauty implied in origin and purpose that the building initially enjoyed as the Schoenborn Palace.

"I'm not sure. I haven't seen him in two days. It's hard for him to get away, I imagine."

"What did he have to say two days ago?"

Baier shrugged. "He was not optimistic."

The ambassador let a barely audible laugh slip free. "I would think not. I take it you haven't heard the latest news then."

Baier was puzzled. He stepped closer to the desk, close enough that he almost brushed against the front.

"Heard what? Have the security forces or the National Police grabbed him?"

The ambassador's laugh was louder and more forceful this time. "Hardly. Well, maybe they have. But that's not the news I'm thinking of." He paused. "Beneš has given in. He approved the new Communist-controlled cabinet. The KSC—and Moscow, by extension—have succeeded."

Baier stepped back and inhaled a deep breath of disappointment and shock.

"So, the old man just gave up? There were no conditions attached?"

"Apparently not," the ambassador replied. "He is very ill, and he did not look at all well when I last saw him a week ago." Steinhardt sighed. "His strength is clearly fading. I doubt he'll survive this setback. I'd give him a few months. No longer."

"Before he dies?"

The ambassador nodded. His eyes sank and remained fixed on his desktop.

"Is that why he caved, do you think?" Baier asked.

Steinhardt nodded. "I'm sure that's part of it. Perhaps he retains his allusions regarding the sincerity of the Communists and the future of Czechoslovakia's democracy. More important, though, in my view, is his concern about not giving the Red Army an excuse to occupy his country. The memory of the war years still burns pretty brightly in his mind."

"That occupation will probably happen anyway," Baier added.

"Yes, I suppose so. Or at least close to it. The Soviets like to have their forces just on the other side of their western border. As near as possible. Just in case. However, there's another invasion and occupation that carries a lot of influence in their thinking.

"The Germans?"

The ambassador nodded once more. "It is amazing when you think about it." He shook his head. Baier could almost feel the frustration and sadness buried deeper in the ambassador's breath. "It's what, just under a week since the twelve non-Communist ministers resigned on the 20th of this month?" Steinhardt continued. "Here it is the 25th of February, and they've succeeded in their coup. And without an explicit show of force. They simply outmaneuvered the opposition. Of course, they've been building towards this since the end of the war."

Baier thought of Hašek and his parting words about leaving the country. Baier also wondered about the fate of the young diplomat Havlíček. Would this be enough to push him back to London?

He turned to leave. "Thank you for sharing your thoughts, Ambassador. I've got a few things to look into."

"Good luck."

The ambassador's words drifted past Baier's shoulders as he stepped into the hallway.

• • •

Baier didn't have to wonder for long about the fate of his contacts in Prague. When he got to the front entrance of the Embassy the following day, a security guard handed him a slip of paper.

"A local left this note this note for you, Sir."

Baier thanked the guard, then glanced at the note. It asked him for a meeting at a café down the street. The words conveyed a sense of urgency— "as soon as possible"—and it was signed simply "H."

Baier glanced up at the security officer. "How did you get this? And can you describe the individual who gave it to you?"

The guard stood at attention, stiff and clearly uncomfortable. He reminded Baier of Marines he had met during the war.

"And you can relax," Baier added. "I appreciate your help."

"Sir, the gentleman slipped it to my colleague on duty at the front desk. I was about to relieve him, but I thought you'd want to see this immediately. I was just on my way up to your office."

"Yes, thank you. And the man? How did he look?"

"He was tall, about your height. And thin, with brown hair a bit longer than yours."

"His age? Did you get any impression of that? Roughly, I mean."

"I'd say he was in his late twenties, maybe early thirties."

"What was his state of mind? Could you tell?"

"Yes, Sir. He looked worried. Very nervous."

"Thanks again. You've been very helpful."

Baier turned and ran out the door, nearly tripping on the front steps in his rush.

• • •

"You've heard?" Havlíček asked. He shifted his weight in the small metal chair, unable to sit still when Baier approached. The young Czech diplomat had chosen a table at the back of the café, presumably to keep as far away from the window as possible.

Baier stared for a moment at the young man. He was seated with a clear view of the door of one of the cafes down the street from the American Embassy, its front shaded by the row of stone archways that lined the sidewalk. Pedestrians rushed by, presumably heading for the large crowds growing in the Old Town and at Wenceslas Square, the main gathering points in Prague's city center.

Baier sat. "About the new government?"

Havlíček nodded, his eyes moving about the room.

"Yes, I have heard," Baier said. "Unfortunately."

Havlíček was silent, his eyes focused now on the table in front of him. His lips were thin and tight, pressed together in anxiety and confusion. Baier wondered just what the man had done, what he had to fear. His hair hung in greasy strands along his sides and over his forehead. The skin had gone pale, and his fingers twitched in a nervous spasm. He tried unsuccessfully to light a cigarette. Baier took the matches from his hand and struck a flame for him.

"I received your note and came as quickly as I could." Baier was silent for a moment while he studied the young man at his table. "My God, Jaroslav, you look terrible. What is it? Have they threatened you? Do you expect to be arrested?"

Havlíček shrugged and shifted his weight again. "Thank you." He inhaled a balloon's worth of cigarette smoke, then blew it out across the room. "Who knows? Those people have long memories and heavy grudges. Anything could happen."

"But why you? What have you done?"

"Don't you see? That doesn't matter. I was associated with the London exile government. That is cause enough for suspicion."

"But were you high and important enough to catch their attention?"

"I refused to work for the Communists when they asked back then. In fact, I immediately reported the pitch to my superiors, and they were the ones who had me agree to work for them initially and act as a double agent. But that nearly destroyed me, and I refused to do it any longer shortly after I returned."

"How long was it?"

Havlíček paused and stared at the ceiling. It looked as though he was formulating a difficult math equation or solving some problem requiring long division.

"Oh, just a few months, maybe three, and almost entirely back in London. But I am sure it was long enough for them to remember and build a grudge."

Baier sat back and tried to think. "Let's order some coffee. We'll look too conspicuous if we don't drink anything."

"Sure, fine. But I could probably use a beer instead."

The two men sat in silence until their drinks arrived. Baier stuck with the coffee, but Havlíček had one of the excellent pilsners found in Prague, this one a Budvar. Baier was tempted, but given the surge of events and excitement, he thought it best to stay as sober as possible.

"So, Jaroslav, what do you want me to do?"

"Can you help me escape? Do you even do that sort of thing?"

Baier sat silent for perhaps a full minute. He studied the young Czech, realizing that he knew next to nothing about the man. In fact, all he did know had come directly and only from him. Baier had not had the time to investigate the man's background. He seemed sincere, but then again, one always needed to be cautious.

In the worst case, this could be a dangle from the local security service, or even the Soviet service, the NKVD.

"Are you sure it's as bad as you say? What about your colleagues at work? Do they feel the same way?"

"Oh, they all oppose the regime change. But no one I know feels as threatened as I do. Then again, none of them have the same background. At least none of my close colleagues."

"Do you mean that you are the only one among your peers who returned from exile in London?

"No, no. Of course not. But the ones I know personally or work with have been more open to changes like this. They usually say something convenient, like how the years have shown us that governments come and go. But the Czech and Slovak people stay. We will always survive."

"And don't you agree?"

Havlíček shook his head violently. Baier was afraid he was going to spill his beer.

"It is so much more complicated than that. I mean, how much suffering can one endure? Besides, I believe I could do more for my country working from abroad. Certainly, in a situation such as this."

"I see."

Again, Baier was silent while he considered the young Czech's plea and his situation. After about another minute, he had made up his mind.

"Let me ask around to see what I can do. It's not the sort of thing I normally do, but perhaps I can find someone with some experience. Or who may know others who can help." Baier thought for a moment, keeping his eyes focused on Havlíček. "I'll have to check with Washington as well. Do you have someplace safe to stay?"

Havlíček's face brightened and his muscles seemed to relax. Not by much, but enough to allow him to sit back against his chair.

"My God, thank you so much. I did not know where else to turn. I think my apartment is still safe for now. When will you know?"

"I'm not sure. But I will contact you in a few days, at the latest. I doubt this is something you can put together overnight."

Not only that, Baier thought to himself, but he had someone else he needed to think of.

CHAPTER SEVEN

The two men walked quickly through the streets of suburban Prague, stopping only to check for possible surveillance. It was the first week of March, and the cold, damp night air let them know in no uncertain terms that spring was still a long way off. That particular message was reinforced by the occasional blast of wind from the east. They were strolling past a row of large apartment buildings, most of them four or five stories tall and covered in a dust coat of dull brown or somber gray. Sparks of yellow peeked through at spots, survivors of a previous era, before the advent of soft brown coal as the major source of heat. The limestone facades seemed to swallow even those modest beacons tonight, as though saving them for a resurrection at some later date.

"Do you get the impression that the new regime has increased its surveillance of foreigners lately?" Peter Jackson asked.

"Oh, hell, yes," Karl Baier replied. "I noticed the occasional guardian in the past, but it always seemed halfhearted. The coverage now is usually a lot more intense and much heavier."

"Then why aren't we seeing much of it tonight?"

Baier nodded and paused in front of a grocer's window. "Well, I did catch a couple of teams working on us earlier. Back near the city center. It looks like it's dropped off out here, though. They could be busy keeping track of all the local opposition figures. My guess is that the number of those targets has grown exponentially in the last few weeks."

"Well, hopefully, they figure us for some smaller fry. Much better fishing elsewhere, you know."

"Didn't you say you live out this way?"

Jackson nodded. "Yes, I did. I can't remember when I said it, though."

"That doesn't matter. They may have thought we were just going to your place."

"Let's hope so."

The two men resumed their hike, this time at a slightly faster pace. For his part, Baier was confident that they were free of unwanted company, and he did not want to give any stragglers time to catch up. Besides, it was too damn cold for a leisurely stroll. If anything, that might draw attention.

"Tell me again why we are adding this Czech diplomat to Hašek's exfiltration," Jackson asked.

"You mean Havlíček?"

Jackson nodded as he shivered.

"You should have dressed more warmly. That light jacket and sweater don't seem to be helping much." Baier pulled his *Lodenmantel* tighter around his body, thankful for the dry woolen comfort it provided. "In any case, Jaroslav Havlíček claims he was active with the government-in-exile during the war, and that he worked for the allies—our Western allies, not Moscow—as well. You guys did check him out, didn't you?"

"Yes, of course we did. And his story does ring true, as you say. Although we have had no contact since he returned to Prague."

"Yeah, well, the war is over," Baier said.

"With a new one on the horizon, apparently."

"God, let's hope not. We still don't know how this could all play out. And these two guys are the kind of people who can help us figure out just what the next few weeks and months could hold."

"Hašek, for sure," Jackson agreed. "I'm not sure what the other one has to offer, given his low status, even if he does work at the Foreign Ministry."

"I don't really care at this point. The guy was scared shitless when we met, and I think he deserves our best efforts." Baier swept his arm up over his head and around in a broad circle, as though he wanted to encompass the entire city. "The people here have gotten the shaft on a pretty continual basis over the last decade. They all deserve whatever breaks we can give 'em."

"Yeah, whatever." Jackson stopped and turned towards the entrance to a four-story apartment building. "We're here."

Baier halted and scanned the street in both directions. The row of apartments with facades of faded color and chipped limestone seemed to hover over the sidewalk and reinforce the ominous presence of a darkened night and the mystery it held. An occasional streetlamp threw a splash of light on the intermittent fronts of the buildings lining the street in either direction. The meager illumination was of little use, helpful mainly for hiding shadows. Baier shivered, but only partly from the cold.

The apartment they wanted was on the third floor, towards the back of the building. Both men paused at the door, noticing the light that peeked out from underneath the door. They ascended as quietly as possible, one step at a time, but the occasional scrape of a shoe was impossible to hide. Each noise reinforced the sense that their slow climb was taking forever. Jackson held his right forefinger to his lips and gripped the door handle. He nodded, then threw the door open, leading with his shoulder as they burst into the room.

Hašek sat silently at the table, his face masked with a look of fear and complete surrender. There were even tears in his eyes, and a drop or two had begun to run down his pale skin. Next to him sat a bulky thug, who covered Hašek with a scowl of contempt on his unshaven face and a semi-automatic gripped tightly in his right hand. A CZ52 Baier guessed, one of the knockoffs the local service had copied from the Soviet standard model. The thug let a deep laugh escape from somewhere in his abdomen.

"That's right, it's one of ours, and it still uses the original parabellum rounds. Why don't you try something, Yank, so we can all see what kind of damage it can do?"

Baier blew him a kiss. "Not tonight. I've got other plans. But I'd be happy to see you again sometime, alone."

"Oh, come now," another, lighter voice announced from the doorway. "There is no need for such dramatics."

Baier kept his eyes on the more immediate danger, the man with the gun. The invisible voice continued. "Karol, that will be enough. This is not some game or wrestling match."

"Dramatics?" Jackson asked.

"Yes, exactly. For example, you could have broken the lock or even the door frame. Haven't you Americans learned to knock? In any case, you will have to change your plans for this evening, I'm afraid."

Baier turned toward the sound and discovered that the voice came from a man standing just inside the doorway. Fortunately, he was unarmed. Then again, there was no telling what he might have hidden under the long, black leather overcoat that stretched nearly to his ankles. He swept the door closed, then stepped to the table, close enough for Baier to reach out and grab him.

"Who are you? And how did you get in here?" Jackson asked.

The thin man laughed. "Who we are should be obvious. We are the police. The National Police, actually. And the door was already open. Presumably by this gentleman here." He pointed at Hašek.

"Then why are you here?" Baier pressed. "Why would the police, especially the National Police, be interested in two Western diplomats and a government official?"

A laugh escaped from somewhere deep inside the police officer. "And why would you be interested in this particular civil servant? And why did you think it necessary to meet him here, of all places?" He glanced at his wristwatch. "And at this hour?"

"That is none of your business," Jackson interjected. He almost screamed his reply. Baier noticed that he had started to sweat, despite the chill in the apartment.

"Mister Hašek here is being arrested as a spy. I assume you two are his handlers. In that case, we may have to come looking for you as well. Later, of course."

"Why not now?" Jackson pressed.

A smile escaped from the thin one. It barely covered the laugh behind it. "Because we have more pressing business with this sad gentleman here." He nodded in Hašek's direction.

"Don't be ridiculous." Jackson did scream this time. "You have no proof. This case will be tossed out of court in no time. And you know it."

The Czech security officer moved closer to Baier's British colleague. He stood just inches from Jackson's face.

"We do not need any proof. And this case will never come to trial." He paused to think for a moment. "Well, maybe when he gets to Siberia."

"Not only is this man innocent," Baier broke in, "but this all serves no purpose. I would even say it goes against your new government's interests."

"Oh, how so?"

"Because it's in your interest to show the world that you're not mere puppets of the Kremlin, and that you will respect the rule of law and democratic freedoms."

The officer laughed again. Not as loud as before, but it still carried the sounds of contempt and dismissal. "What a nice speech. Meaningless, but nice to hear. However, you can save that for an American audience, Mister Baier."

"How do you know my name?"

The smile turned to a sneer. "Really? Are you that naive?" The National Police officer stepped away from the table and the two foreigners. "This arrest serves our purpose in ways you obviously do not recognize. This man," he pointed again at Hašek, "not only worked for the German puppet government during the war, but he was also an agent of the Gestapo."

"That's not true," Hašek shouted. Those were the first words he had spoken. It was good to hear that he was still able to speak up in his own defense.

"Yes, that is ridiculous," Jackson stated. He spoke the words heavily and carefully, trying to give them added weight. "I seriously doubt you have proof for that either."

"We don't need any proof. He was arrested and then released by the Gestapo. Why do you suppose that is?"

"That's still pretty shy of proof," Baier said. "That can be explained in any number of ways. For example…"

The Czech officer shrugged and waved his hand. "No matter. His arrest will send an important message that serves a more important purpose."

"And that is?" Baier pressed.

"That we will not tolerate anyone from the old regime here. Let us just say that this arrest comes in the service of a higher cause."

"Which is?" Baier persisted.

"The cause of the people. And the leadership of their party in creating a new Czechoslovakia."

"Oh, please," Jackson interjected.

That apparently was too much for the thug sitting at the table. The rounded hulk of a man stood, walked over to the Brit, and slapped him across the face. He still held his pistol but had moved it to his left hand, freeing his right fist. The better, apparently, to discipline the British officer.

Baier started toward the heavyweight but halted when he saw the pistol aimed at his midsection.

"I think we will leave you now," the taller, thin officer said. "Enjoy your walk home, gentlemen. If you wait for daylight, it will probably warm up some. And I'm sorry that I do not have a forwarding address for Mister Hašek. I doubt that he will be receiving much mail in any case."

With that, the two policemen and their prisoner left the apartment. Baier listened to their steps echo in the stairwell, followed by the slamming of the building's front door. He looked over at his colleague.

"How?" It was all he could say.

Jackson slumped in the chair Hašek had occupied. He stared at the tabletop. "I...I don't know. I said nothing about the specifics of this operation to anyone." He looked up at Baier. "Did you?"

"Of course not."

"Then there must be a leak somewhere. I'll have to look into it." He was silent for a moment as his gaze returned to the table. "I'll raise it with Philby when I get back to London." Jackson chuckled. "That should be soon after this fiasco. I just hope I'm still employed at that point."

"Philby?" Baier asked. "Who's that?"

"Oh, he's one of the people who oversee operations in this part of the world in MI-6. He's highly thought of. He should be able to get to the bottom of a mess like this."

Jackson paused long enough to take in the room where they sat before returning his attention to Baier. "Poor Hašek. I guess we've lost him for good now. He was a good man. Always wanting the best for his country."

"That's going to be little consolation where he's headed."

Jackson's face brightened. He looked up at Baier again. "Whatever happened to the other gent?"

"You mean Havlíček. I don't know. That's what I'll have to find out next."

• • •

Baier found out soon enough. Two days later, in fact. Havlíček showed up at the American Embassy, asking specifically for Baier. A security guard called Baier from the front entrance to tell him about his visitor. Baier sprinted down the stairs to meet the young Czech in the reception room just inside the entrance.

"You must grant me asylum here," Havlíček urged. "My life is in danger. I want so much to return to London, where I'll be safe." He paused. "At least, safer than I am here."

Baier was struck by the young man's nervous energy and his obvious fright. The wringing hands, the restless eyes, the uncombed and apparently unwashed hair, all gave Havlíček the look of a man lost and confused—not to mention desperate. Baier tried to settle his uninvited guest in the hope of finding some kind of coherent thought and a rational request.

"So, which is it you want? Asylum in the Embassy or a return to England?"

"Both. I need to be safe while I'm in Prague, and then I want to get out of here, back to London."

"So, I take it your apartment is no longer safe?"

"No, of course not."

"Why? What has happened to change your view on that?"

"Because I am certain I saw the police patrolling my neighborhood. And they spent a lot of time in front of my building or just across the street."

"Okay, but first tell me what happened two nights ago," Baier said. "What happened to you? Why didn't you show up? And where were you?"

The remaining bits of color drained from Havlíček's face. Sweat beaded along his forehead, and he stammered as he tried to respond.

"Are you kidding? I saw what happened. I thought I had been followed, so I hid in the shadows across the street from the address you gave me. I assumed it was a British or American safehouse, so I thought it would be safe. I was wrong."

"How did you know that?"

"I arrived early to make sure it was safe. I wanted to check things out. It was a good thing I did. I saw the security agents arrive and enter the building. Then I saw a light go on in the apartment upstairs on the same floor you told me to go to."

"How did you know they were security agents?"

Havlíček stared. "Of course, they were from the police. One can tell when you've been here long enough. The long black overcoat confirmed it. Especially at that time of the night. Who else could they be?"

"And? What then?"

Havlíček wrung his hands together hard enough to polish them. "I saw another man come along, and I thought it might be the other person you said you were going to exfiltrate. I tried to warn him, but I was too afraid to speak louder than a whisper. I hissed at him. He must not have heard me."

"Did he enter the building?"

"Yes. He was the same man the two agents escorted outside later. It looked like they had begun to beat him even before they left the building." Havlíček shuddered. "It was horrible."

"Did you see me and my British colleague?"

"Yes, of course. But by then, I was too terrified to do anything. I hoped you two would be able to rescue the poor fellow."

"How long did you stay there?"

"I...I am not sure. It felt like hours before I decided it was safe enough to wander out again." Havlíček stared at Baier. "You must help me. I went home to change and gather a few things. I've been hiding at the train station with other refugees."

"The train station? That sounds like you've got more than a feeling. It also sounds pretty desperate."

Havlíček shook his head. "I cannot return to my place. At least I seriously doubt it. In any case, I cannot take that chance. I will not."

Baier thought for a moment and paced around the small room. Havlíček sat glued to his seat by the conference table, his rigid posture suggesting he would have to be forcibly removed if Baier wanted him to leave.

"Let me check with the DCM."

"The what?"

"The Deputy Chief of Mission. He's the number two and the one who actually runs things here. I'll see if there's anything I can do."

"But can't you just sneak me out like we planned before?"

Baier shook his head. "Not really. That had been set up by the Brits. I doubt we could replicate that this quickly."

"Why not?"

"Well, for one thing, we do not have the false documentation our friends had prepared. That's why it took so long to prepare for your escape. When you didn't show up, my British colleague took the documents back to his office. And I'm not sure we even have the transportation available."

"Please ask about it. Can I stay here in the meantime?"

Baier nodded. "Probably. But I'll have to ask about that as well. Just stay here for now. I'll get back as soon as I can. I'll see about a sandwich and some coffee. I assume you're hungry."

"Yes, thank you."

"And you might want to change some of your clothes. Maybe even take a shower. I'll check on that, too. I know it has been difficult for you, but you might not want to look—or smell—like a man on the run."

Baier asked the security guard to keep an eye on the Czech asylum seeker and perhaps see if he could use the locker room in the basement. He then went upstairs to see what he could arrange. Baier realized that an added advantage to keeping Havlíček here would be to prevent him from communicating with anyone on the outside. Baier was not sure at this point just whom he could trust, or whom the young Czech diplomat might try to contact... if anyone. Even his family could pose a risk if they found out. Baier paused for a moment to catch his breath. He hadn't realized how much his adrenaline and the excitement and danger of the night's events had quickened his pace and his breathing. His new profession certainly had its moments. None of that, though, could match the danger and ruin that threatened his two Czech contacts.

• • •

In the end, Baier was able to find a car big enough and loaded with a full tank of gas. He bundled Havlíček into the trunk of a Ford sedan for the drive through Prague, a cautionary move that he later realized was probably not necessary. The streets were calm. The police presence was no larger than usual, although there did appear to be an extra squad or two around the Embassy, mostly strolling back and forth along Tržište Street at the front of the Embassy. They were presumably stationed there to prevent any particularly important opposition figures from gaining access to the American outpost. Just how Havlíček managed to get through that semi-serious siege remained a nagging question for Baier as he drove through the city. But he'd have to wait to clear that up later. Once he was certain they had the city—and its police presence—behind them.

The drive west and then south through the Czech countryside to the Bavarian border took around five hours, which was quicker than Baier had guessed, given that they were traveling in the dark. He couldn't be sure of the total time because he forgot to check his watch when they left. He had been pretty damn nervous. This was his very first exfiltration attempt, at least on his own, and he had not had much time to prepare. Actually, he didn't have any. He realized he still had a lot to learn, especially since his British colleague had not been much of a teacher. Then again, he doubted there were many back in Washington, or anywhere else for that matter, with much experience in this sort of adventure.

Once they had left Prague about an hour behind them, Baier pulled over and let Havlíček out of the trunk.

"Thanks," the passenger said. "That wasn't so bad."

"Seriously? Have you ridden in cramped car spaces before?"

"Not really. It was stuffy, sure. But considering the alternative…" He looked over at Baier. "How much longer?"

"I'm not sure. This is my first trip along this route. First, though, can you tell me how you managed to evade all the police outside the Embassy when you arrived this evening?"

"Of course. There was no visible police presence when I arrived. They had not set anything up yet. The new government must not have thought it necessary at first. I mean, there were no army units involved. The arrests had not begun yet. At least, not any large-scale ones. So, there was no real danger of massive flights." Havlíček shrugged. "I guess they're still busy organizing the new government. Their focus must be on the political opposition in Prague and in Slovakia. The American Embassy will get its share of attention later."

"Then why all the panic on your part? You were pretty desperate when I saw you."

"I was worried about what was to come. I knew the calm wouldn't last. That's why I returned to my apartment for only a brief moment. I knew it would be dangerous to linger." Havlíček paused. "That and the police presence, of course."

"Well, it doesn't seem to have taken the new government much time to remove really important figures. Like Jan Masaryk. And permanently. The new government clearly thought he was a danger. Dangerous enough to push him out of another window." Baier shook his head and looked over at his passenger. "That seems to be the preferred way of dealing with opponents in this country."

"You mean like the defenestration at the Hradčany Castle back in 1618?"

"Yeah. It's too bad there wasn't a pile of manure to break his fall like the one that saved the Catholic ministers back then."

'I think that's actually the Protestant version of the story. The Catholics say the men were gathered up by the Virgin Mary and placed on the ground unharmed."

"Well, whatever it was, I'm guessing we haven't seen the last of that method of assassination in this part of the world."

Havlíček nodded. "Perhaps. But Masaryk's killing showed me how dangerous and desperate the new regime must be. Then again, I am no Jan Masaryk. After all, he was the foreign minister and the son of the founder of the independent Czechoslovak Republic after World War I. He had to be eliminated. I knew I had more time. But I could not be certain how much."

"The new government is claiming it was a suicide."

Havlíček glanced over at Baier. The young diplomat laughed. "Of course, they'll say that."

"So, you don't believe that story. He was, after all, found in his pajamas."

"So what? You know the history. They must know it as well, and what most people will think. They almost certainly want to arrange things so they will have some piece of plausible deniability."

It was Baier's turn to laugh. "Yes, I am aware of that. And just for the record, I am very skeptical of the suicide story as well."

"Then I would suggest that we both avoid spending too much time in front of windows, open or closed."

"Agreed. Although I don't think we have to worry about that at the border."

They drove in silence for another two hours. Havlíček slept for most of the trip, communicating in a series of snores and snorts. Baier's anxiety was enough to keep him alert.

They sped past Pilsen on their way west, its skyline outlined by a moon that showed little light elsewhere, certainly, not along the road they were traveling. Baier figured they were more than halfway to the border, and he was glad Havlíček had left him to his own thoughts. In some ways, Baier regretted the darkness despite its helpful cover. The region was supposedly a beautiful one of rolling green hills and farmland that would transform itself into the Bohemian Forest as they neared the German border. Maybe some other time, Baier sighed.

About an hour past Pilsen, Havlíček awoke with a start. He shook his head and sat up straight. Struggling to escape his slumber, Havlíček appeared to be confused, worried even. He looked over at Baier, then seemed to relax, as though he had found a source of reassurance.

"Did you forget where you were?" Baier asked.

Havlíček shook himself and nodded. "Yes, actually. I'm sorry if I startled you."

"No, that's all right. It helped me stay awake."

Havlíček studied Baier for about a minute.

"May I ask you a question? It's a bit personal."

Baier resettled himself in his seat and gripped the steering wheel. "I guess so. Go ahead. Just don't make it too personal."

"Why are you doing this? It's not like we are old friends or colleagues."

Baier was silent for a moment. "That is true. But these are unusual times. They call for unusual measures. I guess you could put it in that drawer. You believe in a Western, democratic Czechoslovakia, like so many of your countrymen. You all have had a pretty painful and oppressive decade. So, I can sympathize with that. It's what we would want for your country as well."

"Yes, that is true. But why me? You know relatively little about me."

"Let's just say I decided to take a chance," Baier replied. "You know, you get a certain feeling about someone and then use that to fill in the gaps. I was confident enough in your story, so I wanted to do what I could to help." Baier glanced over to study his passenger. "Maybe you'll have the chance to pay me back someday."

"Yes, let's hope so. But thank you all the same." Baier reached over and patted his passenger on the back. Then he pointed at the small crowd and the guard post up ahead. "We're nearly there. How do you plan to cross?"

"I will throw myself at the mercy of the border guards if necessary. They are probably sympathetic to my plight. But just in case, I have my passport, which I retrieved when I went by my apartment."

"I thought you were avoiding your place."

"I was. I swung by when I left the apartment where you were the other night. I did not stop for long. Just long enough to grab a few things."

"Well, good luck then."

Baier drove almost to the guard post, about twenty yards short of it, to let Havlíček out. When the border guard approached their car, Baier showed the soldier his diplomatic passport. The guard nodded, then moved to the other side of the car. Havlíček ignored him as he strode to the crossing. The guard did not try to follow Havlíček or demand to see his identification. The young soldier—Baier guessed he could not have been out of his teens for long, if at all—swung his rifle from one shoulder to the other. The guard's eyes and the frost in his breath were all that followed Havlíček's passage. There were already several dozen people waiting, and Baier stayed to make sure Havlíček got through.

Then he drove back to Prague, stopping periodically to stretch and slap himself awake. As he approached the capital, the sun was just starting to peek over the horizon. The sky shot a blend of yellow and red stripes that merged into a band of bright orange set against a deep blue background as it splashed across his windshield. Baier pulled over to stop on the shoulder of the road and watched the rest of Apollo's ascent. In his exhaustion and confusion, Baier was unsure whether the display in the sky harbored a promise or a threat in its uncertain future. He grinned, shook his head, then drove the rest of the way home.

PART III
PRAGUE 1968

January 5: Alexander Dubček replaces the discredited Antonin Novotny as First Secretary of the Communist Party.

January–February: Eduard Goldstuecker becomes head of the Union of Czechoslovak Writers and chief editor of *Literarni noviny* and begins accepting uncensored articles critical of the past regime.

April: Dubček launches his "Action Programme" which includes freedom of the press, freedom of speech and movement, an emphasis on producing consumer goods, and the possibility of multiparty elections and government.

CHAPTER EIGHT

"So, how long did you end up staying in Prague back then?"

It was late June, and Paul Krohn had retained his initial enthusiasm and curiosity. It was a good sign, in Baier's view, for a young officer to hold on to that first rush of enthusiasm over a new adventure. He just needed to make sure that the sense of adventure did not lead to carelessness in terms of personal and office security. "Stay alert" was something that senior officers like Baier reminded their junior personnel—and often their more experienced employees as well. Always be aware of your surroundings.

"Oh, I left in early June of that year. Around the same time as now, if twenty years later. Some things, like the setting and the history of this place feel the same. Together they still evoke a sense of majesty and meaning. The politics and the popular mood are a lot different, though. Back then, we clung to an almost desperate hope that President Beneš would not give up his dream of an independent and democratic Czechoslovakia, something he had worked for all his life. But when he retired on June 2nd and was replaced by Gottwald..."

"The Communist Party head?"

Baier nodded. "That's right. Once Gottwald assumed the presidency, we knew it was all over."

"So, the old guy just said to hell with it?"

"Not exactly. He had been quite ill and weak over the last few years, and he probably saw that it was hopeless. To resist would have no doubt led to a civil war and a Red Army invasion."

"I see what you mean when you say things look and feel a lot different now. I mean, just look at all the changes Dubček has instituted since he took over from Novotny last January as the Party's First Secretary."

"Oh, hell yes," Baier continued. "Dubček enjoys the support of most—and I mean most, not all—of the party leadership, as well as that of the new president Svoboda, who replaced Novotny in that job in March. And the people really love the new regime. Hell, they've got a free press here to rival that of any in Western Europe." Baier paused to smile and look out the window. "And the spread of television here has helped spread the new liberal and reformist message. The people are loving all this, as best I can tell. There's an enthusiasm now that was not here in '48."

"What was the mood back then?"

"Oh, twenty years ago it was mostly one of confusion and uncertainty. And a healthy dose of fear with a bit of resignation mixed in"

Baier leaned forward. His own enthusiasm now matched that of Krohn's. That feeling and a new confidence were infectious. One could see it throughout what had blossomed as a more open and lively Czechoslovak society. It was as though the coup of 1948 had been nothing more than an interlude. "There's even talk of free and multi-party elections," Baier added. "Not right away, of course, but a couple of years down the road."

"But they'll probably have to stay in the Warsaw Pact, right?"

"I would imagine so. To pull out of that would be a step way too far, if you ask me. I think that was one of the mistakes the Hungarians made back in '56."

"But then why has Dubček and his crowd gotten away with so much this far?"

Baier sat back and shrugged. "Good question. I think the government and the party here are taking advantage of Khrushchev's policy shift back in the 50s, claiming that the socialist revolution had evolved far enough to allow a more open form of socialism, one that need not fear the interests of the bourgeoisie because the workers and their interests and prominence have become well-established. I guess they've been arguing that the economic and societal evolution here is under control, that the Revolution has already succeeded to an extent."

"Is that true? You've had a lot of experience in this part of the world."

"Who cares? If it works as an excuse to continue with the reforms, then so be it." Baier thought for a moment. "I think it's really too early to tell. The changes are still new. You know, not all that well established. Not yet, anyway."

"Gosh, you almost sound pessimistic."

Baier shook his head. "Not really. This country has been building toward this for a while now. The old regime lost a lot of credibility when the Stalinist show trials of the early 1950s were exposed later that decade and in early sixties. And the first real liberalization move came back in '63 when the Writer's Union re-evaluated Franz Kafka's life and work. He had been discredited by the old Stalinist regime, but now he's celebrated as a national hero of sorts."

"And the Soviets?"

"That's the sixty-four-thousand-dollar question. And that's where we probably can make our biggest contribution as an office. It looks like there is still a big debate going on in Moscow. You know, over how much latitude to allow the locals. This country occupies a very important strategic position in Europe, situated on the German and Austrian borders. And it also functions as a bridge between the northern and southern halves of the Pact. You're aware of how much the Soviets fear another invasion from the West. It's one reason they like to demonize West Germany so much. It plays well at home. Probably always will. 'Comrade, have you killed a German today?' is something you still here occasionally in the USSR."

"And then there's the neighborhood."

"Absolutely. Whatever happens here could become contagious to the other Warsaw Pact states. It's happened before. You gotta believe that that is on the minds of all those old farts in the Kremlin."

"So, where do we come in? What do you have in mind for me?"

"We need to be out on the street, meeting with local officials. And not just those in the government. You served in the Army, right? Drafted?"

Krohn nodded.

"As I recall from your personnel file you were able to avoid a tour in Vietnam, right?"

"Yeah, I lucked out and got to do my time in Germany."

"Then you might be able to chat up some former or current soldiers here. Leave any actual Soviets to the more experienced among us." Like myself, Baier thought. "They can be a tricky and dangerous group. I think it would be a good idea for you to team up with Frank Kehoe. This is his second tour. That still makes him a rookie of sorts. But his last tour was in Warsaw, which also puts him miles ahead of you on knowing how to operate in this environment."

"Anything in particular you want me to look out for?"

Baier thought for a moment. "We have picked up rumors from the Brits about a KGB plot to infiltrate more hardliners into various institutions and government departments. The real focus, though, appears to be the other non-communist parties, like the Social Democrats and Christian Democrats. Those two no longer play the loyal role of fellow travelers, something imposed on them after the coup in '48. They're now acting like real and independent political clubs. The KGB move, if true, shows the Soviets are still worried about where all this will lead and the need to build barriers."

Krohn stood to go. His wide smile suggested his enthusiasm remained undimmed. Baier hoped it didn't infect Kehoe as well. Then again, everyone seemed to have fallen prey to the contagion known as the Prague Spring…or almost everyone.

Baier stood. "Oh, there is one other thing."

Krohn stopped just short of the door to the anteroom, where Baier's secretary sat typing away with furious concentration. The tip of her tongue sat between her lips, almost like a schoolyard parody.

"Yes?"

"The guy who stopped by the consular section the other day, the one the State guys there called us about."

"You mean the walk-in? Who just as quickly walked out?"

Baier nodded. "That's right. See if you can find out who that was and what he was all excited about. What drove him to come here and then run away again."

"From what I've heard, it sounded like the guy was nervous as hell."

"Could be. But that's all the more reason to investigate. I'd hate for us to miss out on a possible contact or someone with a valuable piece of information. Did the folks in consular pick up anything else on him, any information that could help us track him down?"

"I think they got a name. If it was a real one."

"Well, we'll never know until we start looking. Take Kehoe with you. He should be able to tell you where to look. Start with a government directory to see if he has a post somewhere and what kind of access he might have."

"Sure thing, Boss."

Krohn almost skipped out the door and passed Baier's secretary. She did not bother to look up. The keys of the typewriter beat out a familiar staccato rhythm as Baier shut his office door.

• • •

Baier decided to follow his own instructions and called the Foreign Ministry. He had been cultivating the deputy chief of the European and NATO division since the beginning of March. Gustav Pillar was a career diplomat who had initially advanced in the Foreign Ministry thanks to his loyal service to the Communist Party. At first, Baier had been dismissive of the man's potential as a source of information on internal government planning and deliberations, as well as relations with the Soviet Union. It was almost as though the man had feared that his last name—similar to that of a Communist Party functionary—raised suspicions about his competence and loyalty, as though his career might have progressed through some form of nepotism.

Pillar must have held a similarly negative opinion of Baier, who no doubt had made it onto the local security service's list of suspicious Western diplomats. He had studiously avoided all possible contact with Baier—as well as every other American in Prague. In fact, the State Department diplomats had told Baier to feel free to chase the guy, since they did not plan to go beyond the formal exchanges that would allow both sides to keep contact to a minimum. "A royal waste of time" was how they had labeled the man.

As it turned out, however, Pillar soon proved to be a big fan of Dubček and the reforms underway since the First Secretary's elevation in January of this year. It was almost as though he had suddenly seen the liberal light or remembered the idealism of his youth. He had spent the war years in exile, first in France, then in Canada—not Moscow—which distinguished him from so many in East European party leaderships. Most of that latter crew had been built of a similar stamp: Stalinists like Gottwald, East Germany's Ulbricht, and Hungary's Kadar. Pillar's background and initial exposure to world affairs must have been of a more liberal kind. It was also showing itself now in his enthusiastic support for the Prague Spring and its new openness to the West. He also appeared to have bought into the open and free cultural and political expressions that had become so common in the changing Czechoslovakia.

"I guess this Pillar character played the party loyalist as a means to promote his career," Baier explained to his deputy chief one day.

"So, the guy was a cosmetic Commie," the deputy, Steve Garrity, had responded. "Can you trust the man if he's that superficial?"

"There's only one way to find out," Baier said.

The catalyst for opening up to Baier had been the meeting in Dresden on March 23, where the leadership of the "Warsaw Five"—the USSR, Poland, Hungary, Bulgaria, and East Germany—had pressed the Czechoslovak delegation to explain and justify the new "Action Programme" that Dubček planned to release. The pressure and clear distrust of where the Dubček Government was taking Czechoslovakia had surprised and worried the Czechoslovak leadership. It had also created a lot of resentment in Prague.

"Well," Baier began, "your neighbors may not be happy, but your government is still moving forward. I haven't seen any sign of a Red Army buildup on your border."

The two men sat in a small café about a mile from the Ministry's seat near the Hradčany Castle complex and just blocks from the Charles Bridge. It was tucked around the corner along a cobblestone path that ran from the bottom of the long stairway that rambled down the hill from the Castle walls above. Perhaps it was the long walk back up that kept other Czechoslovak bureaucrats from visiting the café. Whatever the reason, the locale provided a comfortable cloak of privacy. It was also part of a neighborhood where Baier had ample opportunity to check on—and lose, if necessary—any surveillance. They had agreed that it would still be wise to avoid being too open about their budding friendship, and this location would give them a convenient and secure spot to avoid any curious or suspicious eyes.

Pillar had arrived first, and he had chosen a table in a corner near the back where they sat out of sight of passers-by on the sidewalk but still had a good view of anyone who walked by or decided to come inside.

"Ah, yes, so far so good. But one can tell that the suspicion and unhappiness are still there, especially in Moscow."

"Only there?"

Pillar waved a free hand in the air. "Oh, no, no. All our neighbors are nervous. Well, except maybe Yugoslavia." He leaned in close enough to give Baier a close look at his friend's dark red tie that appeared to have a couple of food stains on it. "I believe Tito enjoys seeing anything that brings discomfort to the Kremlin."

"But why are the others in your neighborhood so uncomfortable? One would think they'd welcome the chance to make their own regimes more popular. It's not like their subjects are enjoying much in the way of prosperity and cultural freedoms."

"Ah, but you see, that is a big part of their problem," Pillar explained. "They realize how fragile their hold on power is, and that without the support from the Soviet Union, not to mention the presence of the Red Army, to suppress any troubles…"

"Like in East Germany in 1953 and Hungary in 1956?" Baier interrupted.

"Yes, yes." Pillar lit a cigarette and, in his excitement, leaned in even closer to Baier. It was so close that Baier had to move back about a foot to escape the cigarette smoke that drifted towards him from the table, reinforced by new streams that poured from Pillar's nose. "That is exactly right. And don't think the Kremlin is unaware of their concerns and fears."

"Are there any meetings coming up, similar to the one that took place in Dresden in March? I can't thank you enough for the information you provided on that gathering. Our policymakers in Washington found that truly invaluable. And I am including the President in that group."

Pillar sat back and let another stream of smoke loose, but far enough away to drift safely over Baier's head. This time, he also turned his head to the side to spare his new American friend any more discomfort. "Are you telling me that your report made it all the way to the President of the United States?"

Baier had no idea who had read his reports, or if any of them even made their way out of CIA Headquarters. "Absolutely. Especially as it was straight from the horse's mouth. Or kind of. And I can assure you that more reporting along those lines would be highly appreciated. Well rewarded, too."

Pillar stayed silent for about a minute, maybe longer. He finished his cigarette, then slowly lit another. This time, he did not bother to turn his head. Instead, he let the smoke slip from his lips as he studied his American guest.

"What kind of reward? And why would that be necessary? Since you are an American diplomat, I am happy to provide you with information and insights on developments in Czechoslovakia. Your country is very important to us. It is in our interests to see that you are fully aware of what is happening here." He smiled as he brushed a long ash from his cigarette. "Besides, your money is no good here. There is nothing to buy. Or almost nothing. Not yet, anyway."

Baier sat for a moment. He knew he must move cautiously. He did not want to scare the man off by making a pitch too early…or at all. "At the least, I could keep you supplied with good American cigarettes."

"Marlboros? Or Winstons?"

"Either. Or both."

Pillar smiled again. "That would certainly be nice. But I would not want any American beer."

It was Baier's turn to smile. "I can certainly understand that. Given what I've been drinking over here for the last year."

"Good then," Pillar said as he stood. "I need to get back to my office. Shall we meet again in a week or so? Perhaps I'll have more information on a meeting that is being planned."

Baier stood. "Another meeting? When and where?"

"I'm not sure. I do not think a decision has been made yet. But when I find out, I will be sure to let you know. Let's talk next week. Perhaps I will have more information for you then."

"Perfect."

Baier extended his right hand. He wanted some sort of assurance that they would continue their cooperation, maybe even expand it.

Pillar stamped his cigarette out in the white porcelain ashtray on the table. He studied the blue and white pack of local cigarettes in his hand before shoving it into the pocket of his blue sports coat. "I will leave first. Then you should wait a few minutes before you leave. It is probably best if we do not depart together."

"Of course," Baier replied. He had been thinking the very same thing.

• • •

As he entered the street, Baier felt very good about two things.

One was the sunny weather that promised to carry over into the weekend. He had promised his wife Sabine that they would escape for a weekend away at a mountain lodge in the Slovakian highlands. He had wanted to give them both the chance to spend some time together, away from Prague and away from the pressures of his job.

Both had been happy when Baier took his assignment to Prague, since Sabine would be able to accompany him on this posting. None of the European positions were considered too dangerous, certainly not dangerous enough to prevent a tandem assignment for an officer and his or her spouse. Sabine had been supportive throughout Baier's career, and that had continued ever since their arrival in Prague the previous summer. The assignment had been a reward of sorts for the work Baier had put in as the Director's adviser for strategic affairs during the previous three years. Moreover, Sabine clearly cherished the opportunity to return to Central Europe, and to a post right on Germany's doorstep, as it were. After all, her parents were not that far away, tucked into a pleasant housing development for refugees from the east outside Hannover. That city was in northern Germany and on a direct line west from Berlin—and it was in West Germany, the good Germany.

But the excitement of their time in Prague with all that was going on—and especially for the last six months—had meant less time at home together. Even without the excitement surrounding the Prague Spring, Baier's position as Station Chief meant that he had to make himself available for all sorts of emergencies and personnel issues that left even less time for a home life. They needed this little vacation.

The other thing that made Baier smile was a sense of satisfaction that he was moving his relationship with Pillar onto another plane, a higher level of confidence. It promised to be a significant source of information from a man who appeared to have access to decision-making and communications in Prague, and possibly with Moscow, access that could be invaluable in the days and weeks ahead. Baier was sure that Pillar did not need to be a recruited and controlled asset to provide valuable information, and he did not want to jeopardize a source of such quality by playing the numbers game of recruitment. Then again, Pillar was behaving as though he knew there was more to Baier's role than that of a traditional Foreign Service officer—and it did not seem to bother the man at all.

That good mood, however, the sense of satisfaction that was almost sublime, disappeared in a moment. There on the sidewalk, just two blocks ahead, two familiar faces loomed. They were two faces that sent a shock wave down his spine, where it buried itself with a nauseating landing in his stomach. Jaroslav Havlíček stood facing Baier in a prosperous-looking blue pinstriped suit, his overcoat dangling on his shoulders and a cigarette resting between the fingers of his right hand.

And he was looking straight at Baier, a smile as wide as the Vltava River on his face.

Standing next to him was a German—an East German, to be exact—an East Prussian aristocrat by birth and one who had served faithfully in the *Wehrmacht*, only to join the East German Stasi after the war. Alexander von Hoehn was the German's name, although he had dropped the aristocratic 'von,' a wise decision given the way things turned out in his part of the Fatherland. He, too, was looking straight at Baier and with a smile as wide as the Elbe.

Both men resumed their conversation. Then they shook hands and disappeared into the crowd. What they were doing in Prague and apparently together was something Baier knew was about to keep him awake at night.

CHAPTER NINE

The Tatra Mountains really were beautiful. At least, Sabine thought so, and that's what was most important at this point. She had complained on several occasions of being imprisoned in Prague ever since their arrival on Baier's new assignment the previous summer, when he joined the CIA's Prague Station as the new chief. Baier had found a small but cozy cabin on Štrbské Pleso, a lovely lake in the Tatra range, which ran close to the Polish-Slovakian border. It was also quite popular, but their cabin was isolated enough to give them the privacy and relaxation both needed. Aside from boating excursions and meals in nearby restaurants and cafes, the Baiers encountered no one who could invade their solitude. Sabine expressed her appreciation for the chance to catch up on her reading—mostly German postwar novels like Siegfried Lenz's *The German Lesson*—something Baier tried to do as well.

That was until the third day of their vacation. They had decided on a brief road trip to see the Gerlach Peak, reputed to be the highest mountain in Czechoslovakia. It was about an hour's drive from the cove where their cabin sat, and it had been well worth the drive. The soaring peak of stone that rose just above a tree line of pine caught and reflected the sunlight like a beacon. It was surrounded by similar, although slightly smaller, mountains that ranged across the horizon like some sort of natural fortress, one that was almost impenetrable to the surrounding region and the challenges of the Cold War.

They stopped at a small café along the road back to the lake for a light lunch. It had that idyllic look of a cross between a log cabin and a stone house, which seemed to fit perfectly with the surrounding scenery. Baier and Sabine had discovered that the word 'light' could rarely be applied to the Czechoslovak diet, which relied primarily on heavy dishes of schnitzel, potatoes, and the occasional vegetable. Since that was what they were expecting for dinner, both were hoping to find something akin to a salad or sandwich on the menu.

The waitress had just delivered their plates—a beet salad for Sabine, a cucumber companion to a sliced chicken sandwich for Baier—when a tall, thin man approached their table.

"I am glad to see you are able to enjoy some of our beautiful country this time. I doubt you had such an opportunity twenty years ago."

Baier stood and held out his hand. "Sabine, this is Jaroslav Havlíček." He turned his face toward the unexpected visitor. "So, that was you on the street the other day. It has been quite a while, and a lot has transpired." Baier gestured toward Havlíček with his free hand, nodding at the fashionable mountain hiking outfit. "You seem to have gotten on well. I would have said something back then, but you disappeared so suddenly."

Havlíček took Baier's hand. "Yes, I apologize for that. But there was an emergency that needed my attention.'

"Well, I hope it wasn't too serious and that everything turned out all right," Baier said. "But how did you come to be here at this café and at this precise moment?"

Havlíček smiled. "Just luck, I guess. I was hiking in the area and driving back to my cabin when I saw you two get out of your car. So I worked up the courage as I drove past to swing around and say hello. It really is a small world, you see."

"Amazing." Baier turned again to Sabine. "Dear, do you recall that time I had to come to Prague back in 1948? It was right before we married."

"Yes, of course," Sabine answered. "You left me to make all the wedding arrangements."

"Yes, you're right. And I have apologized several times. In fact, I expect to be doing so years from now. But you did such a magnificent job. In any case, after the communist coup, I helped Jaroslav escape to West Germany. I even drove him to the border."

"Actually, he saved my life. And I shall be forever grateful."

"Tell me then, Jaroslav, what became of you afterward? Obviously, you survived the crossing and made your mark in a prosperous and free country."

Havlíček smiled and waved his hand at nothing in particular. "It wasn't so bad. There was a bus there to take refugees like me to an internment camp near Regensburg. They helped us find lodging and work, which was pretty difficult at first. As you are both no doubt aware, there were also many German refugees in need of the same thing. And many of those came from the old German settlements in Eastern Europe, including the Sudetenland. So, as you can no doubt imagine, Czech refugees were not a high priority."

"No, of course not," Sabine agreed.

"Ah, but that's where the United States came in. The Army and civilian organizations were naturally able and ready to help those fleeing from communism. They provided me with a job at Radio Free Liberty for broadcasting into Czechoslovakia."

"How lucky for you," Baier said. "Do you still work there? If so, then you must be taking a terrible risk to come back here."

"Oh, no, not anymore. I became a West German citizen and eventually secured a spot in the Foreign Ministry. I guess my diplomatic background helped, as did my mother's German heritage." Havlíček's face, too, had a serious, even grim look. "You are also aware that the Germans have a blood, or sanguinity, requirement for citizenship."

"Yes, I am aware of that as well," Sabine said.

"Still, what are you doing back in your old county now?" Baier asked. "I would imagine that you must be on some kind of list of escapees, or even nefarious traitors to the proletariat."

"Well, if so, an arrest would be difficult to execute. You see, I have diplomatic immunity. I am here on official business. I work in the department that addresses the claims of the German expellees from Eastern Europe."

"I see. But I can't imagine there's much sympathy in the East for those kinds of claims. It's not like the Germans left behind much in the way of goodwill in those territories."

"No, of course not. But you can probably understand that the German expellees represent an important voting bloc in West Germany. So, we have to make an effort."

Baier thought for a moment, then nodded. "Oh, sure." He paused, chewing his lip and studying Havlíček for some kind of clue, something to indicate the plausibility of his story. He glanced down at his sandwich resting on the table. It looked more and more appetizing with every word that delayed his lunch. Then, he looked up at his guest.

"But how is it that you are able to work here as a West German diplomat? Your country has no embassy here. Doesn't the Hallstein Doctrine make that sort of thing nearly impossible?"

Havlíček nodded and glanced around the café. Oh, I carry a diplomatic passport and visa that allows me to travel separately. True, there are moments when governments in the region are less than hospitable, but they generally find it in their interests to be accommodating. Eventually."

"Interesting. So, no long prison spells or expulsions? You know. Getting yourself declared *persona non grata*?"

"Well, that would be the worst of it. The latter, I mean." He shook his head. "But nothing like that has happened here. Not yet, anyway."

"Well, I'll let you get back to your work. Are you researching some claims in this area? I don't recall there being many Germans in this part of Czechoslovakia."

"No, actually. I was enjoying a day off and decided to see some of the Tatra range. It really is beautiful here. I've just rented a cabin for the night and will probably return to Prague tomorrow. Perhaps we could have lunch sometime."

"Yes, of course. Just give me a call at the Embassy, and we can set something up." Baier started to sit, then stood up again as Havlíček turned to go. "Oh, yeah, who was that man you were talking to the other day? He looked vaguely familiar."

Havlíček smiled. "That man? I doubt you know him. He's an East German, working at their Embassy here."

"His name?"

"Alexander von Hoehn. He no longer uses the old aristocratic title, although I get a kick out of using it when I see him. He comes from East German nobility. Prussian, to be exact. As you can imagine, I'm sure, he lost his family's holdings. There are only Russians settled there now."

"Well, in any case, good luck with those claims. I'll see you back in Prague."

Afterward, Baier sat in silence, staring at the door through which Havlíček had disappeared. Finally, Sabine spoke up.

"It really is a small world."

"Not that small."

"I was wondering about that. That last name sounds familiar. Are you sure you've never met the old Prussian?"

"Oh, but I have. Our paths crossed on a number of occasions in Paris when I was working to get the man you refer to as 'that fucking Russian' out of Europe. Von Hoehn was trying to prevent it. He works for the Stasi."

"What does that say about this Havlíček fellow?"

"That, Sabine is a very good question. And I do wonder about his explanation for his diplomatic mission here. It sounds kind of far-fetched."

"Yes, he does appear to be exposed in a country like this, especially without an embassy to turn to in the event of trouble."

"Yeah, I'll have to add that to the list of questions I am going to try to answer as soon as we return to Prague."

CHAPTER TEN

For the next two weeks, Baier's Czech contacts had gone silent. It was already early July by the time Baier heard another word from any of them. Baier had little time to worry about Havlíček or von Hoehn, as events began to move at a quicker pace in Prague. Several days after he and Sabine returned from their Tatra vacation, they attended a chamber music concert at St. Vitus Cathedral in the Hradčany Castle complex.

Begun in the 10th century as a Romanesque church, it was redesigned as a Gothic cathedral in the 14th century. Due to the Hussite Wars, however, construction was halted in the 15th century. Work resumed in the late 19th century. It was finally completed in the 1920s, and the church was consecrated in 1929. Like so many buildings in Prague, it reminded both locals and visitors of the city's tremendous historical legacy. This one, though, spoke especially loudly of that heritage, with its vaulted aisles and the numerous chapels that lined the walls along both sides of the cathedral. Each one had its own history, but perhaps the most outspoken and symbolic was the vault of Wenceslas, the early medieval ruler who had done so much for Prague and the Czechs during his reign. Not only did it hold his tomb, but the crown jewels as well.

"Those look pretty vulnerable resting there," Sabine had whispered on an earlier visit.

"Ah, but the spirit of Wenceslas is said to protect them," Baier had responded.

"Good luck with that," was all Sabine had said.

When Baier and Sabine entered on this occasion, they were struck again by the enormous and elaborate Neo-Gothic interior that stretched for yards and yards. Baier would have given the length of the thing as half a mile, such was the optical impact of the long nave and high altar at the back. It was the kind of setting that did justice to an evening of Mozart's chamber music. If Baier remembered correctly from his time in Vienna, the young genius had also spent some time in this city and probably in this very church. The only drawback was that the hard wooden pews were not all that easy on the rear end. Certainly not for two-to-three hours of polite sitting. Mozart's Piano Concerto No. 40 did make up for it, though.

The church—actually the entire Castle complex—embodied so much of what Baier loved about his job. As a devotee of history, he loved the opportunities to dig deep into the past and the culture of the countries in which he served. That same feeling usually occurred when he visited the Foreign Ministry in the former Černín Palace, a living tribute to Prague's and the Czechs' and the Slovaks' place in one of the great European empires. To be sure, the locals did not always see it this way. They were often too busy trying to survive the consequences of their country's troubled history, especially over the last twenty years. For Baier, places like St. Vitus and the Hradčany Castle grounds were a tangible link to the region's history and the people who inhabited it.

As they strolled out of the Cathedral's side entrance with the large crowd of fellow music worshippers once the final notes drifted into the evening air, Baier felt a light tug on his elbow. When he glanced behind him, he saw his friend from the Czechoslovak Foreign Ministry, Gustav Pillar. He, too, was accompanied by his wife, Marianne, an attractive blonde nearly as tall as her husband. Like Sabine, she was attired in a woolen dress of dark blue, warm enough for a mid-summer night in northern Europe, one that had yet to make up its mind about where to take the coming days and weeks. It was also formal enough to impress an audience of the city's elite. Both men wore similar suits of deep navy, giving off the impression of serious scholars in a popular academy of classical music.

"Come, walk with us to our car. We parked just outside the castle walls near you," Pillar said. "I recognized your vehicle when we arrived."

"Of course," Baier answered. "Did you enjoy the concert?"

The question was addressed as much to Pillar's wife as to the diplomat.

"Oh, yes," she agreed. "We attend these events whenever possible. There are so many in churches around the city. It is one of the few ways the regime allows us to enjoy them."

"The churches or the concerts," Sabine asked.

"Both," Marianne replied.

As the foursome approached the entrance to the castle complex, Pillar slowed and let his wife pull ahead. Sabine recognized the implied signal and hurried to catch up with Pillar's wife. Baier lingered to match the Czech diplomat's pace.

"I would love to engage in pleasant chitchat about the music this evening, which was marvelous, by the way. The Bratislava Chamber Orchestra is really quite good, although I am sure you experienced superior performances during your time in Vienna."

Baier smiled. "If you say so."

"My real purpose in coming here tonight, though, was to meet with you." The Czech turned to study Baier's face. "And I must apologize for not returning your calls this week."

"I have to confess," Baier explained, "I was a bit surprised by that after our last meeting. I was hoping we had come to an agreement. Of sorts."

Pillar stopped. "Yes, yes. About that. I have decided to give you as much help and information as necessary, but I will not need any sort of reward. And certainly not a monetary one."

"I am sorry if I alarmed you. I just thought if you did have to take the risk, you should be compensated. It would also make clear the sort of business relationship I had in mind, one that we are already close to establishing."

Pillar frowned. He started to speak.

"I brought the subject up in hopes of building even more trust between us," Baier added, "and quickly."

"I believe that our mutual interests in a free and hopefully soon-to-be democratic Czechoslovakia will ensure that."

"Yes, let us hope," Baier agreed, halfheartedly. "But I would still prefer to arrange the timing and location of the meetings when you have information to exchange. Also, to be able to inform you of what interests Washington has. Particularly if they are specific."

Pillar thought for a moment. He looked ahead to see where their wives were waiting in the street just across the bridge that spanned the old moat to the castle.

"Yes, I suppose that makes some sense. But I may have to make changes sometimes. Or contact you first if something comes up."

"Okay, but let's see how things work out."

"And I want you to be aware that I am speaking to you with the knowledge of my superiors." Pillar took Baier's arm. "They agree that this could be a valuable avenue for communications between our governments." He paused. "In any case, I do have information to pass along tonight," Pillar continued. "Now, in fact."

Baier noticed that the man suddenly appeared to be nervous. Very nervous. He repeatedly surveyed the crowd as it thinned, as though he were watching for familiar faces. Possibly dangerous ones as well.

Baier stepped closer. "Okay, what is it?"

"There has been a new meeting scheduled for later next month. I heard references to it at work just yesterday."

"Another meeting? Like the one in Dresden?"

"Yes, certainly with the Soviet leadership. It may take place in the Soviet Union, which, as you can no doubt imagine, has me and others worried. People have a habit of disappearing there."

"Yes, that's true. Do you have dates, an exact location?" Baier pressed.

Pillar shook his head. "No, not yet."

"Well, we'll need you to try to get them. And as soon as possible."

"Yes, yes, of course. But you must give me a day or even more. It could be difficult this far in advance."

"But we're already nearing the end of June. If the meeting is supposed to take place in July there are only a few weeks or days to go."

"This is true. I can read a calendar, Mr. Baier. But it could be as much as a full month further on. Perhaps even more."

"Okay, okay. Let's try to meet again in two days."

"Three might be better."

"All right. But no later."

Pillar nodded his assent, then ran to catch up to his wife. Baier walked more slowly if only to give the Pillars time to separate themselves and depart alone. When Baier got to his car, Sabine was already seated in the driver's seat. She held out her hands for the keys, which Baier passed to her. She started the engine, then passed a folded slip of paper to her husband.

"This was on the passenger seat when I opened the car. I see you did not lock it."

Baier shrugged. "You never know who may call." He took the slip and read the message. "Be aware. You are being followed by our friends." It was signed simply 'H'.

"So, what does it say?" Sabine asked. She pulled away from the curb and started to drive west, away from the Old Town and toward the suburbs where many diplomats resided.

"You haven't read it?"

"Of course not." She glanced at her husband. "You know better than that."

"Sorry. It's kind of dramatic. It says I need to be careful. I have company these days."

"Well, of course you do. That goes with the territory."

"Yes, but this sounds different, more ominous."

"It doesn't say who, does it?"

"No, but it isn't difficult to imagine whom the author could mean."

"Perhaps that's the real mystery and message. It could be someone other than the locals or the KGB."

"Hmm, yes. That's the beauty and the downside of it. Written like a professional. But leaving me wanting to know more. Signed, for example, with no more than an initial."

"How intriguing. Which one?"
"H."
"Your friend from the Tatra Mountains?"
"I would assume so. I can't think of another 'H' I would recognize so quickly."

CHAPTER ELEVEN

His two young protégés—if you call first- and second-tour officers whom he had never met before this tour such a thing—sat across from Baier in his office. Both were visibly nervous, shifting their weight in their chairs every few minutes.

"We've made contact with the KGB. And not just one of them, but two."

Frank Kehoe was almost bragging. Krohn wore a look of concern, sorrow almost. He had more trouble than his colleague getting settled, and his downcast eyes spent most of their time concentrating on the carpet.

"Together, or separately?" Baier asked.

"No, we reached out separately."

"How did that happen? I told you guys to work on your outreach together on this." Baier frowned, his lips tight and his eyes hard. "And I told you to leave those Soviet creeps to someone more experienced. You were supposed to concentrate on the locals."

"Well," Krohn began, "we wanted to reduce our footprint, so to speak. And we thought branching out separately would allow us to spread a wider net."

"I'm not sure I understand." Baier stared at the more junior officer. "Why were you chasing Soviets? And why do you look as though you've just lost your dog?"

"We wanted to increase our targeting pool," Krohn explained. "You know, run across more possibilities. We also thought we wouldn't stand out as much if we occasionally operated apart."

"Okay, that answers one of my questions. But again, why the Soviets? They're a difficult target. For one thing, I doubt they're operating in that wide a net of their own. They don't generally have a lot of freedom when they serve outside the USSR. In fact, they're probably comparing notes with each other as we speak."

"Yeah, we realize that. But we thought it might be worth the risk. If even one of them is genuinely interested, he's unlikely to let on to the other guy," Kehoe said.

"And even if one or both are interested, they're unlikely to betray that to the other one," Krohn added. "Besides, those sorts of guys are likely to have the information you want on Soviet infiltration of government ministries and political parties."

"Okay, okay. But at this point, you don't know if either one gives a damn. You have their names?" Both officers nodded. "And you've sent them back to Headquarters for the background search?"

They nodded again. "We wanted to see what the 201 files had to say before we proceeded any further."

Baier thought back to his own battles with the guardians of the 201 files, so named because of the numbering code attached to reports involving the broad array of people Agency officers contacted or investigated during their official duties. They provided a ready source of information on an individual, as well as the opportunities—and risks—he or she could present for possible recruitment or even simple contact.

"Good," Baier announced. "But now that you've made contact, let's proceed cautiously. The Soviets are good at dangling people for potential recruitment, when their real goal is to expose our activities. And they are undoubtedly very concerned—and active—with developments moving along the path they're on here and the pace of change."

"But, as you said, Sir, this is really important now, especially with reports from our British friends about that active KGB campaign to infiltrate the liberal parties." Kehoe paused. "Not to mention the government ministries."

"Yes, that's true," Baier agreed. "And don't forget our own wall of obstruction in headquarters."

"You mean Angleton?" Krohn asked.

"Yep," Baier replied. "James Jesus himself."

Krohn started to stand but then fell back into his chair. Baier studied the young man and walked slowly around his desk. He leaned back against the front of his desk and crossed his arms.

"Is something wrong, Paul? You look like that dog you lost is a puppy."

Krohn glanced up at Baier. His gaze seemed to pass right through his chief and focus on the low, rolling hills just beyond the rooftops outside the window.

"It's the walk-in you asked us to look into, Sir. I found out his name."

"And?"

"Gregor Cirek. He's a junior officer with the security service."

"The StB?"

"Yes, Sir. It sounded like he was about my age as well."

"Have you spoken to him? Did you find out anything more about him?"

Krohn nodded, then shifted his weight again. "Yes. I found out that he's missing. He hasn't reported to work since the day he showed up here."

"And you know this how?" Baier pressed.

"I heard the KGB guy I approached talking to a colleague—at least, I assume it was a colleague. They both spoke Russian."

"And how's your Russian?"

Krohn nodded again, several times. It looked as though he was glad to have a positive answer for a change. Somewhat positive.

"It's pretty good. I took it in college and got some intensive training back at Headquarters."

"Yeah, now that you mention it, I remember seeing that in your file," Baier said. "How did they sound?"

"Pissed. At least they weren't happy about it, from what I could tell. They complained about some heavy hitters from Moscow taking a tough approach to keep everyone in line.

Baier sighed as he walked back behind his desk.

"Then we should be extra careful. Maybe you two should give a wide berth to any more Russians you've been thinking about approaching. I do not want to have to write any sad letters to your families back home. I haven't had to write any yet, and I do not plan to start now."

• • •

Later that afternoon, Baier forgot about the risks his overeager subordinates were taking as he pondered the reasons for Havlíček's return to Czechoslovakia and his relationship with von Hoehn. None of his thoughts were encouraging. And there were other problems.

Baier had tried on two occasions to meet with Gustav Pillar after their encounter at the concert at St. Vitus Cathedral. On both occasions, he arrived a half-hour early after a two-hour countersurveillance run to wait for Pillar at the restaurant just south of the Charles Bridge in Prague's version of a modified and much smaller Venice. The first time had been three days after the musical evening, and the second one day later. Pillar had been AWOL both times.

That alone could be explained. Pillar was not a recruited asset. So, he was not bound to follow the protocol of an espionage operation by adhering to a strict schedule and practicing the countersurveillance techniques that Baier would gladly teach him. Although Headquarters had approved Baier's recommendation to try to establish a closer relationship and see if the Czech diplomat was ready for a pitch, Baier still had reservations. Now they had grown.

What really bothered him, though, was the note Pillar had left with the head waiter for him. It simply said, "Sorry." No explanation. All that did was set Baier's imagination loose to conjure up images of Czechoslovak security officers surrounding Pillar at his desk to prevent him from taking lunch outside his office—or something worse.

Baier had tried twice to call Pillar at his office, only to be told that the deputy director was not available. Baier thought back to the man's sudden nervousness after the concert. Had he noticed surveillance? Had it been an issue all along, something Baier missed because of the beauty of the evening and its entertainment?

Because he had grown overconfident of the regime's popular support and strength? He sighed. None of this was helpful.

On top of this, Baier had discovered that he had come under much heavier surveillance of his own. The note in the car had not really been necessary. Countersurveillance was a natural part of an intelligence officer's daily routine, and the more he thought about it, the more the fact that Baier had discovered an increase in his own company on the street was no surprise. There were obviously people in Prague who were uneasy about all this new freedom and the prospects for the country's future if these developments continued.

The real issue of interest for Baier, however, was who the hell had penned that warning, and what it was meant to convey beyond the few words inscribed.

• • •

The ambassador's office looked much the same as Baier had seen it in 1948. Twenty years on, and American diplomatic tastes in Europe remained unchanged—pretty much. The Columbia University mementos, personalized photographs, and souvenirs from Ambassador Steinhardt's tenure were gone. In their place—in fact, not far removed from the very spots where Steinhardt's had kept watch—were those from the distinguished career of Jacob Beam. What first caught Baier's eyes—and those of every visitor—was the orange and black Princeton pennant that hung on the wall behind and a little to the left of the ambassador's desk.

Baier had to admit that he preferred the new university decor. Not because of the university itself, but because Beam's father had been a professor of German Literature there. Ambassador Beam, a career Foreign Service Officer, or FSO, also spoke the language, a skill that Baier recognized as such and appreciated. He wasn't sure how the locals felt about that, though.

"So, *Mein Herr*, to what do I owe the pleasure this morning?" the Ambassador asked.

Baier smiled. The title was one Beam often used with Baier, an acknowledgment of their shared interest in that country's history and culture.

"Well, Sir, I wanted to bring you up to date on what we've been hearing and our efforts to get additional information. Hopefully, some specifics as well."

Beam leaned back in his chair as Baier took a seat on the edge of the sofa that stood to the side of the ambassador's desk.

"Sounds good to me. Is it anything my own staff hasn't heard or reported on?"

Baier nodded. "I think so, but I can't be sure as yet what the implications are. We're still hoping to flesh things out."

"Okay, go on."

"Well, it all remains pretty preliminary at this point, but there are some troubling signs regarding Soviet pressure on Dubček and his government."

"Like what?"

"Like a KGB effort to infiltrate government ministries and political parties to ensure they have the lackeys they need in places of influence and authority."

"Do you have any specifics yet?"

Baier shook his head. "Unfortunately, no. But we are trying to find assets that could help us. I also have a contact that might be able to provide me with some additional insight and details."

"Who is this contact?"

"I'd rather not say, Sir, at this point. Let's just say things have become a bit more difficult than before. That's one of the things that has me worried. He's become more cautious lately. And his behavior is more erratic. Basically, he has a nervous look these days and is a lot less forthcoming. He's also been a no-show several times. The man is clearly bothered about something."

"Okay, I can understand that." Beam leaned forward, covering the back half of his desk with arms that had the shirtsleeves rolled almost to their elbows. "And I will add that this does clash with the reassuring material we've been getting from our diplomatic and governmental friends. They all sound pretty confident and comfortable these days."

"Sir—"

The Ambassador held up his right arm with the hand open and facing Baier. "I'm not saying you should sit on your information. But given its potential impact—not to mention that it conflicts with what we're still hearing—I'd like to see some more substance to it."

Baier leaned forward in turn. "Of course. I agree completely. We'll continue with our efforts, and I'll let you know as soon as we have something we can source appropriately."

Baier left the ambassador's suite with a sense of determination and concern. He had initially assigned his two junior officers, Krohn and Kehoe, to an operation that he had considered more of a sideshow when he first heard of it. The fact that the Brits had found little themselves before tossing the issue to their cousins now looked to have been a misleading signal. Not only that, but now the Ambassador was aware as well. That probably meant that he was likely to develop a growing interest in the chief of station's operations and suspicions. Particularly if the material that Baier and his people were picking up ran against the grain of the Embassy's State Department reporting. Baier realized he had to move quickly, given the importance of any early warning signs on an issue so critical to US policy and interests; he also needed to move with caution. He did not want any of this to blow up in his and his Agency's face.

CHAPTER TWELVE

The weather continued to warm as June moved on to July. The politics grew even more heated. That came with a personal stamp for Baier as he studied the two young case officers in his office.

"So, tell me just how the hell this came to happen."

Krohn and Kehoe sat uncomfortably on the sofa across from Baier's desk. He could see that both men were not only sore and bruised, but also embarrassed. Neither one could look Baier in the eyes for more than a second or two. Both wore the scars of their recent encounter. From what Baier could see they had come out on the losing side. Then again, he had yet to see the other guys—but he was not optimistic.

Krohn was the worse for the wear that had been inflicted. He had a deep bruise over his left eye, scratches along his right cheek, and wads of cotton stuffed in his nostrils; Krohn repeatedly rubbed his left shoulder and upper arm.

Kehoe, on the other hand, had only a split lip and a scratch along his forehead. His right hand, primarily the knuckles, was scraped and red. It looked as though he had been in a fight with a sheet of sandpaper. Baier hoped he had done some damage with that fist at least.

Krohn glanced over at Kehoe, who leaned forward.

"Well, Sir, a gang—"

"A gang? How many?"

"Four, I guess."

"You guess? Were some invisible?"

Kehoe laughed lightly. He looked too sore to do much more.

"No, Sir. But it all happened pretty fast," Kehoe explained. "They came at us from an alley and immediately dropped Paul here, " Kehoe glanced over at his companion, "and started kicking him. I jumped in and got in a few good shots. But a couple of others pulled me off the one doing most of the kicking."

"How many of those were there?"

"Two." Kehoe held up two fingers from his left—and undamaged—hand. "Then these other guys worked over my midsection with a couple of tough punches, probably so the beating wouldn't show." He nodded, his eyes on the wall to his left. "They knew what they were doing. Undoubtedly professionals."

"How long did it go on?"

"It seemed like hours but was only about five minutes," Krohn answered. He winced as he spoke, and his gaze stayed focused on the floor.

"So, who do you think did this? They didn't take anything, did they?"

"No, Sir." Krohn spoke up again, but this time he looked at his chief. "It was obviously a message for us."

"What do you think that message was. And who did it come from?"

"Hard to say, Sir. They didn't say much. And when they did speak, it was definitely not Czech or Slovak. It was pretty garbled. You know, lots of dialect. Or so it sounded."

"Oh, I'm pretty sure it wasn't Russian," Kehoe added. "I also took some during my undergrad years at the University of Oregon. It sounded a lot like that, but it was still different. If you know what I mean.."

"But you two are not sure? Even with some background in Russian?"

Kehoe glanced over at his colleague. "We talked about it afterward, and we both think it was probably not Russian. Just not absolutely positive. I mean, it could have been Ukrainian or another Slavic language close to Russian."

"But you're definitely leaning toward something from the Soviet Union?" Baier pressed.

Both officers nodded.

"Well, then, my guess is that the message was to warn you guys off any of their people here in Prague. You must have made too much of a splash from your approaches to those other KGB officers. I take it neither of those two were involved."

Both men nodded, looking at each other like wayward pupils.

Baier paused as he spun around to look out the window at his rear. He shook his head, then returned his focus to his two junior officers. "Goddammit. I blame myself for this. I should not have let you out there on this kind of target without more explicit instructions. The environment is a lot more open and congenial in Prague these days, but that does not mean that a target like this is any easier."

"I think there was something else, Sir," Krohn added.

"And that would be?"

"Well, one of them whispered to me just as they were leaving that if we didn't mind our own business, we'd get what Cirek got. He said those words in English, too. Pretty heavy accent, but I could still understand him."

"You mean that walk-in we lost?" Baier asked.

Krohn nodded. Kehoe stared at his colleague, shaking his head.

"Yes, Sir," Krohn continued. "And we also found out why the guy is missing."

Baier stepped to the side of his desk, hands on his hips.

"Go on."

"He's dead. His body washed up on the banks of the Vltava a couple of days ago. About a mile south of the city."

Baier sighed and shook his head. He stood, then stepped around his desk to get a closer look at his two officers.

"Is that why those Soviet assholes came after you? Were you pressing to discover more about that walk-in?"

"That's probably part of it," Kehoe broke in. "We didn't want to give up on the guy. You thought it was important enough to ask us to check his story out."

"Yeah, but I also told you to stay away from any Soviets. At least for now." Baier returned to his seat behind the desk. "Do you think the Soviets killed him? And if so, why?"

Both officers shrugged. "We can't say for sure," Kehoe continued. "But he must have been on to something pretty important."

"We'd both like to find out just what that might have been." Krohn looked over at his partner, who nodded in agreement. "Not to mention a chance to get even."

"Let's back up a step, guys. I want you both to back off this target for now. Let me look into this to get a better idea of just what we're dealing with, and what it means for us and our operations here. I also want to be sure that none of the locals were involved. I don't doubt that there are still some unhappy campers in the intel service here who no doubt think their glorious battles for the proletariat are under assault by the Dubček Government."

"What do you want us to do in the meantime?" Krohn asked.

"First of all, I want you to check in with the medical office to make sure your injuries are not any more serious than they look. Get bandaged up, grab some painkillers if you need 'em, and have someone check to make sure you don't have internal injuries." Baier pointed to the door. "I will speak with Gruzsauskas, the Regional Security Officer, to see what he has to say. He's pretty discreet, so I think we can keep this affair under the Embassy radar."

• • •

The RSO, Ralph Gruzsauskas, was as surprised as Baier by the recent assault.

"We haven't noticed much in the way of gang or even basic criminal activity here in Prague. That doesn't mean, of course, that it doesn't exist, but your case sounds pretty intense."

"Thanks, Ralph. That was my initial reaction as well."

"Initial? Does that mean you've had further thoughts on who might be responsible?"

Baier shrugged. "I've got a few ideas."

"The Soviets? KGB?"

"Maybe. But I need to run a few things down before I come to that conclusion."

"Really? That would be my first guess. I mean, who else would it be?"

"But it would mark a departure for them. We generally follow a hands-off policy regarding each other's officers. If that's changed, I need to know why and who made that decision. Plus, how far that's going to go."

"Well, let me know what you come up with. If those creeps are going to start beating on our personnel, they need to be warned."

Baier nodded and turned for the door. "Of course. I'll be sure to keep you in the loop as much as I can."

• • •

The following morning Baier dropped by Peter Mikulski's office in the Station. Mikulski, the son of a steel worker who grew up outside Pittsburgh, was the station's CI, or Counterintelligence, chief. He had the best idea of who and what was operating in the local KGB *rezidentura*. After all, that was his job.

"That would be a real departure," Mikulski agreed. "At least from years past."

"So, what, the KGB gang wants to play rough now? And if so, how is that going to change the operating environment?"

Mikulski held up his hand to settle his chief of station. Both men stood in front of Mikulski's desk. His office was one door down from the chief's, and Baier had nearly thrown himself through the doorway in his rush and excitement. They braced themselves just a few feet apart, as though they were discussing a conspiracy. It was certainly something very sensitive and, Baier suspected, a whole lot more real.

"There was a cable from Headquarters a few months ago," Mikulski continued. The desk got together with some analysts to research a new GRU, or military intelligence, unit that was formed a couple of years back. In 1963, to be exact. Their official nomenclature is Unit 29155."

"So, we're not looking at the regular KGB?"

"We're not looking at the regular GRU either. These guys appear to be butt-kickers. I doubt they're collecting much in the way of military intelligence."

"No order-of-battle stuff and equipment?"

"Probably not. If it is this bunch. We haven't had any indication that people from that relatively new group are here, but it's something we definitely want to look into. Anyway, you are well aware from your own experience that the GRU often does a lot of the Soviets' dirty work."

Baier thought back to his confrontation with the Ukrainian assassin in Paris and Rome.

"Oh, yeah. Like assassinations, kidnappings, and so on and so forth."

Mikulski smiled and nodded. "Exactly. It looks like this group is dedicated to just those sorts of things. But until now, their activities have been geared mostly to turncoat Soviet officers and officials, as well as the occasional dissident."

"So, you think they could be going after opposing forces, as it were. People like us."

"It's a possibility. We can't say for sure. At least not yet."

"But if that is the case, it changes our work here considerably."

"I would say so. That's why I think we need to nail this down as soon as possible."

Baier thought for a moment as he paced the short space in front of Mikulski's desk.

"I'll have Krohn and Kehoe swing by to give you their story and look at our mug book of Soviet officers assigned here."

"Good. But I'm pretty sure this crowd that jumped our guys is unlikely to be in that. They're probably brand new here." Mikulski studied Baier to see if he could read any sort of reaction to this new information. "Which raises other questions, of course."

"Yeah, of course," Baier agreed. "Like why now and to what purpose? I doubt they roughed up members of our team for sport. Or practice."

"No." Mikulski agreed, "they probably don't need any of that."

CHAPTER THIRTEEN

Two weeks passed with little or no movement—on anything. Baier was growing increasingly frustrated, a mood that affected his work and even the atmosphere at home.

"Can't you at least enjoy some of this beautiful weather we're having?" Sabine complained. "It's well into July already. I'd hate to see this summer go entirely to waste."

"Should we plan another trip to the Tatra Mountains?"

"No, of course not," Sabine replied. "You've got work to do. I just don't like seeing you so restless and bothered. Besides, I do not need or want another vacation. I want you to stop wasting your time with all this fretting and anxiety."

"It's not a waste, Sabine. The mood in this town is shifting. I can feel it."

"Well, you're going to have to do something more than work on a feeling, Karl. You know that as well as I do."

"Believe me, I most certainly do."

A week later, Baier had an opportunity to do just that. He finally made contact again with Gustav Pillar.

Baier had tried to introduce a secret means of communicating, something his colleagues—and Baier—often established once they had a fully recruited asset. Pillar recognized Baier's proposal as a step in that direction, something he had tried to avoid. He had firmly resisted the suggestion during their brief encounter at the musical evening in St. Vitus Cathedral. Even so, when the telephone calls went unanswered, Baier decided to take a chance. He left a message in a sealed envelope with an Embassy stamp for Pillar one evening. Baier had waited for his contact to leave work at the Foreign Ministry and thrust the envelope in his hand as he walked past Baier near the front gate and the long downhill path from the castle complex.

Baier had suspected—or hoped—that Pillar was resisting his efforts at establishing a regular system and calendar for contact because of the strong possibility of surveillance and observation inside the Ministry, especially if KGB efforts to infiltrate the political parties and government offices were making any progress. This exchange would allow them to arrange a meeting without the risk of someone overhearing their conversation or being warned by some bothersome busybody or sycophant. The note simply suggested a mark on the base of one of the statues on the Charles Bridge. The statues would alternate according to the week and the day with periodic rescheduling to avoid the risk that came with predictability. In any case, both men would have an easy excuse to stop at that place, given the popular attraction of the site.

It worked.

"Thank you for coming, Gustav," Baier said as soon as they were seated at the small restaurant in the quaint neighborhood nestled under the Hradčany castle and near the Vltava. "I am so glad you answered my call." Baier held up his hand when Pillar started to protest. "I understand your position completely. This does not mean that you are an asset of any kind. As I see it—and I hope you do, too—we are friends in touch to discuss important matters of state, just like other diplomats. It's what we do."

"And yet," Pillar replied, "you are the first diplomat I have met who wants to establish a regular means of communication, and that in a surreptitious manner."

"Well, given the developments and continuing tensions in your country, I really do believe that we need to take certain precautions."

Pillar smiled and nodded. Then he gave Baier a look of acknowledgment and shook his head. He slipped out of his dark gray suit jacket, which he spread over the back of his chair.

"Yes, I quite agree. I guess it will not surprise you to learn that there are tensions within our government on the path forward with the reform movement. Even in our Ministry itself. And let us ask no further questions about our respective assignments."

Now, it was Baier's turn to smile. He ordered a bottle of the local white wine and waited for the waiter to leave to search through the wine cellar.

"I would expect as much. These are monumental times. Historical, even. So, it can't be easy. Can you tell me more about these tensions and divisions?"

"Yes, that's why I decided to take you up on your offer to meet again. These are things I think your government needs to be aware of." He paused to make sure the waiter was not approaching their table. "As you can imagine, a big issue right now is our relationship with the Soviet Union, but there is also our position in the Warsaw Pact."

"Of course. That's an awfully big and threatening neighbor you have."

"Don't I—I mean we—know it. We keep trying to reassure the Kremlin that we have no intention of leaving the Warsaw Pact, but they are finding it difficult to accept our assurances."

"Well, they probably remember that that's where the Hungarian reformers wanted to take their country back in '56. I don't suppose you can say at this point that others—perhaps after Dubček leaves, whenever that might be—might not decide on a more western alignment for the defense and security of your country."

The waiter returned with a chilled bottle of sauvignon blanc. Pillar waited for the man to fill their glasses and then leave. He looked over at Baier and nodded vigorously. The wine glass in his hand even shook, sending small ripples against the rim.

"Yes, yes. That is it exactly. Brezhnev and his crew worry that we have started down a slippery slope, and they worry about reaching a point of no return. I believe that is why they resist just about everything we're doing, even on purely domestic matters, like our free press." He sighed. "And don't get me started on the issue of free and open elections."

"But surely they understand that stasis is not an ally for them. Things change; times change, along with expectations.

This will be especially the case as Western Europe grows more prosperous."

"Yes, of course. But despite the Marxists' claim that they look to the future, I do not believe that any Marxist government—including ours, or at least the previous ones—have had any vision of the future beyond confronting all challenges to their hold on power. It's a fallacy to assume that a socialist future and regime stability are mutually inclusive. At least, not the current system of socialism imposed by the Soviet Union. That is what we are trying to change."

Baier sipped his wine, thinking of how to get to the particulars that consumers in Washington would really want to hear. In the end, he pushed straight ahead.

"Can you tell me who might be arranged on which side in all this?"

"Certainly, you understand if I wish to keep the names of my colleagues at the Ministry out of this for now."

"Yes, of course," Baier agreed. "As you wish."

"Within the Party, though, I believe there are two schools of thought on the way forward. We have what I would call the radical reformers grouped around people like Smirkovsky, Cernik, and Kriegel. Then you have the old hardliners around Bilak, Kolder, and Svestka. It would undoubtedly help your government understand who has the upper hand by following who among these men and their followers move into positions of authority and responsibility."

Baier jotted down the names on a paper napkin. "Thank you very much, Gustav. This is certainly very helpful. Can you say which group has the upper hand at the moment?"

Pillar shrugged, then emptied his wine glass. Baier poured him another. The ice cubes in the silver metallic holder rattled like dice on a bare table.

"I would have to say that right now the reformers are the stronger group. That, of course, is because of the leadership of Mr. Dubček." He held out his hand, the index finger extended. "But in the end, I believe it will come down to the position of the Kremlin. And that remains a mystery. For now."

Baier looked up. "One more question before we eat."

"Yes?"

"What about the Soviet troops still stationed here? They came in for some joint maneuvers, as I recall. Yet, they haven't left for home."

"Ach, those bastards. Yes, they are still here, but there are plans for them to depart soon." Pillar smiled. "Now, if they were American troops, no one would be pressing for their departure. That is, as long as they brought blue jeans and rock and roll with them. All the Russians bring is vodka and theft with some occasional rapes."

"You mentioned the name of Cernik. I was wondering if you'd heard that name before. A younger man, possibly with the security service?"

Pillar savored his wine for about ten seconds, rolling it around in his mouth while he studied the ceiling. When he put his glass down, Pillar stared at Baier for several more moments.

"Why do you ask?"

"I understand his body turned up on the riverbank a little while ago. A tragic end to such a young life. Don't you agree?"

"Yes, I do. The man did not work at our Ministry, although he did have some liaison responsibilities with us for the security service."

"Any relation to the reformer on the Politburo?"

Pillar shook his head. "No, none at all."

"Interesting timing, don't you think?" Baier added.

"In what way?"

"Just when things are opening up in your country. I hope there wasn't a political or security issue involved."

Pillar took another sip of wine and spent another ten seconds testing its quality and aftertaste.

"Yes, I agree. I will see what I can find and pass along any relevant information. Please do the same, Karl."

"Of course." Baier tried to sound reassuring, but he had to ask himself why his guest had suddenly become evasive and withdrawn.

The two men ate their dinner when it arrived and spoke no more of world affairs. The tables around them filled with other diners, and neither felt comfortable carrying on their conversation. Baier certainly did not think the time was right to press for more information. He had to admit, though, that his *duck á l'orange* was excellent. The Czechs apparently could cook more than sausages and schnitzel.

• • •

When Baier returned home later that evening, he found a note taped to the front door. It was from Sabine. It simply said, "You have a visitor waiting for you inside. Be careful."

After he pocketed the message, Baier stepped through his front door, alert for any sudden movement behind or to either side of him. Instead of an attack, he found the visitor seated on the far side of the sofa by the bay window in front of the living room.

He nearly swallowed his tongue. Sitting back with his legs crossed and a cigarette in his right hand was Alexander von Hoehn, the former Prussian Wehrmacht officer and current East German Stasi Colonel.

"I was wondering when you'd get around to calling on me," Baier said.

CHAPTER FOURTEEN

"To what do I owe the dubious pleasure?" Baier asked. "I don't believe you have met my wife, Sabine."

The East German stood and bowed. He responded in German, a modest nod to Baier's heritage and comfort with a common language for both men and Sabine.

"Not until tonight. I have heard of her, as you can imagine. She has an excellent reputation as someone who is strong and has helped you on several occasions."

"Are you referring to our adventure in Berlin?"

Von Hoehn nodded. "That and others. Budapest, Vienna. There are probably more." He turned toward Sabine. "Perhaps someday she will get to meet my wife. I am afraid, however, that she is Russian. I understand that you do not care for those people."

"Just certain ones," Sabine replied. "I am sure your wife is lovely and charming."

"So, what do you want at this late hour?" Baier pressed. He was certainly not in the mood for a casual conversation, or even a modicum of hospitality. He noticed that von Hoehn did not have a drink, and he silently thanked his wife for not offering one to their visitor.

Von Hoehn resumed his seat and crushed his cigarette in the brass ashtray on the end table.

"I appreciate your desire to get right to the point, Herr Baier. As you have surmised, this is not a social call. After all, it would hardly be appropriate, seeing as how we represent two opposing sides in world affairs."

"Yes, something like that. And our last meeting in Paris was hardly cordial. Or cooperative."

"Ah, but you did escape unharmed from that hideous little flat my Soviet colleagues had preserved as a safehouse, of sorts."

"After you killed a man I was trying to bring home with me."

"But didn't Comrade Chernov escape as well? Wasn't that your original mission? I would have thought you would see that the death of that fat Ukrainian assassin was, as you say, icing on the cake?" The Prussian smiled. "Besides, I had motives of my own, which I will leave for another day."

Baier sighed in exasperation. He slid out of his coat and tossed it over the opposite edge of the sofa from von Hoehn's seat. He dropped into the armchair at his side, as his whole body seemed to slide from tense anxiety to relaxed caution. He knew that this was a dangerous position to be in with the man sitting across from him. Baier leaned forward. Sabine excused herself and walked into the kitchen.

"I think that's enough history for one evening. What is your purpose in calling on me at this hour this time around?"

"Well, as I said, this is not a social call. My purpose is more professional." Von Hoehn smiled and opened his suit jacket wide so that Baier could see what might lie inside. There was nothing: no weapon, no wire—nothing beyond a white dress shirt and the silk lining of an expensive suit jacket. The inside jacket pocket lay flat against the coat.

"Other than showing off the expensive tailoring, which I presume you acquired in West Berlin, I don't see any point in that maneuver."

"Let's just say I wanted to demonstrate that I come in peace."

"That's reassuring."

"In fact, I come with a friendly warning."

"Friendly?"

"Yes, friendly. You will understand, of course, if I must remain a bit cryptic. No mention as to the source of my information. And I would also expect complete discretion on your part."

"Doesn't sound like this will be of much use then."

"Oh, but it is. Or it should be. You see, you are under close surveillance these days."

Baier sat up and shrugged. "I hardly find that surprising. I expect—and have found—surveillance of some sort to be a constant in an environment such as this one. We are, after all, behind the Iron Curtain."

"Do not misunderstand me, Herr Baier. It is not the local service. Nor is it my service. In fact, the KGB has been operating here with a light hand against your people these days, as they have a great deal to do otherwise."

"Like infiltrate the government ministries and political parties that have re-emerged under Dubček?"

Von Hoehn smiled and sat back against the sofa. He pulled another cigarette from the pack in his shirt pocket. Baier noticed that the cigarettes were Winstons. The East German lit the cigarette, inhaled a lungful, then let the smoke escape from his mouth and nose. The space around von Hoehn's head filled with the smoke and perfume-like scent of the American cigarette. He did not answer Baier's question.

"You and your people are the subject of a new group that has recently arrived in Prague. They are just now beginning to operate outside the USSR, and this city is a new proving ground of a kind."

"Would it be the GRU team we've spotted? This new 29155 unit?"

"Ah, good." Von Hoehn stamped out his half-finished cigarette in the ashtray and leaned forward.

"It is a good thing that you are aware of their presence. But you may be surprised that you have become a target. And it is not because you have grown so close to that Czech diplomat. What is his name? Pillar?"

"Why would a GRU team worry about that? Our exchanges are entirely diplomatic."

Von Hoehn almost laughed. "Oh, of course they are. But no, they do not care about that. I believe he is quite safe. As you say, there is a convenient diplomatic cover for your relationship. No, they have bigger and more strategic worries."

"I see. And what might those be?"

Von Hoehn stood. "I will let you figure that out for yourselves. I am sure you are more than capable. But please, do be careful. I think some of your people have already had a run-in with that crew."

Baier stood in turn. "Thank you, Herr von Hoehn, for the information and the warning. But why would you want to reach out to me on this? I mean, those thugs are your allies."

Von Hoehn started for the door. "I find people like that distasteful. You should have learned that much in Paris, Herr Baier."

"But it's not like your own service is all that light-handed. In fact, they've been known to be pretty damn brutal. You know, kidnappings and the like in Berlin. One of your stars, this Markus Wolf, has proved to be a master at that sort of thing."

"You should also know, though, that we are not a monolith, Herr Baier."

"I've never found any gaps."

"Perhaps you never knew where to look."

Von Hoehn smiled. Baier would almost have said that there was a twinkle in his eyes. Then again, he never knew a Stasi officer to throw off a sparkle of any sort—unless he was arresting someone, or crushing them for a sarcastic remark or some anti-party humor.

"And some of us have other equities we carry," the East German added.

"Like what?"

Von Hoehn gave only a slight and quick response as he hustled out the door.

"I have said enough for one evening. Good night, my American friend."

"What can you tell me about the death of a young man named Cernik?" Baier shouted after the Prussian as he strolled down the front walk.

"There is a letter."

"About what?"

The only answer Baier received was a brief, cold gust of wind that seemed to blow in from the steppes to the east.

• • •

Baier stood at the window and watched the man disappear in the street outside. An old saying came to his mind at that moment…something about having friends like that and not needing enemies.

As soon as the door shut, Sabine rejoined her husband in the living room. Together, they watched the Stasi officer amble down the street and disappear into the dark night air.

"Do you think you can trust him? I mean, it all sounded so friendly and solicitous."

Baier's gaze stayed with the street outside. "But if it was that, then what was he trying to solicit?"

"Probably anything he could get."

"I do wonder about his motives in coming here, though, and how this might fit into his end game. Whatever that might be."

"Well, I wouldn't spend too much time on it. Have you ever known anyone from that group to have a subtle game plan, and one that could help you in any way?"

"Not so far. But I get the sense that this one is keeping his bets open."

"About what?"

"About the future. It has to look fairly uncertain these days."

• • •

As soon as he arrived at work the following morning, Baier trotted down the hallway to Mikulski's office. The chief of the counter-intelligence branch bolted out of his chair, surprised by the rush of the station chief through his door. Baier strode right up to the edge of Mikulski's desk.

"I had a very interesting visit last night," Baier said."

"Night or evening?"

"Oh, it was late. Really late. It was after ten."

"Jesus, I hope everything's all right. Is Sabine okay?"

"Oh, hell yes. She's seen and gone through much worse than a late-night business call."

"So, who was it? And what did he want?" Mikulski paused. "I'm assuming it was a man."

"Damn right it was," Baier almost shouted. "It was a fucking Stasi officer. Our paths crossed during my operation in East Berlin, and we had a real-life showdown in Paris. Just ask Pittman. I'm assuming he's not still the chief in Paris, that he's moved on from there. But I'm sure you can find him."

"I will. If you say so. What did he want?"

"He came with a warning. About the GRU hit team, or whatever they are. He confirmed the suspicions from Headquarters about this new unit formed just a couple of years back. In 1963, right?"

Mikulski nodded.

"Then you can send that bit of data back to Headquarters. He went on to say that we are in their sights. He didn't say why or what they plan to do. But I think it's safe to assume that the beating Krohn and Kehoe got were part of whatever damn plan those assholes have brought from Moscow."

"Well, that also suggests to me—and probably to you—that Moscow has something bigger in the works. I mean, why push that envelope further at a time when the Dubček Government is pushing its reform program full steam ahead?"

"You're probably right. But my guess is that Moscow still hasn't made up its mind about what it wants to do, or believes it needs to do. That's where we come in."

"What do you want me to do, Chief?"

"My first step is to find out more about the East German presence here, and this contact in particular. We may need to reach back to Headquarters."

"We haven't really concentrated on that bunch of East Germans, as you well know. We just don't have the resources right now to go after even a second-tier target right now." Mikulski paused for a second. "We do have a photo collection on the Stasi station here, however. The ones we know of anyway."

"Yeah, I'm sure you do. I want to know just where this guy fits in. And let me work on the approach. This character is a clever, complicated bastard. Believe me, at times I think I was lucky to have escaped with my life when we confronted each other in Paris." Baier thought back to the sudden turn of events, triggered by von Hoehn, in that small, cramped safehouse on the Montmartre. "The guy's got motivations we can only guess at. At this point, anyway."

"Should I get Headquarters to do a 201 search?"

"Yeah. I need to know what else he's been doing in the interval. And have them check on his wife. He mentioned her to Sabine last night. Somehow, I get the sense that he was being more than just polite."

Mikulski sat back down at his desk. "What's the Kraut's name?"

"This one is Alexander von Hoehn. At least he was born with the 'von.' He doesn't use it anymore, at least not officially. Too much baggage for the workers' paradise." Baier almost laughed. "However, I do get a kick out of throwing that title at him every once in a while."

"Any impact?"

"Nope. He just ignores it. Probably had to learn to do that to survive in his present environment."

"In any case, the last name starts with an 'H,' right?"

"Yeah, that's right. So?

"Didn't you say the note in your car toss was signed with an 'H'? Do you think he was the author?"

"That would make sense. The messages were very similar. He probably intended for that to pique my curiosity, so he could deliver the main part in person." Baier smiled. "Thanks, Pete. I told you he was a clever bastard. Probably pretty damn good on tradecraft as well."

"Yeah, and like you said, complicated, too. Be careful, boss."

CHAPTER FIFTEEN

Nearly a whole week wasted. Only four days actually, but they felt like more, given the hassles and boredom of trying to sit or stand unobserved and remain inconspicuous while still holding a fix on the target. He and Mikulski had taken turns surveilling the East German embassy, hoping to catch a glimpse of this von Hoehn character, chart his movements, and get a sense of his routine and preferences.

The embassy's location on the banks of the Vltava made the job easier and more difficult at the same time. There was a steady stream of pedestrians that flowed along the street out front, allowing Baier and Mikulski to blend in with a crowd, such as it was. There were also benches across the street underneath a small row of trees that gave both men, working the site alternately, the chance to grab a seat now and then. Even then, the corner location and the warren of streets behind the building gave them little opportunity to arrange a thorough stakeout.

Still, the scenery was beautiful, especially the building's architecture. The East Germans had scored one of the more interesting buildings in Prague, an elaborate art nouveau-style thing with medieval-looking figures arranged along the red-tiled roof, which provided a convenient resting place for small flocks of live birds, all of them looking down on wonderful designs that framed the windows and front entrance.

The façade was certainly better looking than anything Baier had ever seen in East Berlin. Of course, the commie Krauts had draped everything here in a pale gray paint that blended with the brown soot and looked as though they were trying to get everyone depressed despite the elaborate figures. It probably worked well back home. Even then, Baier found himself staring at the decorations from time to time, only to remind himself that he needed to give his full attention to the comings and goings of the Embassy personnel.

Von Hoehn, however, appeared to have become a ghost. Or maybe he had taken a mid-week vacation. Baier doubted it.

"I told you the guy was good," Baier explained. "Real good."

"You can say that again," Mikulski shifted his coffee cup on the end table in Baier's office. "But don't." Mikulski paused, as he studied the floor at his feet. He looked up. "Maybe he isn't assigned to the embassy here. What if he's here on some kind of unofficial cover?"

Baier blew out his breath and played with a pen on his desk. "I kind of doubt the Stasi would do that. I think an official presence carries more weight, especially in a Warsaw Pact country. There still isn't much love lost among these East European allies—if you can call them that."

"Well, the alliance is pretty official," Mikulski replied. "There's even a treaty and all that."

"Any word from Headquarters on this guy and his past?"

Mikulski shook his head. "Nope, nada. The guy's been a ghost, or pretty close to one."

"Well, in any case, I doubt very much if he's here on some unofficial posting. The national and geopolitical animosities run pretty deep, given the brutal history in this part of the world. I'm sure the Czechs and Slovaks do not want undeclared Germans of any stripe roaming their country. Whether it's in the interests of the international proletariat or not."

"You're probably right. I guess we'll just have to keep beating our heads against this particular wall."

• • •

Two nights later, Baier and Sabine were enjoying dinner in the Old Town when Havlíček made another unexpected appearance. He was dressed more formally, more businesslike, this time in a dark blue suit and light-yellow cotton dress shirt, but without a tie. Baier guessed that Havlíček was probably more relaxed and informal now that the evening hour had struck.

"Did you just get off work?" Baier asked as the former Czech diplomat approached their table.

"As a matter of fact, yes," Havlíček replied. "I can't believe I've run into you both again. You must think I'm following you." He pulled a cigarette from the side pocket of his jacket and held it up. A Lucky Strike. "May I?"

"The thought has come to mind," Sabine said. She nodded toward his right hand. "Not about the cigarette. And, please, go right ahead. But these coincidences, yes. At least to me. I can't speak for Karl, however."

"An interesting brand, don't you think?" Baier pointed to the cigarette. "Are they still smoking those in West Germany these days? You are probably aware by now that those things were ubiquitous right after the war and even became of form of unofficial currency."

Havlíček laughed. "Yes, they carry a nostalgic weight nowadays. But I happen to like them, so I grab some whenever I can find them."

"Well, good. But this is stretching the limits of coincidence, wouldn't you say, Jaroslav?" Baier added.

Havlíček pointed to an empty chair at the side of the table. "May I? I promise I won't stay."

"Certainly," Baier answered. "What can I do for you? Or should I say, what can we do for you? You don't need help for your German refugees, do you? Has Bonn left you dangling here?"

"Oh, no, it's nothing like that. As you can no doubt imagine, the government here is hardly in a position to anger people at home or in the region by doing the Germans—at least the capitalist Germans—any favors. I keep coming here mostly as a formality."

"Then what is it?"

"Well, mostly I wanted to say hello. I feel as though I still owe you for helping me escape those twenty years ago. You may well have saved my life."

"That's quite all right. I'm happy I was able to help. After all, it was the right thing to do." Baier paused to sip a mouthful of pinot gris. "I do wonder, though, why you're so willing to keep returning to Czechoslovakia. And all alone, as it were. Isn't there a danger in that? Especially if you were in such deep trouble before."

Havlíček waved the thought away.

"I don't think so. As I mentioned earlier, I'm a West German citizen now, and I have diplomatic immunity."

"Of a sort. That is lucky for you, in a way. I believe we mentioned before that there is an ancestry or some kind of blood test for German citizenship. Remind me, where does your German descent come from? Is it prevalent enough?"

"As a matter of fact, it is. It stems from my mother's side. You see, my maternal grandfather was a Sudeten German."

"How lucky for you. But that is also something unlikely to endear you to your hosts here," Sabine observed.

Havlíček laughed. "That sounds a bit odd, coming from Germans like yourselves."

Baier leaned forward and almost leaped from his seat. "I am an American. Granted, one of German heritage. But an American all the same. And my wife is an American citizen now."

Havlíček leaned back, as if he were dodging a blow. "Oh, I am sorry. I didn't mean to offend either of you. It's just that you are both well aware, I am sure, of how long local grudges can linger in this region. I certainly never meant to question your loyalties."

"Forget it," Baier said. "Is there something else you need?"

"Not at the moment, but who knows what sort of future lies in store for this country these days. But I would like to offer my services, should you ever need them. I am, as I have said, still in your debt."

"Well, in that case," Baier began, "what can you tell me of the East German I saw you with the other day? A certain Alexander von Hoehn."

"Who?"

"You know who."

"Ah, yes. You must forgive me. That was not quite 'the other day.' I believe it was some weeks, maybe even more than a month ago."

"Okay then. How do you know him?"

"That was the man the East German Embassy introduced me to for my assignment. I gather he is also a refugee, from East Prussia. They claimed he might know of someone I could approach in the government here."

"So, the East Germans were willing to help refugees who fled to the western and capitalist part of Germany?"

Havlíček shrugged. "They were probably hoping to help defuse a potential dispute over compensation and even border issues. The Soviets would not be happy if their gains from the last war ever came into question."

"I see. And was he helpful?"

Havlíček shook his head and crushed his cigarette in the table's ashtray. "No, not all. He told me my countrymen—the West Germans, I mean—would just have to accept their loss. Like he has, apparently."

"Have you had any other contact with him?"

"No. Nothing more than a passing nod the last time I was at the East German Embassy."

"When was that?"

"Last week. Why?"

"Just wondering." At least Baier knew now that man was still in town, if nearly invisible. It was just as he had imagined.

"Do you have an address or some kind of contact information?"

"No, I only met with him at the Embassy." Havlíček glanced around. "I really must be going. I was supposed to meet a young lady this evening, but she seems to have stood me up."

"We're sorry for that," Sabine said. "I hope it wasn't any fault of ours."

"Oh, no, of course not." Havlíček rose to leave. "My American friends can do no wrong, as far as I'm concerned."

As Havlíček walked to the door, he looked over at a gentleman seated alone at a table by the bar. It was also close to the door.

Baier had the distinct impression that Havlíček wanted the glance to appear to be one of casual curiosity—but his eyes lingered for a moment too long for that. The diner was also the only patron wearing a black leather jacket. Baier had noticed him shortly after he and Sabine had arrived—and he had yet to order anything to eat. He was still nursing his first Czech pilsner.

• • •

"I hope you heard more than a discussion of family pleasantries and past adventures," von Hoehn said.

"Of course, Comrade."

"Then let's hear it."

"Their talk about the past did have some interesting elements, Colonel."

"Such as?"

"Such as the assistance the American provided to Havlíček when he escaped in 1948."

"What did you find so interesting about that?"

"Our friend expressed a continuing gratitude to the American. This Baier gentleman tried to dismiss any sort of debt, but the Czech insisted. Enough that I wondered about where his loyalty sits."

Von Hoen dismissed the officer's concerns with a wave. He studied the young Stasi spy, one of the *Wunderkinder* recruited by Markus Wulf, a rising star in the service, especially its foreign intelligence branch, or HVA. It would not pay to be too casual about a colleague's counterintelligence concerns, not from someone who appeared to be well plugged in at the *Normannenstrasse* in East Berlin.

"Listen,....what is your name again?"

"Herr. Friedrich Herr, Comrade Colonel."

"Okay, Herr. Actually, may I say Friedrich?"

"Please."

"Comrade Friedrich, you will discover over the course of your career that counterintelligence issues such as this will arise in nearly every case. The trick is to learn how to read them properly and establish your control over the asset. This former Czech diplomat burned his bridges to his homeland when he fled to the West in 1948 after the coup. He became completely dependent on the Bonn Government, only to discover that they are nothing more than lickspittles for the Americans and their aggressive imperialism. We have been able to appeal to his sense of fairness and interest in a peaceful future for Europe. Believe me, I have dealt with his kind before. I know what I am doing."

Von Hoehn paused to let this little lesson sink in while he studied the young man. "Is this your first assignment outside our Republic?" he continued.

"Yes. Why?"

"Well, Havlíček could have been freelancing as well."

"Free what?"

"It's an American term. He could have been trying on his own to get closer to the American, this Karl Baier. Get in his good graces, in a manner of speaking. I doubt it will work. This American is too experienced and too savvy, from what I've seen."

"As you say, Colonel. But I also found one element of their conversation at the end very interesting. Especially for you."

"And that was?"

"They closed with a discussion of you."

"Oh, really?"

"Yes. The American was interested in finding out more about you. Where you live, where you work, what your habits and routines are."

"I have none of the latter. You would be wise to do the same."

"Yes, I understand that. But the American clearly wants to contact you. Have you encountered him before?"

"Yes, as a matter of fact, I have. Before you came on board. We had a standoff during an operation in the West. Paris, mostly."

"And how did that turn out?"

"Well enough. Although he did succeed in getting his KGB defector out of the hands of the assassin sent to eliminate the problem. I did succeed in preventing further damage."

"And what was that, if I may ask."

Von Hoehn stood to go. He studied the young man seated across from the desk in one of the hard, wooden chairs von Hoehn had arranged primarily to keep his guests uncomfortable and their meetings short. The room suddenly felt too small, too confining. He had been distracted by the noise from the street all evening, traffic mostly, but drunken yells and shouting, too, plus they had had to keep the windows closed to avoid drawing attention or being overheard, despite occupying a flat on the second floor. Von Hoehn had even begun to sweat some in the stuffy and overheated air.

He thought the young officer was too damn smug. He must be closer than a promising recruit to Wolf. Hell, he acted like he was a relative. Von Hoehn wondered if this young pup was one of the Moscow crowd, like his reputed mentor. He was too young, naturally, to have been one of the crowd around Mielke and Wolf, but maybe his family had been one of those foreign communists living in the Hotel Lux during the war.

Von Hoehn thought of his own sometime mentor, Johann Gracchus. He had emerged from the Lux at the end of the war as well, but others—like Wolf—had apparently outmaneuvered him. Gracchus had been stuck in what many in the service like to refer to as a series of 'horizontal' promotions. Not the rapid rise men like Wolf enjoyed. Then again, even Gracchus had told von Hoehn on several occasions that he was a bit too independent-minded, something that came out during the crisis surrounding the Wall's construction.

Well, we'll see who maneuvers best in this crisis, he thought. It was certainly a different case, not like the earlier outbreaks of distrust toward the Kremlin elsewhere behind the Curtain. He thought of East Berlin in '53, and Hungary and Poland in '56. This was much more challenging, and it called for sensitive hands and deft handling. In any case, von Hoehn decided it would be wise to keep an eye on the young prick.

The bigger problem was the American's plans...not to mention Havlíček's. If he truly did have any of his own. Von Hoehn reminded himself that he would need all his experience and insight, the skills acquired through years of patience, practice and observation, to handle the new challenges in this shifting and dangerous environment.

"I'm afraid that is beyond your security clearance level. Maybe when you're older." And wiser, he thought. And if you survive.

CHAPTER SIXTEEN

It was July 10, approaching the middle of the month. The days seemed to be flying by with all the excitement and tension in the air. The television programming was full of open, almost subversive debate on the future of the country, its corrupt and static political system, and its dull economy. Theaters and films broadcast incisive themes and narratives that would have been forbidden just months ago. It was pretty heady stuff, and Baier was excited to see what new surprises Dubček's reform program might bring to the country and its citizens. More important, though, was the question of whether Dubček's government could continue to play the Kremlin as well as it had so far.

Baier's ruminations were interrupted by a call from Gustav Pillar, which came over an open line. It was as though his fears and worries about meeting with Baier too openly had all but evaporated.

"Can you meet me at our usual place for lunch two days from today?" Pillar asked.

Baier readily agreed. The Czech diplomat's voice sounded relaxed, almost casual—just like one might expect from a foreign diplomat engaging with his American counterpart.

"Of course," Baier instantly agreed. "It won't take much to rearrange my busy social calendar."

Pillar laughed. "That's one of the things I like about you Americans. Your relaxed and ready sense of humor." There was a moment's silence on the line. "Unlike some of the others we have to deal with."

Baier replaced the receiver with an uneasy feeling that his friend had not taken the time to check to make sure that no one was in easy listening distance before his closing remark.

Baier still made sure that he arrived for their lunch about an hour early to survey the streets and the restaurant's entrance to ensure that Pillar did not bring along any unwanted company. The man was not what Baier would consider an asset, more of a foreign colleague willing and even eager at times to provide insights and information of value to a representative of the United States. That was all good and welcome, of course. However, that also meant that Pillar was not a controlled source, one that had undergone a thorough vetting and a modicum of training on how to detect and evade surveillance. Baier dropped a comment now and then about the sorts of things Pillar should be aware of. Baier was pretty certain of the man's motives and loyalties. That was the most important first step, of course. He just wanted to make sure they avoided unpleasant surprises.

A few minutes shy of noon, Baier was seated at a table at the rear, one that was isolated enough to provide minimal security and a clear view of the front entrance. Pillar entered about ten minutes later, a warm smile and loosened collar paving the way past the other diners. He had even left his suit jacket in the office, apparently, which Baier hoped was a good omen.

"Greetings, Mr. Baier." Pillar nearly shouted his welcome. He thrust his right hand forward and pumped Baier's like he had installed a piston in his elbow earlier that morning. "I am really happy you were able to free yourself today."

Baier laughed. "Anything for a good friend like you, Gustav. And please, I suggest we agree to use first names. We certainly do not need to be so formal anymore."

"Yes, yes. I believe we should."

Pillar seated himself across from Baier, spread his utensils, and flapped his napkin open like a circus entertainer. "I have good news." He flattened the napkin on his lap, then looked up at Baier. "Well, I hope it is good news. I believe so, anyway."

Baier leaned forward and pulled his own napkin free. He let it settle over his lap without his guest's flourish, however. "So, Gustav, I am all ears." He smiled at Pillar's look of confusion. "It's an American saying. What is your good news?"

"There has been an agreement for a meeting with the Soviet leadership." Pillar leaned forward in turn, and his voice dropped to a whisper. Apparently, he hadn't thrown all caution and suspicion away. "No date has been set yet, but it looks as though the place will be Čierna nad Tisou."

Baier sat back and ordered a plate of pork schnitzel for both men, as well as a glass of white wine. When the waiter had left with the order, Baier sat forward, his elbows set almost in the middle of the table.

"That's in Czechoslovakia, isn't it?"

Pillar nodded eagerly, "That's right. It is near the Soviet border, but it is still in our country. That means, or it suggests to me, that the Soviets may be coming around. At least we haven't been summoned to explain ourselves or answer for our crimes." He reached across the table and grabbed Baier's hand. "It's a negotiation, Karl!"

"Do your colleagues in the Foreign Ministry share that opinion?"

Once again, Pillar's head bobbed like a fishing line that had snagged one of the good-sized brown trout that swam in the country's mountain streams. "Yes, most do. At least those with whom I have spoken. Of course, there are a few old die-hards, but no one listens to them anymore."

Baier sat back and freed his hand. He waved it in the direction of the Foreign Ministry. "Well, I hope you're right, Gustav. Still, it is a bit of a leap for the Soviets. I doubt they've given up on trying to pull your government back from its reform program."

"Ah, but as I see it, they have accepted that we cannot go back to the beginning, back to the way things had been done before Dubček arrived."

"Will there be anyone else there? I mean, representatives from any other Warsaw Pact countries. You know, like the meeting in Dresden in March."

Pillar shook his head, paused, then shrugged. "I do not think that has been decided yet."

"Do you think your country can negotiate well enough alone with the Soviets? Would it help to have other members of your alliance present, someone who might be able to moderate Soviet views, especially if they can provide a different perspective—a more European one—from Moscow's? Say, someone like Hungary's Kador?"

"I like the way you think, Karl, but I doubt that your viewpoint is shared in many other capitals here in Eastern Europe. True, Hungary is the most likely to support us, but it stands pretty much alone now. The others are probably more concerned with securing their own power. And popular reforms and past protests in Poland and East Germany are keeping those leaders particularly resistant to change."

The waiter brought their dishes, refilled the wine glasses, and then returned to the kitchen. Both men chewed and sipped in silence for ten minutes or so, but Baier could see that the Czech diplomat was bothered by something. He glanced at his food and ate only the occasional small bite. In fact, he spent most of his time stirring the food on his plate and glancing around the room.

"Is something the matter, Gustav? Your mood seems to have changed. What happened to the elation you displayed when I first arrived?"

"Well, there is something else, Karl." Pillar paused, his eyes focused on a particularly large slice of pork that occupied the center of his plate. When he glanced up at Baier, the Czech was squinting, as though he was trying to bring the American into focus.

"Does it help for you to know the location of the meeting?"

"I'm not sure. Help in what way?"

"Well, could you...could you perhaps bug the location? You know, listen in?"

"Gustav, why would we take that risk? That's a very tall order for that kind of location. It will be swarming with security people from both sides. Besides, your people will no doubt answer all our questions. You know we're on your side here."

"But Karl, I am not talking about listening to us. I...we would like to know what the Soviets are saying among themselves. That will be the great mystery. Before, during, and afterward."

Baier sat back and drained his wine glass. He shook his head when the waiter came by with the bottle, his face a question mark as he held the bottle aloft. Pillar covered his own glass as well.

"That is an interesting question. Would your people, the security service, I mean, be able and willing to help?"

Pillar stared at Baier for a moment. Baier could not be sure how long the silence lasted. He was too busy listening to his accelerated heartbeat.

"I am not sure whom to trust among that service. It would probably be better for you to do it alone," Pillar explained.

"I see."

They finished their lunch in silence. Baier did not provide an answer by the time they left the restaurant.

• • •

The very next morning Baier convened a meeting in his office with Mikulski, the CI chief, and Fred Garrity, the deputy chief and head of the Station's technical operations. He briefed both men on his luncheon conversation with Pillar from the day before.

"He really suggested we take this leap?" Mikulski asked.

Baier exhaled and nodded. He leaned back in his chair.

"Yes, he most certainly did. I haven't informed Headquarters yet. But I'm pretty sure they'll want me to give the Ambo a heads-up. As you guys can imagine, there is a considerable risk here."

"Political?" Mikulski again.

"Hell yes, political. This is a delicate time in Czechoslovakia. I'm sure you guys are aware of that. Not to mention in the world at large."

"Technical and operational as well," Garrity added. "I mean, we're not even sure it's going to happen in this town. What's the name again?"

"Čierna nad Tisou," Baier replied.

"And where is that exactly?"

"Near the Soviet border."

"That's even worse. It's not like we have a home-field advantage there. Even if the new regime likes us. The United States, I mean. The verdict, from what I can see, on the part of the local service is still out. That group is probably loaded with old Stalinist types," Garrity said.

"There are some heavy logistical challenges, too," Mikulski added.

"Oh, I'm aware of that," Baier said. "Not only is the town still not locked in, but we don't know which building will hold the discussions or negotiations. Or whatever's going to happen there. And if we're to get any devices installed, we'll need a blueprint of some sort, or at least a thorough inspection to prepare the spot and the cleanup afterward. None of that would be easy, no matter where these folks get together."

"So, Chief, where do you want to go from here?" Mikulski pressed.

"All that aside, the rewards would be massive," Baier said. "Insight into Soviet thinking and discussions would be a bonanza for the Czechs and probably cement a solid cooperative relationship with this regime. It might even help move some of those old Stalinists you mentioned," Baier nodded in Garrity's direction, "into early retirement." Baier smiled at the thought of what he was about to say next. "And you can also imagine how that material would be appreciated in Washington."

"Good Lord, yes," Garrity exclaimed. "Insight into Soviet thinking about reform among its East European satraps. I mean, the plans and preparations for future challenges like these would give our team a definite leg up in the Cold War. Hell, it might even allow us to get more proactive in supporting change in the region."

"So, what do you want us to do?" Mikulski asked.

"Start drawing up some contingency plans, but be sure to work out the risks and rewards. Someone above our pay grade is going to have to make the decision on this one. And I want to be able to present a clear picture to the leadership back home. And to the ambassador. He'll need some warning on this if we're to move ahead. But above all, we must have a realistic picture about how feasible this is if we want to convince people who will make this decision. This can't look like some pipe dream we came up with because a local official got excited over some wine and schnitzel."

All three men stood. They stared at each other for about fifteen seconds, smiles broad and deep. Baier recognized the pleasure and excitement that came with the prospects of a valuable and challenging operation like this one. It was something people in the Directorate of Operations loved and lived for. It was precisely this that brought so many to work for the Agency. Than again, he also recognized the need for a cautious and sober approach. Failure or exposure—especially if it became public—could do more harm than most officers could imagine. But, damn, this felt good.

• • •

Baier felt pretty confident that he could call Pillar directly at his office to set up a follow-up meeting. The man had exuded confidence at their lunch yesterday, and he obviously felt safe enough to suggest what was clearly a clandestine operation directed against the most powerful neighbor and the greatest threat to his country's independence. True, Pillar had hesitated and seemed to have lost some of his exuberance when he raised the idea of a bug at the big powwow later this month. But then, who wouldn't have?

Pillar answered immediately and agreed to meet Baier on the Charles Bridge later that evening. Baier did not want to select another café or restaurant, preferring instead to take a leisurely stroll through the Old Town, like any other visitor to the city. Only this was unlikely to be a stroll and certainly not a leisurely one.

"Yes, of course," Pillar had agreed. "Have you given any more thought to my suggestion?"

"That's why I'd like to see you," Baier answered.

Baier waited for the diplomat just outside the Hradčany complex at the base of the long, winding set of steps that descended from the Castle to the streets below, where he picked up the diplomat as he left the Foreign Ministry. Baier did not greet Pillar at once. He chose the spot so he could follow the man to the Bridge, hoping to ensure that he arrived without a tail. If Baier did spot surveillance, he would use a brush pass to drop a note in Pillar's pocket, explaining the problem and proposing another meeting for the following evening.

Fortunately, Pillar appeared to be unescorted but also unaware. Baier smiled to himself, remarking that despite Pillar's reluctance to become a real-life clandestine asset, circumstances in his country and government were ironically pushing him in that very direction. It would probably be a step too far in the man's mind to receive actual training in subjects like surveillance detection, but continued suggestions and hints here and there should help the diplomat operate in what was becoming a more dangerous environment.

"Ah, Mister Baier, you are late. Not by much, however. I see you are being infected with a Czech's more relaxed approach to time. Not at all like your ancestors in Germany."

Baier shrugged and held both hands out at his side as he walked toward Pillar. Both men stood for a moment under the shadow cast by the evening lights across the statue in the middle of the bridge on its upriver side.

"What can I say? I do apologize, however. I needed to take care of something first. I hope you haven't been here long."

"No, not all. Just a few minutes," Pillar said.

"Good. Come, let's walk a bit."

Baier touched Pillar's sleeve, and the two men turned and headed for the heart of Old Town. Once they had left the Charles Bridge about a block behind, Baier spoke up.

"I discussed your surprising proposal with several colleagues yesterday."

"Oh? And what was their reaction?"

"Interested but concerned."

"About what?"

"Oh, a number of things. The location for one. Are you certain of the town?"

"Yes. That has been confirmed."

"So, I am pretty certain that your service and the Soviets have already begun to establish a security perimeter of sorts."

"That may be the case. I am not privy to those discussions."

"You see, that's one big problem. We would need to have access early enough to study the layout, especially of the rooms and their assignments…"

"Assignments?"

"Yes. It's a question of which ones will be used for what purposes. That would dictate where we plant any listening devices."

"I see. And other concerns?"

"Yes, there are a few more. How, for instance, could we guarantee access for our people to do the work? It would almost certainly require hours of operational activity. If a listening device is planted in the building's structure, it would require some carpentry, painting, and the like to make sure it was not discovered. And that takes time."

"Hmm, I hadn't realized that."

"And then, there is the general matter of time itself."

"I'm not sure I understand."

"Time is already of the essence, as they say. The conference is not that far off, and the clock is ticking. We can be pretty flexible and agile, but this would be a big, big challenge, as you can no doubt imagine."

"Have you mentioned these issues to your superiors?" Pillar asked.

"Not yet. If I do communicate with them—as I will, of course—they will have expected me to have thought these things through. I can't just dump everything in their laps. Not if it's my operation."

Pillar was silent for several blocks as the two men navigated their way around the clock tower and town hall. The gothic towers of the Church of Our Lady Before Týn loomed before them. After about a minute, Pillar sighed and steered them in the direction of the far corner behind the Jan Hus monument.

"Those are certainly important matters that we will need to resolve. I am not sure how much help I can be myself. But there is someone I believe I might be able to engage for this."

"Oh, really? And who might that be? Another diplomat?"

Baier did not mean to sound condescending or abrupt. But just relisting the challenges and problems had made him more frustrated and even discouraged than when he had discussed the proposal back in his office.

"No, no, of course not," Pillar said. "But there is someone in my building who might be in a position to provide some assistance. Or at least some suggestions."

Baier halted in mid-stride. "Gustav, you need to be careful with whom you discuss this. The more people you engage, the more likely you will be exposed. And imprisoned, no doubt."

"I believe this man is okay."

"Why? And how? What is his background?"

Pillar looked over at Baier as they resumed their walk. "You may be surprised to hear that the KGB has liaison officers in nearly all our ministries. They are concentrated in the Ministry of Interior, of course, because that is where the State Security Service is located."

"Yes, I am aware of that. And 'liaison' sounds like a bit of creative labeling. I understand they have the authority to take control of any operation and assets they want."

"Yes, and you can imagine how popular that has made them. Especially now."

Baier laughed at Pillar's obvious sarcasm.

"Well, we have a few in our ministry as well. And there is one in particular who I believe would be willing to help. Or at the least, he would not immediately report us to his superiors."

"And why is that? How does that work? I mean, it sounds pretty fantastic."

"You see, the man is actually Czech. The KGB pulled him from a Siberian camp and sent him back home. With a specific purpose in mind, of course. You will understand when you meet him."

"And when is that supposed to happen?"

"I will set something up. Once I have sounded him out first. I will not put you in danger, Karl."

You may have already done just that, Baier muttered to himself.

• • •

It was Saturday morning, and Baier studied the street below from one of the Agency's three safehouses in Prague. He glanced out the bay window at the front of the building, set in a border of yellow limestone that, when mixed with the heavy air pollution, had assumed the color of faded and patchy urine over the years. It did, however, look out at the medieval Gunpowder Tower that marked the end of the Old Town district, so named because of its previous function as a storage point for just that, gunpowder. Down Celetná Street, the broad avenue that led toward Old Town Square, Baier could see a building that had allegedly been one of the homes of the Kafka family. A few houses further down was where Einstein was said to have delivered the first lecture on his recently developed theory of relativity. Unfortunately, a light rain was falling, leaving the streets and sidewalks with a dark, slippery carpet and showering the historical route in a shadow of depressing forgetfulness. If such a thing was even possible in a city with so much history

It did fit his mood, though. Despite his years of experience and practiced judgment, Baier was relying on a Czech diplomat, allegedly unschooled in the arts of espionage, to bring another individual—one from the other side—into a risky and possibly game-changing operation. His entire career could be on the line, as well as the interests of his country at a time of global upheaval. The ambassador, for one, was clearly worried and unwilling to support such a dangerous endeavor.

"I'm sorry, Karl," Ambassador Beam had told Baier yesterday, "I can't give you my open and full endorsement for something that sounds so problematic and risky."

Baier started to object. The ambassador held up his hand.

"I'm not saying I will forbid it. The rewards are certainly promising. If successful, our country would benefit immensely. But I cannot provide you with cover in Washington if it all goes haywire."

Again, Baier started to say something. The ambassador's hand rose once more.

"The best I can do is say that I was vaguely aware, but that you withheld the details. Which is true. And I do not expect any more from you. I recognize the need for operational security. What I will not do is let you rot in some cell here. I would press for your release until it happened. You would, of course, be expelled. But you already know that."

Baier stood. "That is also all that I can ask."

"Good luck, Karl. I mean it."

Those last words swam around Baier's head as he searched for the two Czechs he was supposed to meet. The rain had dropped to a meandering drizzle, as though to remind Baier just how much his operation depended on luck. And it did not look very promising on that particular morning.

Then, two shadows, moving slowly, emerged from a side street. They appeared to be looking for an address. Baier hoped they were also looking for a possible tail. To blow his contacts and the safehouse in one move would be doubly disastrous. He'd have to spend the rest of his career waiting tables in the Headquarters cafeteria if that happened—and the cafeteria didn't even have waiters. It was all self-serve.

When the two faces emerged under the cloudy sky, they were partly covered by the hoods of their jackets. Baier recognized Gustav Pillar first. That much was easy. But the second face brought a shock to Baier's system. He gasped, his hand flying to his mouth. Baier started to sweat in the clammy, sultry air of the apartment. He threw the window open to get some circulation in the room before he fainted. He almost screamed at the men below.

• • •

"My god," Baier breathed, "I can't believe it. You are actually alive and back home."

Janos Hašek smiled and held out his hand.

"Mister Baier, for my part, you cannot believe how good it is to see you. You know, I never did get the chance to thank you for your efforts twenty years ago to gain my freedom."

"But I failed. You were arrested and shipped off to Siberia, I presume. That was where you ended up, was it not?"

Hašek's smile held. Baier wondered how long the man could hold it. Apparently, quite a while yet, given all that had happened.

"Yes, it was Siberia. And, as you can imagine, it was horrible. But I survived."

"Obviously. But how?"

"I swallowed my pride and crumbled before the overwhelming power of those who held me. I strove to be a model prisoner and a model Communist. Soviet style, of course."

"Is that how you came to be here today? In Czechoslovakia, I mean."

Hašek's smile finally softened.

"Yes, I realize it is difficult to fathom. After many sessions of self-criticism, I was able to convince my captors and their superiors that I no longer posed a threat. Also, because my incarceration no longer served the Party's political purpose. They began to look at me in a different light. Apparently, they decided I could serve a more useful purpose working in a liaison capacity during what so many have aptly called the Prague Spring."

"I see. So, where do you stand on Dubček's reform program?"

"He fully supports it. Otherwise, he would not be here today," Pillar interjected.

"How could you be so sure, Gustav?" Baier asked.

"You recall, I hope, my comments about the generational divide in the Foreign Ministry over the reforms, one that reflects a similar division in the State Security Service."

"Yes, but that would put Janos here on the wrong side of that divide."

Pillar shook his head. "Not necessarily. There is another split. And that includes those who lived and served in Czechoslovakia before the coup of 1948. That is where Janos Hašek comes in."

"And you knew this how?" Baier pressed.

"I knew this because I knew Janos. Or I knew of him. When someone at the Ministry pointed him out to me, I realized I…we had an ally."

"I see. But let me ask the question I should have raised the moment you got here. Were you followed? If so, that could bring our exercise to an end before we've even begun."

"You can rest easy on that score, Mister Baier," Hašek said. "I am familiar with that sort of thing. We made sure we were unaccompanied."

"Good," Baier replied. "That makes the next step easier. Has Gustav told you of our plans, such as they are?"

Hašek shrugged. "Yes, but it does not sound like you have much of a plan. Just a list of obstacles."

"Do you have any advice to offer?"

"As a matter of fact, I do."

"Excellent. I'm sure that will be a great help." Baier started to rub his hands together, then thought better of it. That would probably be too dramatic and possibly sophomoric.

"I suggest you drop the idea entirely."

"What?" Baier stepped back and dropped into one of the armchairs. "What the hell kind of help is that?"

"It is the only help that will allow us all to survive. There is simply too little time to set up a listening and recording operation in the time allowed, given the heavy security and your extremely limited access. In fact, as of this moment, you have none at all."

"So, what then? Do you have an alternative?"

"Yes, I do. I will attend, take notes of the discussions, and steal whatever else you might need. Believe me, it is much safer this way."

CHAPTER SEVENTEEN

"How is this so much safer?" Baier asked.

"Because it involves only me. You do not have to bring in a team. Believe me, I may not have a complete idea of your station's size here, but I doubt you have the personnel available to pull something like this off alone. The KGB, with the help of others, will be able to monitor the arrival of anyone else."

"How?"

"They will swarm to ensure this meeting remains secure. Wouldn't your side do the same?"

Baier had to admit that was almost certainly true. He hated to do so, especially in front of someone allegedly on the opposing team, but now was not the time for false bravado.

"I suppose you're right." Baier's mood was darkening. The euphoria that came with the arrival of this old warrior and the sight of his survival was wearing off quickly. Baier did not doubt that his offer was genuine, and the man was taking almost all the risk on himself. Still, damn it, the thought that this mission would be dependent on him, a man who had only recently re-entered Baier's life and work—in the last few hours, to be exact. This was a man whose last twenty years remained a mystery to Baier. His opinion was not that easy to accept in such a short space of time. "Anything else?"

"Well, yes," Hašek continued. "There is also the issue of access for your people if they did escape notice. I cannot see how that might be possible."

"So, what do you propose? How will you gain access for all this note-taking and potential theft?"

Hašek smiled and took a seat on the edge of a sofa across from Baier. He leaned forward to reduce the space between himself and the American.

"I have thought about this all evening and morning. In fact, I have considered my approach ever since Gustav raised the issue."

'I'm not sure I like the idea of you two conspiring all alone. Especially since I doubt you were actually all alone."

"Please, Mister Baier, you are not the only professional here. Let me explain."

Baier sat back and waved his hand between the two men. "By all means."

"The first step will be to get myself assigned to work on the meeting, which I believe will be possible. If that fails, then of course the operation is over. But in view of my position as a KGB liaison officer in the Foreign Ministry, I can plausibly argue that it fits with my responsibilities." Hašek motioned toward his colleague. "I will also recommend that Gustav go as well, as a representative of the Foreign Ministry. As deputy chief of the Western Hemisphere division and the effective head of the American desk, I…we can make the argument that his views on the possible reaction and plans of your government will be a valuable contribution. Together, our possibilities for success increase exponentially."

"Are you sure?" Baier asked. "You've just doubled the size of your team, which also doubles the risk."

"True. But going from one to two is hardly the same as, say, going from five to ten. Or even two to four."

"Granted. Still, this whole scheme makes me nervous. I'm not sure I can get my people to agree to it."

"What choice do you have?" Pillar interjected. He stepped between the other two men. "You know as well as we do that your original plan…"

"Which came from your suggestion," Baier interrupted.

"…That your original plan is unworkable. Or nearly so. The prospects for the success of this one are immeasurably greater."

"Do you think you can swing your assignment to the meeting? And can Janos get his?"

"We cannot be absolutely certain, of course. But the prospects are good. We have several weeks, between two and three, to work on this. That should be time enough. Remember, the Foreign Ministry and even many in the security service are favorable toward Dubček's reform program. They want to ensure its continuation. And the logic of our proposal to attend the meeting fits with that."

"How so?"

"Voices of reason and support against Soviet pressure will be welcome. I am sure of it."

Baier was silent for several minutes. He stood and walked to the window. The rain had stopped, even the drizzle that seemed to have clouded the entire conversation. At least, Baier's view of it. The clouds remained, however, as though refusing to let the light through and to prevent anyone from coming away with a clear picture of the future. Well, Baier thought, the weather is certainly fitting—and it is also very central European—like this scheme.

Ah, fuck it, he finally concluded.

"Okay, let's give it a try. Remember, though, I cannot give any guarantee that my people back home will approve."

"So, our agreement is tentative?'

"Yes, I'm afraid so."

Hašek stood and looked over at his compatriot, who had joined Baier by the window. "That doesn't really matter. We plan to move ahead in any case. It is too important not to do something to protect the changes here."

"And you think this will do that?" Baier asked.

"At the least, it will help."

The two Czechs walked to the door. Baier followed. He grabbed Pillar's sleeve after the Czech diplomat had pulled on his rain jacket.

"Gustav, can we speak alone for a minute?" Baier looked over at Hašek. "I'm sorry, Janos. There is something I want to raise with Gustav. It will only take a minute."

"Of course," Hašek replied.

Baier waited until Hašek had moved into the hallway. He turned to Pillar and whispered in his ear.

"If things go sour, I want you to know that I will arrange for you and your family to get out of Czechoslovakia. We can do that sort of thing."

"Really?"

Baier nodded

"Then, thank you. That is reassuring. But I doubt it will come to that." He motioned with his head toward his compatriot. "And for Janos?"

Baier looked into the hallway. He knew he had taken a chance to promise such a thing for one man and his family. Not only did Baier not have the approval to arrange something like that for someone who was not a controlled asset, but he had not prepared an exfiltration plan either. Moreover, to promise that for another man, also not an asset of the Agency, was pushing his authority well beyond normal limits. Hell, the new guy was a freelancing KGB officer. Today's meeting had started Baier down a slippery slope without a break or even a berm in sight.

"Yes, Janos, too."

CHAPTER EIGHTEEN

Alexander von Hoehn sat behind his desk in the East German Embassy, staring hard at his guest. Fortunately, von Hoehn's office window looked out over the Vltava, which gave him an unobstructed view of the dim outline of Hradčany Castle about a mile or two away, nesting atop the hill that commanded the city. It allowed him to pursue a more pleasant thought, occasionally.

The Stasi's relationship with the Czechoslovak State Security, or StB, was not always one of socialist brotherhood, something von Hoehn did not, at times, appreciate, and certainly not today. Thanks to its growing reputation as a first-rate intelligence service with a budding list of successful recruitments in the West—largely among gullible and greedy West Germans—the German Democratic Republic's Ministry of State Security, or Stasi, was emerging as the premier intelligence company in the Warsaw Pact. Indeed, even beyond those narrow European confines. Stasi advisors were turning up in far-flung regions such as Cuba, the Middle East, and even Africa.

This success and the reputation it created were not necessarily shared and appreciated elsewhere in the Soviet imperium—as von Hoehn was discovering on this tour.

"Why in the hell should we let you Germans take the lead on this operation?" The protest came from the lips of Karol Bilak, von Hoehn's liaison partner with State Security. "This is our country, and we shall take the lead in any operation ensuring the security of such an important meeting on our soil."

Von Hoehn had expected as much. "Comrade, I understand your position, and I do not mean to remove the main responsibility for the meeting's security from your service. The KGB and GRU will probably have a different view from yours and mine, in any case. But perhaps this would be a good time to point out that the KGB has expressed its desire to have us included in the operation. In coordination with you, of course." Von Hoehn paused to see what effect those words would have. "You should ask them yourselves if you suspect otherwise. In fact, I would encourage you to do so. As you said, this is your country."

Von Hoehn was confident the lie would have the desired impact. He had not raised the matter with the Soviet service, nor did he intend to. Actually, he planned to do everything possible to prevent the KGB from learning of and interfering in his efforts. He had worked closely with his Soviet brethren in the past, largely because those cases had come at critical junctures in the evolution of the East German state, not to mention his own personal history. The KGB's predecessor, the NKVD, had first recruited him during his time as a POW after the war, and von Hoehn had found the Soviet backing crucial to the success of his plans during the crisis surrounding the building of the infamous Berlin Wall. He had also learned that cooperation often came at a cost. The Soviets would have to be involved now, of course.

This time around, however, he wanted to limit their role to protecting the Soviet delegation as much as possible. He wanted to proceed with as little interference as possible to preserve his own initiative and plans. Intrusions by the heavy-handed Russians would inevitably screw things up.

"I am assuming you will use our joint asset for this," Bilak continued. "That would make the most sense, in my view."

"Now," von Hoehn responded, "that's where our views begin to differ. That man does not have the appropriate cover to justify his presence in Čierna nad Tisou. And not for a meeting such as this. Why would a West German diplomat be present? And one not even covered officially by an embassy they do not have."

"I'm sure you will think of something. We can always say that one of the issues discussed would be the necessity for cooperation between us and the Soviets to block German revanchism."

"And why would Bonn send someone to participate in such a ridiculous discussion?"

"Perhaps to argue the West German case."

"Why would we care to hear what Bonn would have to say? We might as well invite the Americans along."

"I am just making suggestions here."

Von Hoehn did not reply. He sat in silence, trying to think of a polite way to ask his Czechoslovak comrade if he had had an education beyond primary school. Failing that, von Hoehn began to think of an excuse for the asset's presence despite the facile reasoning advanced by his guest.

"After all, this asset of ours is a Czech national..." Bilak continued.

"But he is a West German citizen now," von Hoehn interrupted.

"Yes, but he would be at a real advantage in operating in that environment."

"Well, that depends on what I...we would have him do."

"It sounds, Comrade Hoehn, as though you have not really developed an operational plan yet."

Bilak was right, von Hoehn conceded, but he as sure as hell was not going to admit it. Not openly, at any rate. Then again, the more he thought about it, the more the idea began to appeal to him. Using this asset might even help keep the local service at bay, especially if a Czech national was involved. In fact, the StB would probably try to interfere throughout if he used a real German.

Von Hoehn studied the Czechoslovak comrade seated across from him. Or should he say Slovak? Those ethnic, or even national, distinctions still existed in this country. The man had never displayed any open animosity toward his Czech colleagues, but one could never be certain about what was hidden beneath the surface. No, his motivations were probably more ideological. In that case, von Hoehn reasoned, it was surprising that Bilak would be willing, in fact, adamant about using a Czech who had fled the country in 1948 to avoid the communist coup and only returned to the fold as a recruited Stasi asset, which had come from pressure on his relatives who had remained behind...and the money, of course. No, Bilak appeared to be one of those true believers who had joined the party after the war, convinced that only by creating a socialist homeland in cooperation with the Soviet victors over Nazism could this country find its way to a just and prosperous future. Czechoslovakia was still waiting for that and probably would be for a good while yet. That realization—if it ever arrived—was not likely to sway Bilak.

"I will admit that my operational plan is not yet fully formed. But I do have a general outline at this point. In fact, the more I think about it, the more I realize that the pressure points we used in the recruitment—primarily his family's presence in Czechoslovakia—could come in handy. There are times, you know, when I am not sure I can trust his loyalty entirely."

"So, when can I expect to hear further from you? I will need to inform my superiors before giving my approval."

Von Hoehn's eyebrows arched. Approval? What the hell was this clown talking about? Since when did he or the Stasi need the StB's approval for an operation?

"Besides, are you so certain that something like this will be necessary?" Bilak continued. "Are you aware of a Western plan to infiltrate the meeting?"

"Not yet," von Hoehn replied. "Not specifically." He thought of Baier. "But I know our opposition here. We've tangled before. I am fairly certain he is up to something. He can't help himself."

"He?"

Von Hoehn smiled and nodded. "Yes. I would say more, but my information comes from a very sensitive source with whom I have dealt in the past. I must protect his identity at all costs."

That should shut him up, von Hoehn concluded. Despite the fiction about his source, von Hoehn was nonetheless more confident about possible American interference than he was prepared to let on, and certainly not to someone like Bilak.

• • •

Baier spent the next week driving around western and southern Czechoslovakia exploring his options for an exfiltration, should it become necessary. It would probably have to occur in two phases if Hašek was to be included, especially if he had family members he wanted to accompany him. That had not come up. Baier was certain that Pillar would want his wife along. There were no children, though, which made his case a bit easier. The challenge there, he realized, was that such an adventure would require much more psychological work with the Pillars back in Prague than the cosmetic tourism in the countryside he was currently engaged in.

Fortunately, he had Sabine as a companion. Not only was she good company, but her previous experience escaping from Hungary and East Germany had given her a sharp eye for advantageous locations and routes. Plus, traveling as a married couple gave them excellent cover for their excursions. He just hoped that the young face that popped up twice on these trips, almost certainly a surveillant, would be convinced.

"What a pleasant way to see this lovely countryside," Sabine said one afternoon. It really was lovely, not least because of the sunny weather and moderate temperatures in the high 70s. They were driving with both front windows of their Mercedes down. Baier had his elbow resting on the windowsill, as the wind blew his hair around the back of his skull and over his forehead.

"You do not look like the rock star you probably imagine you are right now," Sabine chided him. "But you do look like some overbearing Westerner—German even—driving like that in your big bad Benz."

"Hell, that's what I am. Well, maybe not German but probably overbearing. It's what the StB would expect. If they're watching, that is."

"Of course, they're watching."

Several minutes later, Sabine picked up the thread of an earlier conversation. "Any luck so far? To me, anyway, the forested border areas look promising. The barriers and fencing seem to be pretty haphazard and spotty."

"I thought they had built up their border posts and fencing after the coup in '48 when so many escaped so easily."

"Like our dear Czech friend, you mean?"

"Yes, for example." Baier leaned out the window to get a better view of the wooded countryside on what appeared to be a deserted stretch of road. They had kept to the back streets, which they would presumably use for any escape attempt.

"I was hoping it wouldn't come to that," he continued. "If it does become necessary, I was looking for the lightly or undermanned post. I doubt they're as thorough as the East Germans at this sort of thing. Otherwise, I figure we'll have documentation that we can give them that will stand up to just about any inspection, no matter how thorough. We're pretty good at that sort of thing."

"Have you put in the request yet?"

"No, not yet. I don't even know if it will be necessary at this point. Besides, I still need to get the photographs from Pillar. Hašek, on the other hand, has refused. He claims it won't be necessary."

"Right. We'll see."

"He's probably convinced that his position with the KGB is solid enough to deflect any suspicion. That is, if word gets out about what we're up to, especially if we succeed."

"That sounds pretty damn optimistic, if you ask me," Sabine said. "If the Soviets or any of their henchmen suspect something, that suspicion may well point to our two Czech friends at some point."

"Yeah, I know. Maybe he believes that Dubček will succeed in holding off the Soviets and will continue with his effort to build what everyone is now calling 'Socialism with a human face.'"

"Good luck with that, too."

"For sure. But for now, I've got to rush back to Prague. I have a visitor coming from Washington. Someone I need to convince of the wisdom of our plan."

"Well, good luck there as well," Sabine said.

Baier pushed his speed up to just over 70 miles an hour as they cruised the final 100 miles home.

• • •

The visitor arrived early. When Baier returned to his office late that afternoon, the chief of the Soviet Bloc Division was sitting at Baier's desk, drawing up copious notes on a legal pad and using one of his trademark fountain pens. He must have brought that with him, Baier surmised. He kept only ballpoint pens in his desk drawer.

"Ah, sit down, Karl." The SB chief, Ralph Badger, pointed to one of the two leather armchairs opposite the desk.

Baier was not surprised by the imperial behavior. Most division chiefs in the Directorate of Operations were notorious for their quasi-autocratic approach to management, and Badger was no exception. Baier just wondered how long he would be treated as a visitor, or even a supplicant, in his own office.

"How was your trip?" Badger continued. "Or should I say trips?"

"Fine," Baier replied. "There are some attractive locations, but I still think we should use false documentation if it comes to that." Baier paused to wait until his boss had finished whatever note he was writing. "Sorry, I couldn't meet you at the airport. I take it Garrity handled your arrival like the pro he is."

"Yes, yes, that was all fine. Very smooth, and I appreciate it. But I take it, you mean things like passports? That's probably the best we could do at this point. We're what, two weeks out?"

Baier nodded. "That's right. I've asked Garrity, who is also the head of our technical ops staff as well as my deputy, to look into that. I haven't asked him to send in a request to Headquarters on moving forward with the technical preparations yet, which is why you haven't seen it yet. I was waiting to discuss it with you in person since you were coming through anyway. I'm sure you understand."

"Yes, yes, of course." Badger stood. "Here, take your seat, Karl. I didn't mean to keep you waiting out there like some junior officer. Lord knows, you've had some impressive accomplishments in your time with us."

Finally, Baier thought. He stepped around the division chief and slid into his chair. Badger remained standing, although this time on the other side of the desk. Baier noticed only now that his visitor's dark blue pinstriped suit pants and white cotton shirt were wrinkled. The division chief must have come straight from the airport, eager to get to work. Baier wasn't sure if that was a good or a bad sign. Badger's suit jacket and tie hung on the peg on the back of Baier's office door. When he looked closer, Baier could see the bags under the man's eyes.

"Unfortunately, I can't stay long. I have to leave tomorrow for Berlin, and then it's on to London and Paris. You can imagine how developments here in Prague have gotten our European partners excited and worried at the same time. I'm meeting up with several senior analysts for briefings in the latter two capitals for discussions on where things are heading in Prague and the Kremlin. As best we can tell, of course."

"Good luck with that, Ralph. I'll be interested in hearing what they have to say."

"Oh, you'll be slotted for distribution on the readouts. Not to worry. But that does bring me to the point of your proposed operation."

"I'll bet. If we can get anything from it, it should help immensely in our understanding of where things might go from here."

Badger exhaled, raised his eyebrows, then looked hard at Baier.

"Theoretically, yes. A successful op would give us an enormous advantage. But there are still some issues, as we see them in Headquarters, Karl."

"Such as?"

"Such as the people you want to use. One man, the diplomat, is not a controlled asset, and we have no way of knowing what he'll be able to accomplish in such a dangerous situation."

"True. But I think it's still a risk worth taking. He won't be handling the trickiest part of the operation, in any case."

"I'll concede that point, Karl. But what about the other fellow, the KGB officer? I've read about his background, which does appear to make him amenable to working with us…"

"Amenable? It was his idea in the first place."

"Okay, but how can we be so sure of his loyalties at such an early stage? How can we be sure this isn't some kind of provocation the KGB has cooked up?"

"I agree, Ralph, we can't be 100 percent certain. But can we ever? Besides, I do have some history with the man. True, it isn't that extensive. But I believe I understand what makes him tick. He'll do this for us, if it's at all possible. But most of all, he'll do it for himself and his country."

"I'm not here to kill your plan, Karl. Your past makes me believe I can trust your judgment. And I agree that the potential rewards of this justify the operation. But I do have one restriction."

"And that is?"

"It is that I do not want you directly involved. We've discussed this thoroughly back home, and we all agree—all the way up to the Director—that you need to keep some distance between yourself, your station, and the events in Čierna nad Tisou. We must make sure we eliminate as much of the potential blowback as possible if things go south."

"That will make it difficult for me to direct this thing, to make timely decisions. In fact, it will force me to rely even more on the characters you're so uncertain about."

"I…we realize that. But we believe it is even more important to make sure that the developments, this entire Prague Spring, remain free of any suspicion that Dubček and company are acting at our behest. The potential benefits of the reform program and reduction in tensions in Europe and the world are simply too great. I'm sure you agree on that."

Baier nodded and stood. He held out his hand. Badger took it, then smiled.

"Let's go have some dinner," Badger said. "Can Sabine join us?"

"I'll give her a call."

• • •

Von Hoehn loved Vienna. His heart, naturally, would always rest with Koenigsberg, a city lost to him and the Germans forever, but Vienna lived on. In a way. True, Vienna had lost the empire it had governed for centuries, a much larger swath of territory than Koenigsberg had ever ruled. But Vienna somehow retained its imperial splendor, its streets and buildings still echoing and reflecting the legacy it had left on Central and Eastern Europe, and the people still spoke German…or most of them anyway. It may have sounded funny with its musical dialect, so common to other south German patterns, but it was German all the same.

He also loved the Franciscan church that sat on the square not far from the more famous *Ringstrasse,* as though content to hide its inner glories in the shadows of better-known monuments, like the imperial place, or *Hofburg,* and St. Steven's Cathedral, the wonderful *Stephansdom*. Built in the early years of the 17th century, the Franciscan Church may have been smaller and its treasures more compact, but that concentration lent the church's interior a much more intense beauty. With only a modest stone front facing the square, the visitor was almost overwhelmed by the magnificence of the Baroque interior upon passing through the doors. The plaster and marbled walls, the arches lining the sides and framing the altar, the resplendent religious paintings that spilled their bright colors against the white and grey backdrops, and the hidden chapels along the side walls introduced one to the glories of an imperial and Catholic past that broke forth just a few years later to reclaim lands and inspiration lost during the Protestant Reformation. Even the wooden pews, stained a dark brown to offset all the light around them, seemed to have absorbed and retained the spiritual and historical wealth for future generations. Jaroslav Havlíček sat in one of them, two rows back and about ten feet to the right of the altar.

Von Hoehn wished, at times, that he believed all this. He wondered if Havlíček did. His family came from Bohemia, so there was an even chance he had been raised either as a Lutheran or a Catholic. Lord knew what he believed in now. He had seemed committed to the ideals of Western democracy when he fled his homeland after the communist coup in 1948. Yet he had come over to the side of proletarian socialism easily enough about a dozen years later. Was it because of the threat the regime in Prague—or some working for that regime in cooperation with the East Germans—-was prepared to inflict upon his family that had stayed behind? Was it the money, which he obviously needed to enjoy the pleasures of the consumer society that West Germany offered? Or was he only superficially engaged, ready to switch allegiances whenever the opportunity arose?

"I keep wondering why you chose this church to meet in," Havlíček said. Von Hoehn slid into the pew and rested his rear and back against the hard wooden seat. "Why not one of the tourist spots, or perhaps someplace to get a cup of that famous Viennese coffee and a slice of *Sachertorte* as well? Did you feel an urge to go to confession?"

"No, nothing like that. I just like this church. Besides, I have nothing to confess."

"Well, that's good to hear. I can rest more easily on my ride back to Prague. Nonetheless, no need to visit your bosses in *Normanenstrasse* afterward?"

"No. I know what I'm doing. I'll keep them informed from Prague." Von Hoehn turned sideways and leaned one arm over the back of the pew. "But I did want to talk to you. And in person."

"I thought as much. But why here in Vienna? We could have met somewhere in Germany, you know. Say, West Berlin."

Von Hoehn smiled. The cool air drifted and then hung in the space above the two men. A form of holy air conditioning that kept the sun and the heat outside.

"I thought this town would provide more privacy for us. I can never trust that my visits and travels in West Germany will remain unobserved. And bringing you back into Czechoslovakia poses an even greater risk from there."

Havlíček nodded. "True. I can only push my cover so far. There really are not that many issues involving reparations for the land taken from the Sudeten Germans. I mean, unless the Dubček government wants to institute a reform program in that area as well. You know, all in the interests of the brotherhood of man."

"I seriously doubt that is going to happen. But it would be advantageous for you to find some sort of excuse to visit again."

"When? And what for?

"Soon. In about two weeks."

Havlíček shifted his weight and stared at the East German. "Does this have to do with that meeting coming up between the Dubček people and their Soviet lords?"

"Yes, but not how you might think. You see, I do not need anything in the way of information. But I will need to have someone I trust to observe others there and what they might be up to." And someone I can control, von Hoehn said to himself.

"Do you suspect something is afoot? From the Americans?"

"Yes, I do. I will leave out my specific suspicions for the moment. But you can be sure the Americans are involved."

"Aren't they always?"

Von Hoehn smiled and nodded. "Yes, they usually are. But even if you can't visit there in person, perhaps you can also pick up a scent or two in Bonn. The government there must be very interested in what will come of the meeting and whether Dubček survives. Just think what it would mean to this budding *Ostpolitik* that has everyone—and not just the Social Democrats like Willy Brandt—so excited."

"I'll see what I can do," Havlíček promised.

"See that you do." Von Hoehn stood and inhaled a deep breath of the sanctified air that the church seemed to circulate. He might even try some holy water on the way out. It could contribute to the success of his new mission. He was not one to exclude any possibility out of hand, from any power.

CHAPTER NINETEEN

July 30. The waiting was intolerable. Baier felt as though he had been handed a death sentence, but for someone else. Now, he was waiting for the actual execution. The meeting may have been within the borders of Czechoslovakia, but it might as well have been occurring in Siberia for all the help it gave Baier.

"Stop pacing around your office so much," Garrity had admonished more than once. "You act like there is something dangerous and momentous out there."

Baier had stopped in his tracks and stared at his deputy for a full minute.

"Of course, there is."

"Then don't give it away."

The meeting in Čierna nad Tisou had begun the day before. Both Hašek and Pillar had swung assignments at the meeting, although they would not have direct access to the discussions themselves. Baier had to admit to himself—and convince the minions back at Headquarters—that the operation was still worth the risk. They would still be able to pick up pieces of the conversations and readouts from the various parties, enough for the analysts in Langley to pull together an assessment that would provide a more complete picture of where things stood with the Prague Spring—for Czechoslovakia, sure, but more importantly, for the Kremlin. That alone made the whole exercise worthwhile.

For his part, Baier had remained in Prague, as instructed. He did not want an obsession for control of the operation to jeopardize the mission. That obsession, the anxiety when an operation began to slip away from the officer's ability to retain control over the details and direction of an operation, was typical for Agency handlers. It stemmed in part from the varying degrees of capability and trust the assets had for a particular operation, as well as the obstacle a local service or someone bigger with a larger hand might be able to throw in the way. Admittedly, the officer's ego often played a part.

In this case, Baier was confident in Pillar's and Hašek's abilities to acquire the necessary information without endangering themselves or exposing their relationship with Baier. Hašek's and Pillar's motives were clear and understandable. Baier did not need to add anything in that regard. Pillar may not have had much in the way of clandestine experience, but he would be working on the sidelines, hopefully out of the range of the extensive security established by the KGB. Hašek, on the other hand, was clearly taking the greater risk. His life and current assignment, however, had prepared him well for an operation of this sort.

Still, the waiting and the distance pushed Baier's imagination to wreak havoc with his nerves. Sabine had noticed, and she tried repeatedly to calm him down. She did not have the details of her husband's plans, of course, but she knew that something was up and that it must have something to do with the gathering in Čierna nad Tisou. After all, it was all over the news and the focus of nearly every political discussion in Czechoslovakia. She assumed it was at the heart of the talk about a possible exfiltration as well.

"How was work today?" Sabine had been asking every evening for a week.

"Oh, okay, I guess. We'll see in a short while."

That was about as committal as Baier could get with her.

•••

Alexander von Hoehn sat in his cottage on the outskirts of Čierna nad Tisou, staring out of the bay window at its front and across the manicured shrubbery that separated the cabin from the street. That road and the expansive lawn on the grounds of the estate separated him from the discussions underway between Leonid Brezhnev, Alexei Kosygin, Nicholai Podgorny, and Mikhail Suslov on one side and Alexander Dubček, Ludwig Svoboda, Oldrich Cernik, and Josef Smrkovsky on the other. That the supreme leadership of the Soviet Union was just down the road and on the other side of the lawn discussing the fate of this small, benighted country in Central Europe frustrated von Hoehn more than he could remember, certainly more so than any other past operation. He slammed his fist on the windowsill. He could not even gather a whisper of what was going on.

That was not all that bothered him. True, he may have been the senior representative from his government, but the talks did not affect East Germany...not directly anyway. He understood the nervousness of his country's leadership. Memories of the popular uprising in East Berlin and elsewhere in the newly formed German Democratic Republic in 1953 were still fresh. It had been a near-miss thing. Fears were strong there—and elsewhere in the Warsaw Pact nations—that the Czechs and Slovaks could be entering that slippery slope of reform that would endanger all their regimes.

Von Hoehn, however, was less concerned about that. Let the big minds with big paychecks and piles of privilege worry about those longer-term strategic things. Besides, change was inevitable sooner or later. He could never be sure, but it was always best to keep one's options open.

Von Hoehn's immediate concerns had a more narrow and timely focus. Havlíček had not been able to gain an assignment for this meeting. In fact, he had jeopardized his standing and raised suspicions by pressing for something that was clearly removed from his current responsibilities. His pleas that his interest in the well-being of his native land and family were at play had fallen on deaf bureaucratic ears back in Bonn.

As it was, von Hoehn had been forced to rely on the younger officer Herr, in whom von Hoehn was developing a growing distrust—and a growing dislike. Contrary to his instructions, the young Stasi officer had cultivated a rapport with members of the older generation of Czech and Slovak officials, those who were less committed and less enthusiastic about the reform program in Czechoslovakia. Von Hoehn wondered if Herr was acting at the behest, or outright orders, of people in Berlin like Marcus Wolf, that preening prick who liked to parade his ties to Moscow from his family's time at the Hotel Lux with all the other exiled—and protected—European Communists who had fled the Nazis and their control of the European continent. Wolf did not bother to hide his affection for and attraction to younger female officers either. An early marriage of Wolf's had already fallen victim to the man's shenanigans.

He would say this much for Herr, however. The young man was good, very good. He had already uncovered an operative whose curiosity had outpaced his responsibilities. That fellow was the unfortunate young Czech security officer Gregor Cernik, who had betrayed himself by showing up unannounced and unapproved at the American Embassy in Prague. Now there was this Janos Hašek, the former Czech gulag prisoner the KGB had seen fit to spring from prison after his exemplary behavior and the pressing need for officers to work in an advisory role in Prague. That had made people in Moscow so sure that his return to Czechoslovakia would not raise suspicion about his assignment there.

Good enough. The man would still bear watching, though, and that would also keep Herr occupied. Von Hoehn already had some suspicions about this Czech retread but would not pass this information along to the Soviet team in Čierna nad Tisou, nor to the KGB office in Prague. Not yet. Lord only knows what that GRU goon squad would do with it.

"But Comrade Colonel," Herr had protested, "shouldn't we assist our brother allies in this? It could be important. We want to prevent the Americans from stealing anything and getting a leg up, so to speak."

"From what I've been hearing, I'm not sure any devices the Americans may have installed or people they may have recruited will report anything all that damaging to our side."

"It is a good thing, then, that we swept the buildings so thoroughly."

Yes, it is. Besides, the discussions are going fairly well. The Czechoslovaks are proving to be quite pliable."

"How so?"

"They are agreeing not to jeopardize our security and to retain communist party control over the levers of power."

"But what might the CIA and the American Government be able to do with inside information? What if they fabricate different messages?"

Von Hoehn smiled. "Here's another lesson for you. When you control the messenger, you can also control the message."

• • •

Baier took about two hours for his countersurveillance run this time. The meeting in Čierna nad Tisou had ended three days ago on August 1st, but he had yet to hear from either Pillar or Hašek. He had finally contacted Hašek through the pre-arranged drop site two days ago and found the response yesterday. The long absence worried him. Some delay was understandable, but given the significance of the discussions, no, the negotiations, Baier had expected a quicker readout from his new quasi-agent.

That concern explained his anxious trip to the safehouse near the Gunpowder Tower, where he had first met Hašek upon his return from the Soviet Gulag. Baier was already considering an effort to find a new safehouse, concerned that their earlier meeting there may have compromised the general location, if not the actual building and room, to the local service and any potential KGB allies. There was that Stasi bastard von Hoehn as well, so Baier moved with considerable caution and ventured far from his normal routes to the location. The double sighting of that piece-of-shit black Tatraplan, the almost-sleek Czech car that was the standard transportation for StB officers, had only heightened his caution. Maybe his nerves were getting the better of him— but then, a little paranoia could be a good thing in a difficult environment like this one.

Once Baier was convinced he was black— as they said in Langley—he entered the second-floor apartment and put on a pot of coffee. He did not need any himself, not with all the adrenaline his body was pumping through his system, but given the late hour—ten o'clock—Baier figured Hašek might find it helpful. And what if he brought Pillar along? Then both of them might find some liquid incentive helpful. There was always the bottle of Armenian brandy, or the French stuff, available if different prompts were needed.

"Jesus, it's about time," Baier exclaimed. He glanced at his watch. It was already ten thirty, which told him Hašek and his partner—Pillar had indeed come along—were later than usual. They may have hurried to the meeting and forgotten to check for possible surveillance. In that case, a reminder wouldn't hurt.

"I hope you spent the extra time making sure you weren't followed."

Hašek moved to the kitchen counter, where he poured two cups of coffee. He brought both to the table, holding one in his left hand. His right extended the second cup to Pillar.

"Do not worry, Mister Baier. We are good to go."

"Then why the delay in getting back to me? You can imagine how eagerly people in Washington are looking for reporting on the recent group chat with the Soviets."

"Did your Embassy not send anything back to Washington?" Pillar asked. "I would think they'd report back the very next day. I know I met with someone from your Embassy's Political Section the next day, as did others in my building."

"Yes, they did send their own cables back. But I was hoping to get some additional information and insights from both of you."

"Ah, well, there is the rub." Hašek sipped his coffee and grimaced. "You should keep some cream here, Mister Baier. This coffee needs something else. It is not very good, you know."

"Yeah, I am so sorry about that. It's probably Folgers or an import from Russia. But as to the meeting in Čierna nad Tisou?"

Hašek set his cup down. "Yes, as to that, I am afraid I probably do not have much to add. In terms of specifics, that is. You see, I think it was a minor victory not to have tried to install your bugging devices. You would probably not be any wiser."

"What do you mean?"

"I'm not sure anyone's listening devices would have picked up what was truly important. Unless, of course, you had installed them in the most significant and strategic locations. But there was no way of knowing where that would be in advance. Neither one of us," Hašek nodded in Pillar's direction, "picked up anything in the discussions themselves beyond what was openly discussed and reported through the press."

Hašek glanced over at Pillar again and smiled. He retrieved his cup, sipped some more coffee, grimaced again, then looked up at Baier. "You see, the negotiations themselves, as it turned out, were only of secondary importance. The real importance lay in the atmospherics. That was where the script got sidetracked."

"And what was that script?"

"Dubček and his team appear to have won Brezhnev's approval to continue with his reform program, as long as he agreed to remain loyal to the Warsaw Pact. That, of course, had been one of the Hungarians' big mistakes in '56. He also had to promise to prevent the revival of a Social Democratic party, since Brezhnev knows full well that if truly open elections are allowed to occur, the KSC would have no chance against that sort of group."

"That sounds easy enough. Was there anything else?"

"Oh, yes, there was the matter of the press. Dubček had to promise to control the press more effectively. That is another one of the Kremlin's bugaboos."

"Based on what I've been seeing during my time here, that could be a difficult promise to keep. If you ask me, that particular genie has left the barn."

Hašek and Pillar looked at each other, confused. Both men put their coffee cups on the kitchen table.

"Excuse me?" Pillar said. "I do not understand."

Baier waved at the air. "Sorry. In my anxiety and nervousness, I just mixed some metaphors. It's just that I doubt the press and cultural scene in Czechoslovakia are going to let themselves be stuffed back into the old Stalinist bag."

"Perhaps you are right. And that leads me…no, us, to the next point. And that is that one cannot put too much stock in that agreement, nor the one that was issued after the follow-on meeting in Bratislava."

"Meaning?"

"Meaning that those communiques were worded so that both sides could claim they received what they wanted," Hašek replied. "Dubček may have come away with a sense of victory, but it is not one that appeared to me to have been shared by the Soviet delegation. And Gomulka and Ulbricht, those two preening bastards from Poland and East Germany, were downright contemptible toward the Czech delegation. Wouldn't you agree, Gustav?"

"If I might," Pillar suggested. He picked up his cup, looked at the remains in obvious distaste, set it back down and waved at it, as though he might make it disappear. "Do you have anything more enjoyable? A glass of wine or brandy perhaps?"

Baier walked over to the cabinet next to the sink and pulled the bottle of the Armenian stuff from the cupboard. He grabbed two glasses from the sideboard at the sink and filled them both. Pillar thanked him when Baier carried the two offerings to the table. Hašek held his aloft as a form of toast to the host. Baier smiled and nodded in appreciation.

"Thank you," Pillar said. "And, yes, I do agree. From what I understand, the last day at Čierna was quite bitter and divisive. In fact, the meeting broke up with little agreement beyond that communique, and then a compromise was reached for a follow-on gathering in Bratislava. That's why it took us so long to get back to you, Karl. We wanted to see if there was more information to pass along."

"I was going to say that your people in Washington should not put too much faith in the agreements arrived at either Čierna nad Tisou or Bratislava. The dynamic in Czechoslovakia, and especially in Prague, is not likely to be controlled that easily. As yet, the leadership here does not have a well-thought-out plan for how to proceed. At least not that I have discerned."

"So, you agree with my assessment about the popular mood and aspirations in Czechoslovakia. In other words, the street is driving things now." Baier said.

Pillar sipped his brandy and nodded. "Yes, I do. The popular press and the artistic scene are not about to be put back in the old box."

"Or the barn," Hašek added. "My distinct impression is that Brezhnev is under heavy pressure from Warsaw and East Berlin, not to mention hardliners in Moscow, to bring Prague under control. I think he and the others are only playing for time."

"I did not hear anything specific to confirm this, but I believe Brezhnev and his team see it that way," Pillar added. "The same goes for the new or revamped political parties here. You do not have to label a group officially as Social Democrats to have something similar emerge. Not if the public is looking for that."

"So, we are not out of the proverbial woods yet," Baier concluded.

"What woods would those be?" Hašek asked.

"It's just another expression we use in America. It means we are not home safe and sound yet."

Hašek drained half his glass in one long swallow. "I believe that is correct. And I believe that is especially true after the meeting in Bratislava yesterday, with the Warsaw Five and a Czechoslovak delegation."

"Why exactly is that?" Baier asked.

"Well," Pillar explained, "the declaration declared an unshakeable devotion to Marxist-Leninism and proletarian internationalism, as well as continuing the implacable struggle against bourgeois ideologies and all anti-Socialist forces. The Kremlin also proclaimed its inalienable right to intervene in any Warsaw Pact country that allowed a pluralist system to be established with what it called 'capitalist parties.'" He paused to polish off the rest of his brandy. "Gomulka and Ulbricht almost certainly are taking that home as a victory. The wording is much harsher than what was put down in Čierna nad Tisou."

"But haven't the Soviets withdrawn their forces that were camped here after the last Warsaw Pact exercise?"

"Yes," Pillar agreed. "But only so far. They are still located close to our border."

"Well, shit," Baier mumbled. "I don't feel so good anymore. In fact, I'm more worried than ever. You two sound very pessimistic."

Hašek shook his head and held out his glass for a refill. "No, we're just realistic, aware of the challenges we face." He sipped. "Especially from Big Brother."

"This is all very helpful," Baier said. "But what I need for Washington are hard facts about what we can expect next." He studied both men, his eyebrows raised in anticipation. "Is there any way we can gather something that is more than an impression or an opinion about how the leadership in Moscow, or even Warsaw and East Berlin, plans to move forward?"

Both Czechs looked at each other and shrugged.

"We will see if there is anything further we can learn," Hašek suggested. "But that sort of information will be tightly held, of course."

Baier wondered how he could report this all back to Langley. Without the hard facts on what somebody like Brezhnev or Kosygin, or those two clowns in Warsaw and East Berlin, thought and planned to do about it, Baier would not be able to put anything in official channels. At least it would not be anything that would see a broader distribution outside Agency Headquarters and into the hands of policymakers back home. As it stood, the information did not go beyond the opinions of two men, who were well-informed and thoughtful, but not authoritative. Still, he'd figure out some way to get what he needed. In the meantime, a personal assessment from the field would have to do.

• • •

Outside, standing in the shadow of a building kitty-corner from the apartment block where Baier was meeting with Pillar and Hašek, Friedrich Herr and Karol Krasnor, a middle-aged and often disgruntled Slovak officer with the StB, watched the light peeking out from under the window shade on the third floor. Krasnor raised a camera to take a picture, but Herr pulled his arm down.

"No, I don't want a flash. Besides, a picture now would not tell us or anyone else anything."

"Then you should have let me photograph the two traitors when they entered the building."

"Same thing, Comrade. No flash. And we don't need any proof. This isn't a court of law." Herr smiled and let a low laugh escape. "We've got them now in any case."

"How can you be so sure?"

Herr studied his companion for several seconds. "I think you may be letting your distaste for your countryman's reform program cloud your judgment. We do not need to wade in with clubs swinging. Not yet anyway."

"Why not? I've been waiting for the opportunity to do just that ever since that bastard Dubček got Novotny kicked out of the general secretary job back in January. Betrayed the Revolution, he did."

Herr smiled. "All in good time, my friend. All in good time."

CHAPTER TWENTY

For the next week, the mood was a happy one in Prague—buoyant even—or so it seemed to Baier. Despite the agreement and atmosphere in Čierna nad Tisou and Bratislava—or at least as Pillar and Hašek had reported them—the press remained open, even defiant. The cultural and literary scene was also as free as ever, certainly as free as it had been since just after the beginning of the new year, when the totalitarian chains had begun to loosen with Alexander Dubček's elevation to the post of party first secretary.

"I don't understand why you're still so worried Karl," Ambassador Beam said. Both men were seated together on the sofa that sat in the corner of the Ambassador's office on the second floor of the US Embassy.

"It's just that there are some worrying signs out there. On closer examination, I'd say that the Soviets haven't given up much. They could be stalling for time."

"Or giving Dubček and his allies in the Politburo time to prove themselves," the Ambassador replied.

"But that's also part of the problem. Dubček seems to be almost naive about what he expects from Brezhnev and those around him in the Kremlin."

"How so?"

"He thinks that because he personally remains a committed communist and that his program is wildly popular, Brezhnev won't do anything to upset the situation in Czechoslovakia. And I'm afraid that that is child's play."

"I take it you're basing this view on the opinions of some of your contacts. Are you confident that they have a good insight into the situation?"

"Yes, Sir, I am. And I'm not saying that an invasion or Dubček's removal is imminent. Just that it's still a possibility." Baier studied his chief of mission. "A strong possibility."

The ambassador stood and returned to his desk. He held up a report that looked to be about five pages long, held together by a paper clip. Standing, the ambassador glanced at the cover page, then dropped the packet on his desk blotter. He sat.

"Karl, I'm going to add a comment at the end of your report. This is one of the think pieces you can send in based on your own on-the-scene analysis, correct?

"Yes, Sir."

"Well then, since this is written as your personal evaluation, I have no reason to block its dissemination. But since interest is understandably high in Washington, it is likely to get a wide readership. That's why I want to have the Embassy's—and my personal—viewpoint included. Like you, I realize there are still challenges out there. Serious ones. But I'm a bit more sanguine that Dubček has time to prove himself."

"Of course. I'll have my secretary bring up a finished copy once you've had the chance to write your rebuttal."

"That's too strong a word. Think of it as a more optimistic prognosis. But nothing too rosy."

• • •

Baier's optimism, such as it was, faded quickly two days later. Frank Kehoe stood at Baier's desk, his hands gripping the front as he leaned over the furniture to get as close as possible to his boss. It was as though that would give his words greater weight. Not that they needed it.

"And when did this happen?" Baier asked.

"About an hour ago. Maybe a little bit longer. I didn't think to look at my watch."

Kehoe's eyes were wide, and his hair hung low over his forehead, covering the sweat that pooled just underneath.

"Tell me again just what happened."

"Paul and I had just finished up our morning coffee, taking a break before we went to meet a landlord about renting an apartment. You know, to get a new safehouse like you asked."

"Yes, go on."

"That's when it happened. We had just paid and stood up to go. In fact, we were out on the sidewalk, when this fucking Lada drove up and pulled to the curb with this godawful screech. Then a team of two men jumped from the back seat, grabbed Paul and threw him in the trunk. I started for one of the guys, I even grabbed him by the throat from behind, when this other jerk popped out of the passenger seat in front, holding a Makarov to my chest. Then he says—with this heavy Russian accent—back off. Or you and your friend will get hurt.' So I did just that, I backed off."

"Did you get a license plate number? Can you give a description of the car?"

"You bet. And, Sir, those bastards were definitely Russian. Even if they were trying to speak English."

"I don't doubt it. But why are you so sure?"

"You know I speak some Russian. I was originally supposed to go to Moscow, but that changed when headquarters wanted to beef up our station here."

"And that's what they were speaking? With each other?"

Kehoe nodded vigorously. "Damn straight. Sir." Baier sat back and thought about his first move. It would be tempting to march right up to the Soviet *rezidentura* if only to put his outrage on full display. Maybe even have Ambassador Beam lodge an official protest with the Czechoslovak Government, as well as the Soviet Embassy.

Then again, maybe something more subtle might prove more effective. Moves that could be made behind the scenes, as it were.

"Okay, Frank, I'll get back to you on our next steps. In the meantime, why don't you go home, grab some lunch and try to think of anything else you might remember. You might also want to wash up. It looks like you've been in a street fight."

Kehoe looked down at his front and saw that his shirt had been torn. A couple of buttons were missing, too. His pants had also been scuffed, and one knee was ripped. He looked up at Baier.

"Yeah, good idea, Sir. I forgot to add that I also got in a few good swings at the asshole who grabbed me. He hit me back, pretty hard, too. Tough son of a bitch. We rolled around on the ground some before another prick from the front seat stepped in."

Baier just hoped the other guy looked worse. A lot worse.

• • •

He sat at a corner café down the street from the East German Embassy, watching the little bit of foot traffic entering and leaving the building. Baier was looking once more for Alexander von Hoehn. As it turned out, von Hoehn was almost certainly the local Stasi station chief. At least Baier assumed that was his position. If not, then he acted pretty independently from some kind of staff officer. Baier had no other way to contact the man, and he had been sitting there nursing his second cup of bad Czech coffee and ignoring the unwelcome glances and sighs of exasperation from the waiter over this cheap American customer occupying the table by the window.

This was his second day on this particular job, but this time at a different location. Yesterday, he simply sat in the park out front, reading a newspaper and pretending to nap on and off.

"How long do you plan to sit here? Surely you have more important things to do."

Alexander von Hoehn stood at the entrance to the café in a double-breasted blue suit and white shirt. His yellow tie was loosened at the collar. He walked over to Baier's table.

"Well?"

"That's a pretty bourgeois outfit for a champion of the proletariat," Baier said.

"Think of it as my disguise."

"And actually, I do not. Have anything better to do, that is. Not right now."

"I think I understand why." Von Hoehn glanced out the window. "I will get my car and drive two streets down from here and pick you up. It would be better to have our conversation elsewhere, someplace more private."

"Of course. I'll see you there."

Baier did not have long to wait. Five minutes was all it took for von Hoehn to grab his car and swing by the street corner he had designated for the pick-up point. The off-white Mercedes pulled up next to Baier, and he climbed into the front seat. Von Hoehn immediately accelerated as he turned back into the street and hustled Baier away from the Embassy neighborhood. Baier shook his head and laughed.

"What is it?" von Hoehn asked.

"It doesn't matter which side you Germans come from. You all drive alike. As though you only have minutes left, seconds even, to reach some distant destination."

"Are you frightened?"

"Not in this car. And I have to say that you are full of capitalist surprises today. No Trabi or Wartburg for a representative of the workers' paradise?"

"Knock it off. Are all you Americans so clever?"

"More or less. You'd better watch out."

"Can we get to the point? I think I know why you're here. It has to do with your compatriot, correct?"

"Yes, it certainly does. I take it he was grabbed by that GRU asshole troupe you mentioned earlier?"

You Americans love to use that word."

"Which one?"

"'Asshole.' You know you can be sued in Germany for calling someone that."

"Even if it's true? Like in this case?"

"Well, we could make an exception here. But what do you want me to do? I have no control over those people."

"How about if you arrange a meeting for me? I want to talk to someone in the Czech service. Someone with some authority to make this go away."

"That will not be easy. Making it go away, I mean."

"Well, someone will have to do just that. I mean it. This could touch off a real big diplomatic incident."

"Does your ambassador know?"

"Of course, he knows. You cannot hide something like this for long. And my superiors in Washington know as well."

"What are they saying?"

"They've given me the authority to do whatever is necessary to get our man out." Baier looked hard at his host. "I will repeat that for you. Whatever is necessary."

Von Hoehn nodded and glanced over at Baier. Until then, the East German had kept his eyes focused only on the road. It was almost as though he was too embarrassed to look Baier in the eye.

"I will go one better. I will arrange for you to meet the Soviet chief in their *rezidentura*. He is probably the only one who can make this go away."

"Good." Baier smiled for the first time that day. "I'll look forward to it."

CHAPTER TWENTY-ONE

They met at the same riverside walk near the East German embassy the very next afternoon. They also sat on the same bench Baier had spent several days warming when he first took up a post here in his effort to meet with von Hoehn. Poetic justice? Perhaps. But Baier had to laugh inwardly all the same.

Baier had been waiting for an hour, maybe a little less, when he finally saw von Hoehn approach with a man Baier recognized as the head of the Soviet *rezidentura*, or KGB station, in Prague. He was not tall but also not short, probably well under six feet tall. Baier took an immediate guess of about 5 feet 8 inches. He was overweight, though. Baier doubted it came from too much borscht. The Soviet boss probably had served in several European posts, where he could fatten himself up on the heavy starches and pastries available in the West, not to mention Czechoslovakia. His pale gray suit hung on him like a gift from a bad tailor, and his white shirt was open at the collar, trapped by a striped tie that looked as though it had come straight off the rack at Woolworth's. He plopped himself down on the bench just about a foot from Baier.

"So," the Soviet spy said, "what can I do for you, Mister Baier?"

"At least you know my name," Baier replied.

"Oh, I know more than just your name." He smiled. "I know everything about you that is worth knowing."

Baier leaned back to give himself some space. The Soviet's breath stank of stale tobacco and bad toothpaste. He studied the man's face for a few seconds just to make sure it was the same

Russian as the one whose photograph sat on the front page of his office's mug book.

"Yuri Spekov, let's not get too cute today. You know damn well why I'm here and why I wanted to talk to you."

"Of course. You Americans are so direct."

"Your people have been holding one of my officers for two days now. No, make that three. You have no right and no reason to do that. I want him released immediately."

"Or what?"

"Spekov, you know you've overstepped a red line here, one that has governed our work for two decades now."

The Russian smiled. "Oh, yes, the one that we not harm each other? Your officer has come to no harm."

"Well, I don't know that, do I? And just kidnapping, as you have done, is harm enough."

"Mister Baier. You may have a point when you say that I had no right to do this thing. We can argue all day over who is responsible, and that this has come to pass. However, that will solve nothing."

"Perhaps not. But I think that would be a very short argument."

"There is also the matter of exactly who on my side performed this deed."

"That does not matter to me. You are the boss here. The responsibility rests with you. So, it is up to you to make things better."

"Ah, I wish it were so simple. You see, there is nonetheless a reason."

"And that would be?"

"That we need to deliver a message to you and your people here. You must remember that you are operating on the soil of a valued member of the Warsaw Pact, and that you cannot be allowed to jeopardize the security of our allied brethren."

Baier could feel the heat rising in his face. He thought his cheeks must be glowing red by now.

"Listen, Spekov, my officer was not jeopardizing anyone's security. Besides, I already know why you do not want any of my people working in this city."

"And what would that be, Mister Baier?"

"You do not want them finding anything out about your country's plans for Czechoslovakia and the Dubček Government. Moreover, they were doing what I asked them to do."

"What was that?" Spekov asked.

"I told them they needed to relax and enjoy a morning coffee break. They needed to relax because of the harassment they have been facing from your henchmen."

"Ah, so you are the one responsible. Perhaps you should have been the one arrested. Perhaps you would like to take your man's place."

"No one is taking anyone's place," Baier nearly screamed. He leaned in closer, close enough to smell once again the sour scent of a Russian cigarette and the breakfast herring on Spekov's breath. Baier could have sworn that there was also a trace of vodka there. "You are going to release my officer as soon as you get back to your office."

"Or else?"

"Or else I will do whatever is necessary to free my man by myself. With you or without you, Spekov. It is your choice."

"Mister Baier, your men have been sniffing too closely around a matter that is no concern of yours."

"And that would be?"

"The unfortunate death of a young Czechoslovak officer. His death was an accident. You must leave it at that."

"I hope you will not be insulted if I do not take your word on this."

"Not insulted. Only saddened."

"It looks like we have reached a stalemate."

The Russian stood. "Then let's see what you can do."

He stood and turned to walk away. Baier noticed that a sleek black Czechoslovak limousine had pulled against the curb at the other side of the park. Baier recognized it as the Tatra 603, the finest automobile off the country's assembly line. So fine, it was not available to the average citizen in this worker's paradise. Spekov strolled toward it. Before he was halfway to his ride, the

KGB chief stopped, turned, then held his hand to his mouth to serve as an amplifier.

"We will be waiting for you."

• • •

Baier pondered Spekov's last remark. Then he stood and walked over to the beige Mercedez waiting at the point where he and von Hoehn had met just the day before.

"Did you hear all that?" Baier asked.

Von Hoehn removed the ear plugs he had been wearing and dropped them in his jacket pocket.

"Yes, nearly everything."

"I take it you had the bench bugged."

"Of course."

"Are you going to help me?"

Von Hoehn frowned and shook his head. "You know I can't do that. Not directly."

"But you agree that this is a step too far, do you not?"

"Yes, I do. But you must remember that I told you about the new GRU squad in town. They were probably the ones behind this. Spekov may not have anything to do with it. Those guys are too new, and they think they are a law unto themselves. They are probably testing the limits as to what they can get away with."

"I'm not sure I accept Spekov's innocence in this. But if that is the case, it's good to know it at this point." Bauer waited a minute before continuing. "Spekov brought up the incident of the young Czech officer's death. The guy who was found with his lungs full of water on the riverbank just south of town."

"What about him? And I don't believe his lungs were full of fluid. I have heard that he died before he hit the water."

"What more can you tell me? You mentioned a letter earlier. What was in it that was so important?"

"I do not know. I have never seen it."

"Then what have you heard about it?"

"Only that it is a note about a meeting earlier in the spring to which the Czechoslovaks were not invited. On May 8, I believe."

"And? What was discussed? Or decided?"

"I do not know. As I said, I have not read the letter. But it allegedly discusses options."

"Options about what?"

"The future of this country."

"So, presumably this dead young man got hold of the letter or knew of its contents."

"And he wanted to share them with his new American friends. Not very smart of him," von Hoehn concluded. The East German looked off into the distance and seemed to focus on Hradčany first and then the Charles Bridge, little more than a thin brown line against the sky from this point. "That is all very interesting, if puzzling. But you have more immediate matters at hand. So, what do you plan to do about all this?"

"Oh, you will find out soon enough. But the next time you see Havlíček, tell him that I have found a way for him to pay me back."

"What do want him for? Besides, what makes you think I run Havlíček, whoever he may be."

At this, Baier laughed. He rapped his knuckles on the roof of the Mercedes and started to walk away.

"Just tell him," Baier said as he walked to his own car down the street.

• • •

Hašek was even more excited and angry than Baier. As they walked through Prague's Old Town, Hašek waved his arms in the air as he spoke. Baier kept telling him to keep his voice down.

"This is so typical of those Soviet bastards. I should know. I personally experienced their arbitrary oppression day after day."

"I'm not so sure it's arbitrary. I think they believe they have a good reason for doing this."

"Don't make excuses for them."

Hašek had raised his voice again. Baier looked at the others walking by in the opposite direction and smiled, as though he was simply accompanying some overly excited yet harmless individual on an evening stroll. He glanced behind as well to make sure no one was providing steady company from that direction.

"I'm not," Baier replied. "I am just explaining their rationale in this particular case. I don't doubt that they were a bunch of mean and vindicative sons of bitches during your time in the gulag. I've always wondered why they let you go and then sent you home."

"I told you. They thought I could serve their purpose. Or at least one of them. And I try to make them believe I continue to do so."

"Okay, in that case, can you find out where they're keeping my officer without exposing yourself or undermining that belief the Soviets seem to have in your utility?" Baier sighed and blew out a breath of stale, frustrated air. "And see if you can find anything about a May letter."

"A letter? What sort of a letter?"

"Something to do with a series of options regarding Czechoslovakia's future. It came after a meeting of Warsaw Pact hardliners. Your government was not present."

They walked in silence for about a minute. A heavy, fetid summer air hung above both men, complicating their thoughts while seeming to multiply their problems. Baier sighed and shook his head. "Janos, I'm sorry but—"

"Never mind that. I will see what I can find out. I can always bring it up in a discussion with other KGB advisors. There isn't much I can learn in the Foreign Ministry, but there are actually a few in State Security who might help." He paused to look over at the American. "You are aware, I am sure, that there will not be many privy to any of that information, especially since the new GRU unit is undoubtedly behind this operation. I am talking about your officer's location, not the letter. That is a matter for another time."

"You mean the letter? I would assume that it is very pressing."

"Oh, I'm sure it is. But first things first. We need to take care of your man."

"Yes, yes. Of course, you are right. I most definitely want to get my man out and away from those GRU bastards—if that is indeed who has him. I can't imagine they're likely to be all that sympathetic to his situation. I also recognize the risk involved. That's why I want you to be so careful. But I do not have anyone else at the moment I can turn to."

• • •

It took Hašek only two days to discover where Krohn was being held.

"Please tell me you did not jeopardize your position and safety," Baier said.

"You do not have to worry about that. As I said, I was able to bring the matter up in a conversation with some other KGB advisors, each time separately."

"Jesus, Janos, I hope you didn't go around dropping little time bombs in your daily conversations about something as sensitive as this. That would be bound to raise suspicions."

"No, of course not. The conversations were always about something else entirely. This came up only as an aside. I told you not to worry about me."

"So, where is he, and what kind of security is there?"

Hašek gave Baier the address in an outlying section of Prague, a largely residual neighborhood on the city's northern edge.

"As for security, the GRU unit has given that responsibility to others. They really just want to be out on the prowl. Actual security would be too stationary and boring for them."

"So, how many people are there and what sort of schedule do they keep?"

"That, I am afraid, you will have to discover for yourself, Mister Baier. That would most definitely have raised suspicions if I had probed for that kind of information."

"Yes, I suppose you're right, Janos. But, in any case, thank you for this. This has been a great help." Baier halted and studied the cobblestones at their feet, gathering his thoughts. Then he looked up at the sky before returning his attention to his companion.

"Any word on this mysterious May letter?"

"Funny that. Nobody claimed to know of it, which is not all that surprising. It must be very sensitive. Although one of my Soviet colleagues just smiled and said I did not need to worry about that. I took that as a warning."

"Okay. Thanks for trying. At least you got me some valuable information about my officer."

Hašek smiled and held out his hand. "I am glad I could be of assistance. Good luck."

Baier shook Hašek's hand, then stood and watched as the man moved off alone into the darkening evening.

• • •

Baier decided he would spend no more than two days studying the house where the GRU—or KGB—team was holding Krohn. This had gone on too long already. The house was in a residential neighborhood, as Hašek had described it, which held advantages and disadvantages. Baier and Garrity took turns walking the neighborhood, making sure they did not pass the house itself too often. They also used a variety of cars on the street, parking several homes away in either direction to avoid raising suspicions about their surveillance.

Hašek had mentioned something about the GRU gang having turned over security to a local KGB squad, which gave Baier some hope. This team was likely to be less well-trained and a lot less violent. And as best he and Garrity could tell, there were only two teams of two men who traded off their shifts every twelve hours, So he did not have to worry about being outmanned or outgunned…if it came to that. And if Krohn was not restrained, then they might actually outnumber the bad guys.

The morning of the third day, after 48 hours of watching and waiting, Baier and Garrity approached the house together. The plan was simple. Get inside and overpower the Soviets, grab Krohn, and get the hell out of there. Baier settled his Browning in the small of his back underneath the sports coat he was wearing and then nodded to Garrity to do the same. He knocked.

The answer came in Russian. Baier had expected as much. Since Garrity had the better Czech, he said that he had some papers to deliver from the Czechoslovak State Security office.

The voice inside the house told him in fractured Czech to leave it on the front porch. Garrity refused, claiming he needed a signature.

The door opened a crack. Baier immediately thrust his foot forward and slammed the door against the man inside. The Russian stumbled to the floor, then rolled toward a side table in the foyer. A semi-automatic waited for him on top.

Baier was on him in a flash, his own pistol in his hand. He rammed the side of the gun against the Soviet officer's face and temple, sending blood spurting across the tiled floor.

"Do not move, cocksucker," Baier screamed. In his excitement, he had yelled out his command in English.

The Soviet officer appeared to understand anyway, probably from the force and anger of Baier's voice. He let his right arm drop to the floor and rested his bleeding cheek and temple on the left forearm.

When Baier reached for the rope in his jacket pocket, he looked up to see not one additional team member, but three. All of them were smiling.

"Where did you assholes come from?" Baier asked.

Again, he spoke in English. Baier noticed that Garrity had drawn his Browning and leveled it at the Russian in the middle.

"We've been here the whole time," the Russian said. He also spoke in English, which was almost free of any accent. "And we've been waiting for you, Mister Baier."

CHAPTER TWENTY-TWO

"My first question is why did it take you so long?"
The Russian's smile—at least Baier assumed he was Russian—widened. He grinned at his companions and signaled for them to lower their weapons.

"I do not think these will be necessary now," he continued. "If they ever were."

Garrity shot Baier a confused and quizzical look. Baier shrugged and nodded. He realized that their own guns would be of little help at this point. He stood and looked down at the Soviet he had just beaten and begun to tie up.

"Fine. I'll just turn this poor sod back over to you." Baier shrugged again. "I am sorry, though, that I did not get to finish the job."

"I believe you have done enough damage to that poor man."

Baier looked at the fallen officer again. "Oh, not him. I meant our effort to secure the release of my own officer." He pointed to the Russian on the floor, who now held a handkerchief to his bleeding face. "That was just payback for how you have mistreated my man."

"Ah, but Mister Baier, he has not been mistreated. We have taken good care of him. As you have probably surmised by now, he was not our real target."

The Soviet team leader nodded to the man on his left and motioned with his head toward the back of the house. That officer turned and quick-stepped down the hallway to a room at the rear of the house. After about a minute of silence, the Soviet officer returned with Krohn, who was rubbing his wrists and the back of his neck. The officer marched up to the two Americans and seized their pistols.

Baier glanced up when he heard his officer approach.

"Oh, man, but you guys are a welcome sight," Krohn exclaimed. "Even with these goons still here."

Baier walked up to his man and looked him over. He finished by staring straight into Krohn's eyes.

"Have they harmed you in any way? Tell me the truth. I don't care if these assholes have us surrounded."

Krohn shook his head. "Not really. Only in the food and drink department."

"Come again?"

"The only stuff they offered me to eat was either boiled chicken or super-boiled chicken. And I had to wash that down with vodka, mostly. Every once in a while, I got some tap water."

"Did they touch you at all?"

"No, not after the initial kidnapping."

"How do you feel?"

"Ready and able to get the hell out of here." Krohn glanced around the room. "I've also got some debts to pay." He paused. "I do have one question, though."

"Go ahead."

"What took you so long?"

Baier smiled. "Yeah, sorry about that. But I had to call in some favors to get your location, and then we needed to do some surveillance to put together a plan to get you out."

Krohn turned in the direction of the three Soviets behind him. "They kept saying you'd be along shortly. It was almost reassuring. At first."

"Yeah, like I said, sorry about that. But that was probably what they were hoping for. As it turns out, you are not the real object here. They used you as bait."

Krohn stared hard at his hosts. "Sons of bitches."

Baier turned toward the middle Soviet. "So, are you KGB or GRU?"

The man bowed. "We are GRU, of course. Not like those softies in the KGB."

"I see. Members, no doubt, of the new special unit that arrived a short while ago."

"Precisely. You are well informed, Mister Baier. Then again, I would expect nothing less." His smile had faded, but it returned shortly, brighter than ever. "That is why we needed to have you here." The Soviet's arm waved in the direction of Garrity and then Krohn. "Your men are free to go. Unfortunately, you will have to stay with us."

"Oh, really? And for how long?"

"Not that long. Perhaps a week or a few days more."

"And why is that?"

"Because it serves our purpose. You do not need to know anymore."

Baier looked at Krohn and then turned to catch Garrity's attention.

"You guys should go. When you get back to the office, inform the Ambassador of what happened here. Then send a quick 'eyes only' cable back home." Baier then turned back to the Soviet in charge. "I don't expect this will take too long."

"Perfect," the Russian said. "I would expect you to do and say as much. After all, we have to keep up appearances."

The Soviet chief said something in Russian to his compatriots, and the man on his right walked to the door. He opened it with a flourish and pointed outside. Garrity and Krohn hesitated, looked once more at their own chief, then walked out the door and into the street. After a second or two, Baier called Garrity back and tossed him his car keys.

When he walked back inside, Baier saw that the four GRU officers were busy packing things up. Two men had skipped up the steps to the floor above, while the other two were busy in the kitchen and the back room. Baier thought of simply walking away while they were preoccupied. But as soon as he turned to the door, the chief appeared at his side with his gun drawn. He was also holding Baier's and Garrity's two Browning semi-automatics.

"Believe me, Mister Baier, I will use this if necessary. Our mission is that important."

"Okay then," Baier said. "I will certainly cooperate." Baier smiled for the first time that day. "For now."

When all four men had finished their job, the group strolled through the front door and headed down the street to a pair of Ladas parked at the curb about two blocks away.

"You never noticed these?" The Soviet chief asked.

"Well, it's not like these are the only ones in Prague."

"Of course," The GRU chief replied. "Hiding in plain sight, I think you call it."

"Something like that," Baier answered. "By the way, where did you learn your English? It's pretty good." He paused and studied his antagonist. "And what is your name anyway? It would be nice to know just who my counterpart is."

"My name is not your business. Not yet. And I am not really your counterpart. That would be the KGB chief here."

"Sure. You mean Spekov, right? And your English?"

"Ah, that came from my three years at our consulate in San Francisco. A wonderful city."

The group had reached the two cars, and that's when it happened. A half dozen men leaped from two cars that pulled up in a rush and braked three to four feet from the Ladas. It gave them enough room to block the Ladas but still have enough space to jump from their own vehicles. Thinking back later, Baier realized how surprised he was by their speed and dexterity. True professionals. The Soviets never had a chance. The new bunch quickly surrounded the GRU team with weapons drawn.

"What is the meaning of this?" the GRU chief demanded. "Who do you think you are?"

One of the men was a tall, blond individual in a thin, beige raincoat that stretched to his ankles. He looked to be in his mid- to late thirties. He stepped forward and walked up to the GRU chief. He spoke first in Czech. Then he turned to Baier.

"I told him to release the American immediately. He has no authority here to retain you in our country."

"Well, that is certainly good news."

Then he directed his men to disarm the GRU officers. The Soviet head of the unit stared at the Czech with a cold, hard hatred in eyes that resembled ice picks on a slab.

"You will hear from your superiors for this. I will not forget it," the GRU officer said.

"Gladly. I am acting on their orders." He motioned for his men to retrieve the two Brownings as well.

The GRU man was not about to give up, however. "You know, of course, that this is far from over. In a short matter of time, I will come looking for you."

"As I said before, gladly."

One of the other Czechoslovak officers took Baier by the arm and escorted him to the lead vehicle. Baier climbed into the back seat. He let out a heavy sigh of relief and thanked his companions and newfound friends.

"So, where did you all come from? Are you from the StB?"

Only then did Baier recognize the man who sat in the passenger seat up front. That man turned with a broad smile on his face and spoke in a voice that brought memories from years ago. Those memories were much more pleasant than the times when he had heard that voice more recently.

"I believe we are even now, Mister Baier."

"Yes, Mister Havlíček, I believe we are."

• • •

"I have to say, I am really, really surprised by your appearance, Jaroslav," Baier said. "Pleasantly, of course. But surprised all the same. Just how did you come to be here and at this time?"

Havlíček spoke to the driver, then looked over his shoulder at Baier.

"We were forewarned that you might be at the GRU safehouse."

Baier settled back against the seat. "By whom, and why? And how did you know the right house? The address, I mean."

"Oh, there are those within the StB who work closely enough with Moscow's station in Prague to learn such things. This was one of several that the GRU and the KGB maintain here. Yuri, in the car following us, learned of this particular address through his own contacts." Havlíček looked back at the other car, then turned to the windshield. He smiled at the driver, then focused again on Baier. "We had this one and some of the others staked out days ago. We knew you would eventually show up."

"And you meant to help us all along?"

"Yes, you can say that. Mostly, though, we wanted to prevent the Soviets from having a free hand in our capital."

"Surely not all of those in the StB feel that way."

Havlíček shook his head. "No, you are correct. But I think you have heard of the generational division within the security service. Have you noticed the general age of the men here?"

Baier glanced around the car, then peered through the rear window to get a better glimpse of the others in the car behind. "Now that you mention it…"

"Exactly. They are all from a later generation. They are much less enamored with the Soviet Union, and they support the reform program of Dubček, Cernik, and the others."

"But what are you doing here? Surely you didn't come by that safehouse for a property restitution case for some Sudeten Germans enjoying their newfound prosperity in Bavaria. Or wherever."

"No, officially, I am on vacation."

"Vacation? In Czechoslovakia, the country you fled from in 1948?"

"I still have family here, you know. And with a West German passport and diplomatic status I feel relatively safe."

"So, how did you come to be here with a group from the Czechoslovak security forces?"

"Ah, that is a very significant question. All I will say is that we have a mutual friend."

Von Hoehn, Baier thought. He had passed along the message as Baier had requested. But how had Havlíček assembled the StB team and gotten them to rescue a group of Americans seized by the GRU? And Havlíček's personal role and status remained as mysterious as ever.

"Before you spend too much time and energy trying to solve the puzzle you are so clearly grappling with, let me pass along some information," Havlíček said. "And perhaps a warning."

"Go ahead." At this point, Baier was all ears.

"There is a new commander-in-chief of Warsaw Pact forces now. He was appointed earlier this month, sometime around the 10th of August. General Shchemenko. The man is an old-school Stalinist. And he's been doing a lot of traveling between Warsaw, East Berlin, and Moscow."

"Okay, that was what, four days ago? So? Is this any different from past Soviet appointments and behavior?"

"Perhaps not. But you may find this interesting in conjunction with the recent meetings in Čierna nad Tisou and Bratislava. You should know that Gomulka and Ulbricht were two sources of pressure at those meetings to bring an abrupt end—by any means possible—to what we call the Prague Spring."

"Okay, that is interesting, if circumstantial. I mean, you don't know what they've been saying at these meetings, do you?"

"No, I do not. But you should also be aware that the Politburo in Prague is not united behind Dubček. Moscow has its friends in town."

"Aside from its KGB advisers and the GRU hit squad?"

"Yes. There are still numerous Czechs and Slovaks who support the old Stalinist line. They have been unhappy ever since Khrushchev's speech exposing the crimes of Stalin at the Soviet party congress in 1956."

"Are you saying they are plotting against Dubček and his crowd?"

"I am saying that is something you need to investigate."

Baier was silent for a moment. He glanced out the window at the hills outside the city, watching them roll by as the car sped toward downtown Prague. The sun was high above town by now, and Baier figured it must be close to noon or just beyond. He suddenly realized that he hadn't eaten since yesterday afternoon.

"So, where does the GRU kidnapping of my officer and their effort to hold on to me come in? Why do something so egregious?

It would draw all kinds of attention to their presence and what they are up to."

"Excellent question," Havlíček agreed. "I really cannot say. Maybe you were just a diversion."

"A diversion? From what?"

"From whatever it is Moscow has planned. Perhaps also an attempt to keep you from finding out what they actually do have planned for this country."

CHAPTER TWENTY-THREE

Baier called Sabine to tell her he would be home late that evening—probably very late. Since it was just a few minutes shy of five o'clock, Baier knew that most of the members of the Station would still be at work. He called both Kohn and Kehoe to his office. The two junior officers arrived within a minute. It was as though they were waiting for just this call.

"I'm sorry, Paul, but I think it's best for you and the Station if you went home early," he informed Krohn.

The protest was immediate, as Baier knew it would be.

"No way." Krohn almost shouted. He slid his body far enough forward that Baier thought he was going to fall off his chair. "I mean, why? I haven't done anything wrong."

"I know you haven't," Baier replied. "But you're probably a convenient target at this point. Besides, those bastards have already hit you up twice, and I don't want you to be in any more danger here than you already are. I have a feeling things are going to get increasingly serious." Baier paused to study his junior officer. "And dangerous."

"Sir, with all due respect, I believe Paul can handle himself just fine here." Kehoe also leaned forward in his seat, but not nearly as far as Krohn. Baier was not worried about his balance. "He's learned a lot during his first tour. More than most of us when we first head out."

"I realize this isn't easy for any of us, and I will make sure Paul gets a solid evaluation when the annual reviews roll around. I will also make a point of saying that I would be happy to have him work for me again." Baier paused to let out his breath. "But given all that's happened and going on here, I think this is best."

What Baier did not say was that he wanted to make sure that their work did not get overly influenced emotionally by what had happened. Even for Kehoe, who already had one tour under his belt. Things were going to be difficult enough.

His next move was to mark the drop site on the Charles Bridge that he had agreed to with Hašek and Pillar for another meeting. Their insights into the workings of the Politburo would help steer his own inquiries as to who might be working to undermine the Dubček Government and its reform program. They might also have some information on where the Kremlin was planning to take matters over the next few weeks, or even months. Hašek, in particular.

"Come on, Sabine, it's a lovely night for a walk. Let's stroll through the Old Town, maybe stop somewhere to have dinner."

"Karl, you just got home." She glanced at the clock above the kitchen sink. "It's eight o'clock already. And it sounds like you've had a long and exhausting day."

"Unfortunately, my day isn't over yet."

Sabine walked up to her husband and stared into his eyes. She took hold of both arms and pulled him closer.

"Karl, you're still working now, aren't you? I can always tell by the faraway look in your eyes and how your muscles go so tense. It's like you're planning the next few steps ahead."

Baier smiled. "Yes, yes. I know I can't fool you. But it's only a dead drop of sorts. I need to leave a signal."

Sabine laughed. "Then let's go. But I am going to hold you to that dinner."

Despite the late hour—at least for two Americans—the city center was full of pedestrians enjoying the warm summer evening. Baier actually appreciated the cover this would provide, and he decided to have Sabine leave the mark under their favorite statue—St John of Nepomuk- which would give him the opportunity to check for any surveillance. That was the one disadvantage of having a crowded space. It made it more difficult to single out any individuals you might have seen more than once, as the crowd provided cover for them as well. This time, though, Baier was pretty certain they were free, and Sabine skipped back to her husband in a confident mood.

"Did you rub the relief of that guy falling into the river for good luck?"

"Of course, I did," Sabine exclaimed. "It's a local tradition. If someone is watching, he might have become suspicious if I hadn't."

"Good," Baier replied. "I'll make an ops officer out of you yet."

"You're on." Sabine pushed her forearms against Baier's chest. "When do I start?"

"Well, not here, and not right now." He smiled. "But you are making a good start."

Sabine chuckled. "I will hold you to that. Now, it's time to eat. All this work has made me hungry."

They chose a pleasant café just past the Bridge on the side of the river with the Clock Tower and the city gate. It was still close enough for Baier to have a clear view of the Bridge. After an hour and a half, the two Americans left the restaurant and walked back to where they had parked their car down along the riverbank and just past the old Jewish quarter and the National Opera House. Nobody had walked past the statue and its mark. That was no great surprise for Baier.

"But how long will you have to wait? Is it really that important?" Sabine asked.

"We agreed to try to get by there every other day. And by my counting, today should be that day."

"Well, he could have come by earlier, or will do so later," Sabine suggested.

"True," Baier agreed.

But in the end, it wasn't necessary after all. When they reached their car, Baier climbed in behind the steering wheel. Sabine, however, remained standing by the passenger side. She opened the door slowly and reached in for a slip of note paper folded over three times and resting on the seat. She picked it up very carefully, as though it were a piece of uranium. She handed the message to Baier.

"Someone has been here, Karl."

He took the slip, unfolded the note, and read the message.

"Shit."

"What is it?"

Baier held the note out to Sabine. She shook her head.

"It's from Pillar. Hašek has disappeared."

• • •

Baier did not even get to the front door of his office the following morning. Pillar was waiting for him as he walked along Vlasska Street about a block from the front entrance to the Embassy. Baier could see almost at once that the diplomat was disturbed and frightened. He was without a tie and the jacket had been misbuttoned, giving the man an awkward and worried appearance. His shirt also looked like it had been slept in.

"Gustav, this is one hell of a surprise. On any morning, of course, but especially today, after that message last night," Baier said.

Pillar's head and eyes barely stopped moving to greet Baier as he approached, hand extended.

"Yes, yes, I am aware of that. But this is very important. And worrying."

"Okay, but let's take it a step at a time." Baier placed his hand on the Czech's shoulder, hoping to relax the man a bit and offer some encouragement. He led Pillar away from the Embassy building and began to stroll across the square around the corner so they could talk in private and, hopefully, unseen. "I take it this is all about Hašek's disappearance. I was going to call you as soon as I got to my office."

"I couldn't wait. In fact, I am not sure I should even return there."

"Gustav, just what has happened? No wait, before we get into that, tell me if you were followed this morning."

Pillar's eyes started to dance around the square and the streets behind them again.

"I…I cannot be sure. I have been too nervous, and I rushed over here as soon as I got dressed. I must have waited for you for half an hour."

"Okay. Well, I am here now. What have you heard about Janos? Let us start there."

"He called me last night at home. He sounded very worried, scared even. He claimed that there were men outside his house. They hadn't done anything yet. They were just waiting."

"Waiting for what?"

"He never said. He never got the chance. He just said that they were at the door at that point and that he had to go."

"So, how do you know he has disappeared?"

"I drove over there after he hung up."

"And?"

"The house was dark. No one answered my knocking. There was no one there. It may have been foolish for me to go over there, but I couldn't think of anything else to do."

"Who do you think has him? Your own service or the Soviets?"

Pillar shook his head. "I...I just do not know." His gaze settled on Baier. "I am very frightened at this point. For Hašek, and for myself."

"Has anyone spoken to you about this? About your own activities lately?"

Again, Pillar shook his head. "No. no. Nothing that I recall. But people at the Ministry have been looking at me differently, almost as though they know something is up."

"In what way? Can you give me an example of how their behavior has changed? And does this apply to everyone or just certain people?"

"No, there is nothing specific. No one has said anything. But I no longer receive even the most common greetings or courtesies. It is as though no one wants to be seen speaking with me."

"Okay, Gustav, you need to settle down." Baier went silent for about a minute as he pondered what was best to do next. "All right, Gustav, let's get you back to your normal routine, while I try to find out what has happened to Hašek. I think you should go back to your office and act as normally as possible. Do not give anyone a reason to be suspicious. If you act like you're guilty, people will think that you are."

Pillar's head raced up and down, as though this would settle the suggestion deeper into his consciousness. "Yes, yes. I will do that. And what about Janos?"

"I will ask around. I'll see what my contacts can tell me. I'm not sure I'll be able to do anything at this point, especially if the Soviets have him, which is my suspicion."

"Why is that?"

"Because they consider him one of theirs. They are the ones who let him out of Siberia on the condition that he work for their interests in Czechoslovakia. And, if that's the case, it depends on what they have on him."

"But that would also be the case if it is the StB."

"True, to a point. I think we both might have others inside the StB who would be willing to help us. In any case, our talking about this will not help either of you. Let's get started on our day. Things could look much different by the end of it."

Pillar stopped and grabbed Baier's arm. "I have one more question, Karl."

"Yes?"

"You stated earlier that you would be prepared to help me escape Czechoslovakia, should it be necessary. Did you mean that? Does it still hold?"

Baier nodded. His response was immediate and vigorous. "Yes, of course. If you need to leave I will do everything in my power to get you out."

"And my wife?"

"Yes, of course. Her as well."

• • •

Before he even got to his desk, Baier would be pressed to deliver on his promise. As he walked down the hallway, Baier could hear his telephone ringing. He ran to the door, flipped the lock, then stumbled to his desk. He jerked the receiver from its cradle and pressed it against his ear. Before he said a word, Baier could hear the labored breathing as Pillar pushed his words through the line.

"Karl, Karl, hurry, please."

"Gustav, what is it?"

"They have come for me."

"Where are you calling from?'

"From a telephone booth down the street where we parted this morning. A car with four men rushed to the curb, but I saw them coming when I looked for surveillance. Just like you told me to do."

"Okay, okay. But where are they now? How did they miss you?"

"I am not sure. I ran into an office building and out the back door into an alley. I waited for a few moments around a corner of a building at the end of the block. Then I doubled back when I did not see anyone and called you."

"Good, good." Baier tried to think. "Is there some place there you can hide? Stay out of sight, I mean."

"Yes, I will stay in the restroom of the office building." He gave Baier the address.

"Got it. Please do not panic, Gustav. I will be by shortly to pick you up."

Baier just hoped he could get there in time. And beat anyone else in the hunt for the diplomat.

CHAPTER TWENTY-FOUR

Baier was certain now that the Kremlin and the pro-Soviet contingent in the Czechoslovak government had something afoot. He just wasn't sure who was involved and how far along their plan was. As soon as he got Pillar's wife to the safety of the Embassy, he would turn to that. He hoped he still had time to get the necessary information and send it along to Washington.

For the first part, he asked Ralph Gruszauskas, the Embassy's Regional Security Officer or RSO—the man responsible for the security and safety of the Embassy and its staff–to join him for the trip to Pillar's home. The man was capable enough, but Baier really wanted him along in case he needed extra diplomatic cover. That is, if they were interrupted.

Besides, he knew he could trust Gruszauskas's discretion since he had helped Baier recover Pillar and smuggle him into the Embassy via the trunk of the RSO's car. The RSO had not even hesitated when Baier suggested they use one of the Embassy vehicles, as he was fairly certain his own was on some sort of watch list with the KGB and GRU by now.

"Please. Karl, you must allow me to accompany you," Pillar had pleaded.

"No, Gustav. That would only increase the complications and challenges. We already know you are being hunted, and I am sure there's a team outside keeping watch over this building. In fact, I'm sure of it. That's why we used my colleague's car in the Embassy garage."

"Then how do you plan to leave unnoticed?"

"That's where it gets interesting. You will just have to trust me." Baier smiled with a look that he hoped was reassuring. "It worked getting you in here, didn't it?"

Baier left the poor man standing in the first-floor conference room, his face creased with anxiety and fear. Apparently, the smile was not enough.

"Please, just trust me. I know what I'm doing, Gustav."

While Gruszauskas drove out of the Embassy garage, Baier hunkered down in the back seat to escape being seen by what he was certain would be a team of StB, KGB, or even GRU officers. Maybe all three. He also had a disguise kit for himself and Pillar's wife.

Gruszauskas steered the car clear of the compound and the street in front of the Embassy at a leisurely pace, the better to avoid alarming any watchers. The drive took about twenty minutes through the heart of the city and out toward the northern neighborhood. It was almost a suburb, even resembling an American outpost with small residential lots and two-story wooden-framed or stucco-lined houses. Pillar's was one of the latter, with a dark grey stucco covering and a roof of brown slate tiles. Baier wondered if the color of the stucco was the original one, or if it had been warped by the years of pollution from the use of the soft brown coal that fouled the air of much of eastern Europe.

"How do you want to proceed, Karl?" Gruszauskas asked. "You're the expert here."

"I'm hardly that. Although I do have some experience, more so, anyway, than you State Department weenies."

Gruszauskas laughed and turned to Baier. "Do you want my help or not?"

"Of course, my man. I think we have the makings of a great team." It was Baier's turn to laugh. "Or however Bogie phrased it."

Baier surveyed the street. He was surprised at how deserted it was. That could be a good sign, or a trap.

"Aw, screw it," Baier decided. "We haven't got a lot of time here. Let's just do it."

Gruszauskas parked about a block away. Then the two Americans climbed from the car and walked casually to the Pillar residence. Baier remembered the disguise kit after a few steps and retreated to grab that. A row of shrubbery that reached about a foot beyond Baier's and Gruszauskas's heads marked the front boundary of the property, with a small, white, waist-high gate in the middle. The two Americans glanced around, saw no one, and passed through the gate. Surprisingly, the front door was open.

"I guess we won't need these," Baier said. He held out the keys that Pillar had given him before they left the Embassy.

"Yeah, but let's hope somebody else didn't take advantage of the free passage before we got here," Gruszauskas said."

As soon as they entered the front foyer, Baier realized that someone had done just that. The living room furniture had been pushed to the side wall that looked out over a driveway, and books and papers lay scattered on the floor. A table lamp lay on its side next to an end table, while another remained upright, although the table had been pushed to the entrance of the kitchen. Taped to the frame of the entrance to the kitchen was a large note on an 8 X 11 piece of paper. Baier ripped it down and read the message out loud.

"You are still a step behind, Herr Baier. If want to see Frau Pillar, you will need to meet with me first." It was signed "v H."

"Son of a bitch," Baier shouted. He thrust the note at Gruszauskas.

"What the hell does that mean?"

"There's a long history there," Baier tried to explain. "I am really getting to dislike this guy."

"Can you say anymore?" Gruszuakas asked.

Baier shook his head. "Not right now. But I will need you to drop me off at the East German Embassy."

"Seriously? I mean, what the hell can you do there?"

"The real question, Ralph, is what can I do if I don't go there next?"

Baier slammed the door shut on their way out. He locked it as well.

• • •

Baier had just under an hour to wait, maybe fifty minutes. He wasn't checking his watch. He stared at the entrance to the Embassy of the German Democratic Republic, as the sign in front so gloriously and inaccurately proclaimed, the entire time. He was prepared to stay there as long as it took. He did not want to have to confront Pillar without more information on the whereabouts and well-being of the man's wife.

"We are going to have to stop meeting like this," von Hoehn said as he approached the familiar bench on which Baier sat. "Isn't that what people in your country say?"

"When it's appropriate. How did you ever learn all those quaint American phrases? Shouldn't you be using those hackneyed British ones?"

"I have been studying your American slang. I find it more entertaining."

"Well, in any case, we can stop meeting like this when you stay the hell out of my affairs."

Von Hoehn actually laughed out loud, his head rocking back so that he could look at the sky. He turned his focus back to Baier.

"What makes you think any of this is simply your affair? What is going on here—and especially now—concerns all of us. Don't you realize that we could be standing at one of the breaking points of the Cold War?"

"That sounds a bit exaggerated when all I want to do is reunite a man with his wife."

Von Hoehn smiled. Baier remembered that condescending look from their confrontations in Paris and Berlin. It was even less attractive now. The East German kept his stance at the back of the bench while Baier slid away from him. He wanted more distance since he was uncertain where the conversation was going.

"Oh, is that all you want?" von Hoehn asked. "You don't want to know more about the machinations underway within the Czechoslovak Praesidium? Moscow's efforts to arrest and reverse the reform program of Dubček?"

"Do you have that information?" Baier asked.

The East German's smile widened. "Some. My assistant, some eager young kid from Chemnitz, has been working closely with the conservatives—some of them truly committed Stalinists—and he keeps bragging about what all they are going to do." His smile disappeared suddenly, as von Hoehn seemed to ponder one of life's strategic questions. "You know, our regime has exploited the old chemical industry there to boost our exports to our East European allies, and it has destroyed the quality of life in the area. It's amazing that anyone who grew up there can feel any loyalty to the regime. The stucco on the homes has actually turned black from the pollution. It's even worse than here." He looked quizzically at Baier. "Can you imagine what their lungs must look like?"

"Back to the matter at hand, von Hoehn. What of all this plotting? Where do things stand?"

Von Hoehn shook his head. "Not so fast, my American friend."

"I am not your friend."

Von Hoehn laughed again. "Oh, that's just another one of your cute phrases. But all your information comes with a cost."

"Which is?"

"That you will discover the next time we meet."

"When will that be? And where?"

"Let's meet tomorrow late morning. Say around ten o'clock."

"And where?"

"How about in front of that nice little restaurant below the Charles Bridge that you and Pillar like so much? We'll be in the back having a coffee. But don't come hungry. We won't have that much time."

"Will Mrs. Pillar be there?"

Von Hoehn looked at the sky and pursed his lips, as though pondering his response. Baier had no doubt that von Hoehn had brought the answer with him when he first arrived.

"Yes, probably." He nodded and smiled again. "And perhaps someone else as well."

Baier jumped up. The East German turned to go and started back toward his embassy. Baier hurried to follow.

"Who? Who, dammit?"

Von Hoehn turned and simply shrugged. He did not say a word. The smile returned as he walked away.

• • •

When Baier arrived at the restaurant the next morning, he was early, a half an hour early. It was a habit of his, ingrained from years of training and experience. Always arrive early to secure the meeting site and check for unwanted company. The restaurant was nearly empty, nothing unusual for a late morning assignation, but when the clock registered a quarter after the hour, Baier became concerned…not worried or anxious, but still concerned. After all, von Hoehn was German, and a North German at that.

A Prussian, to be exact. He, if anybody, should be punctual to a fault.

Five minutes later, the waiter brought a note to Baier and excused himself for the misunderstanding. Confused, Baier read the message, which told him to come outside. Baier stood, dropped some change on the table to pay for his coffee, then walked outside. There he encountered the smiling—and annoying—countenance of Alexander von Hoehn.

"I decided it would be best to change our location." The East German held out his hand. "Please, come with me."

He led Baier to another restaurant several blocks away. It sat in a narrow warren of cobbled streets, perhaps a quarter of a mile from the Charles Bridge and still in the Malá Strana neighborhood. Baier followed von Hoehn inside. At the back of the dining room, two women sat at a booth, obscured from any passersby outside. One of them was Marianne Pillar. Bair did not recognize the other woman.

"Please, take a seat," von Hoehn said. He held out his hand again, this time indicating a spot on the bench next to Mrs. Pillar. She smiled and squeezed Baier's hand. Baier wondered if it was a greeting or a cry for help. As it turned out, it was a gesture of gratification.

"Thank you so much for coming," she said. "You do not know how much this means to me and my husband."

Baier stared at her face and nodded. He forced out a smile.

"Are you all right? Have they harmed you in any way?"

Marrianne Pillar shook her head. "Oh, no, no. The Hoehns have been very gracious and understanding. And, I might add, very helpful."

"Then why did your house look like someone had driven a bulldozer through it?"

Her face took on a worried look as a frown and wrinkles spread across her forehead and along her cheeks.

"Then we got out of there just in time," von Hoehn replied. "29155 must have shown up later and tossed everything in frustration."

Baier looked across the table, noticing the other woman who sat close to von Hoehn. She was also holding his hand. The Stasi officer nodded at the other woman and spoke up again.

"Herr Baier, allow me to introduce my wife, Tina Hoehn, nee Chernov."

The name hit Baier like a thunderbolt. Images of his past encounters with a man of the same name rushed back, surrounding him in a web of confusion. The name of his old antagonist and sometime partner from the KGB, and before that, the NKVD, was one he never expected to hear again. He sat there for a moment in stunned silence, his lips parted as though he was waiting for a word or two to emerge, but without the power to push them out.

"I expected as much in your reaction, Karl," von Hoehn said. "Please, excuse me for this sudden change in our company. But I did not know how else to include my wife. Anything else would have been too risky."

Von Hoehn's use of his first name almost brought a smile to Baier's face—not quite, though. Baier immediately tried to figure out what lay behind the East German's use of such a friendly form of address, something unusual in a language governed by a variety of formalities. That faded, however, when Baier considered the new complications that von Hoehn's wife brought with her presence.

"And this is not? And what do you mean by including your wife? Include her in what?"

"That will become clear shortly. But first, let me explain how we came to this position today."

"Yes, please do," Baier said.

"As you may have already guessed, Mrs. Pillar was not seized by the KGB, the GRU, or anyone else. Not even by the Stasi. I myself decided I had to intervene to, shall we say, protect my interests."

"Your interests? And what would those be? Do they differ from those of your employer?"

"Well, today they do, yes. You see, I knew that the StB and the Soviets were about to arrest both Hašek and Pillar. They were aware that both men had been working with you in passing along secrets of various developments within the Dubček Government and the relationships certain people in Prague have had with the Kremlin for some time now."

"Go on."

"You may already have the names of some of the conspirators. Men like Bilak, Indra, Kolder, and Svestka have been working closely with the Soviet functionaries here in Prague to orchestrate a new body called something like a 'revolutionary workers' and peasants' committee' to create the aura of a popular movement—or least a movement within the party leadership—to invite a Soviet intervention or coup to remove Dubček."

"And the good guys?"

"Well, along with Dubček, of course, there are men like Kriegel, Cernik, Mlynar, and Smrkovsky. The two sides are pretty evenly balanced, and much will depend on where the fence-sitters like Husak and President Svoboda come down."

"Who do you think will win out? What are you hearing?"

"It all remains unclear at this point. Today, August 20, I understand that the pro-Soviet faction is meeting before the party plenum meets later today, to engineer support for a proposal to invite the Soviets in, all in the name of this vainglorious 'committee.' The problem this group has, though, is that most of them are cowardly bureaucrats who are clearly opposed to Dubček's reforms because they threaten the positions and power of the conservative faction within the government and the party." Von Hoehn paused and smiled. "I really can't say how it will all turn out."

"Will it make any difference in the end?" Baier asked.

"That is hard to say. I believe Dubček and his backers remain convinced that they continue to enjoy broad popular support and are convinced that reform within the Communist system is still possible. That is, as long as Moscow's international interests are kept in mind. This will make further reforms like those already underway still possible."

"And you? What do you believe?"

"I believe it is a mistake to underestimate the determination of the Kremlin to protect its international interests, and the interests of the more conservative leaders in Moscow. I have even heard that the Soviet leadership made a decision in favor of invading as early as May. But Brezhnev has been holding it as an option, not something that is inevitable.

"You sound pretty confident."

"I know the enemy you face."

"So, how does that bring us to this meeting today?"

"Mrs. Pillar has told me of your promise to her husband that you will assist them in escaping, if that becomes necessary."

The alarm bells were ringing loud enough in Baier's ears to drown out any noise from outside. It must have shown on his face.

"No, do not misunderstand me, Herr Baier. I have no intention of blocking or disrupting any plans you might have had to assist the Pillars."

"Is that where your interests differ from those of your employers?"

Von Hoehn nodded. He glanced over at his wife before looking back at Baier.

"Yes, that is one area where I differ from my own organization. I want you to include my wife in an escape. That is, if you decide to move forward." He paused. "And I think it would also be wise to do so."

"Why is that?"

"Because a Soviet intervention is only a matter of time. And my wife thinks it is also time to reunite with her brother in America."

"And what are your plans? Are you coming with her?"

"No, I will stay here. That, at least, is my plan for now." Von Hoehn stared hard at Baier. "Things, however, have a way of changing."

This was the second shock of the morning for Baier. The first had come, naturally enough, from the woman's name. That could have been a simple coincidence. He had no idea, but 'Chernov' was probably not that unusual a name for a Russian family. Maybe not as common or as popular as 'Weber' or 'Strauss' in Germany, but still likely to pop up occasionally. But this, Sergei Chernov's long-lost sister, the woman who, with the other brother, had allegedly disappeared in the far reaches of South America after the Bolshevik coup, was now sitting across from him and holding hands with her East German—no, Prussian—aristocratic husband. Now that was just too difficult to accept or digest as anything other than extraordinary, or fictional. He sat dumbfounded, unable to process the thought or speak.

"Again, Herr Baier, I apologize for the shock I have caused. Perhaps someday I will tell you how we met and fell in love, but for now let me say that it happened in Paris shortly after I returned from Soviet captivity."

"Okay. This is going to take a while for me. I am sure you can understand that."

"Yes, of course. But surely you can see how this motivated me to help you in certain ways and at certain times."

Baier thought back to Havlíček's recent appearance at his own kidnapping, even the message in the car seat the night of the concert.

"Was the message on the front seat yours that night back by Hradčany?"

"Actually, no. I was going to pass a note to you when you returned to your car, but I saw Hašek toss his own note into your vehicle."

"Okay. I guess this is starting to make sense. But what am I supposed to do with these two women until an escape is attempted? If it even occurs? Surely, Mrs. Pillar is in danger of being seized, since the StB and others are after her husband."

"Whom I hope is safely tucked away in your embassy. In that case. I would suggest that we spirit both women away to your house until the time comes."

"My house? What makes you think that is safe? And why should I jeopardize my wife's safety?"

"Because that is the risk she took when she married you. When she agreed to accompany you on assignments such as these. Do you think she would object? Didn't you arrange for her own parents to escape from the East? Surely, she will understand the precarious time we are in and want to do whatever she can to help."

Baier had to agree. Even if it was to help someone related to "that fucking Russian," as she had labeled Sergei Chernov all those years ago in war-torn Berlin.

"How do you plan to transport everyone to my house?"

"I will take care of that. My wife's and Mrs. Pillar's suitcases are packed in my trunk already."

"Oh, so you knew all along I would agree to this harebrained scheme."

Von Hoehn's condescending smile crept back in. "Karl, I have encountered you, and, yes, your wife, enough to know how you were most likely to react. And if you hadn't agreed, then what harm would a couple of suitcases in the trunk of my car pose?"

"All right. But I will have to follow you home. I will need to prepare Sabine for her surprise. I expect her shock to be almost as great as mine."

Von Hoehn and the two women stood. Von Hoehn's smile carried a more grateful expression this time.

"I never really had any doubt about your wife. In some ways, she is the stronger of you two."

Baier sat a moment longer. He needed a minute to gather his thoughts and to communicate the command to his body to rise and leave the booth. He followed his new companions, his new associates, out the door.

• • •

The Ambassador was skeptical, not disbelieving, but skeptical nonetheless.

"I'm sorry, Karl, but I think you're being a bit alarmist here. Are you aware that the meeting of the pro-Moscow conspirators has collapsed?"

"Collapsed?" Baier asked. "In what way, Sir?"

According to my sources, that group proved to be a pretty cowardly bunch. They failed to push through their proposal at the Presidium meeting. The agenda stuck to the normal run of a weekday business meeting."

"So, what do you or your sources think that means?"

"Well, it's obviously too soon to make any kind of pronouncement, but there are a number of possible interpretations. For example, it could be that the old Stalinists realize that the reforms have far too much support among the Czechoslovak populace to try anything that would subvert Dubček's program."

"Okay," Baier agreed. Momentarily. "But they could try again. Doesn't it all depend on where the Kremlin comes down on this?"

The Ambassador nodded and shuffled his hair in thought.

"Oh, sure. You always have to take Brezhnev and his cronies into account. But it still isn't clear to me just how they plan to address the situation here, especially given the popular mood. Brezhnev could still be pondering a number of options. He may have taken the pressure off his agents in the Politburo in Prague to see what develops. I think he also has to consider the international reaction. Any Soviet intervention—no matter how hard he works to hide Moscow's hand—will meet with widespread protests. That could not look good to a leader of the so-called workers' and peasants' state."

"Okay," Baier responded. "But I have to say I'm still not convinced. Every meeting, every conversation I've had with my local contacts indicates that something bad is in the offing."

"I can't say you're wrong, Karl. Go ahead and finish up that report of yours—or whatever you people call those analytic reports from the field—and send it back to Washington. I can put my own qualifications in a "comment" section. Be assured, though, that I will not try to refute your argument. None of us are infallible. We all deserve a hearing."

"Thank you, Sir."

Baier stood to leave, shook the Ambassador's hand, then walked into the hallway. The Secretary and office manager both gave Baier their usual comforting smiles. The door to the office of the Deputy Chief of Mission at the other end of the suite was open, with the DCM at his desk writing something furiously. The DCM glanced up and nodded in Baier's direction before returning to his own task.

Everyone, except the DCM, looked busy but relaxed at the same time. Baier hoped he would have enough time to finish his cable to Headquarters before what he feared actually happened.

CHAPTER TWENTY-FIVE

He never did get the chance to finish his report.
It was still dark outside when Baier awoke to what sounded like the rumble of heavy traffic and intermittent gunfire. Baier fought his way free of the sheets wrapped around his legs and fell from the bed. He stumbled to the window, brushed back the curtains, and peered into the street below. Nothing but more darkness and the occasional light from a street lamp.

"What is it, Karl?" Sabine mumbled from the bed.

Baier turned and stared at his wife. She was sitting upright, a look of confusion fighting with the remnants of the night's interrupted sleep. Her hair lay like pockets of matted fur along the sides of her head. Baier brushed his own hair toward the back of his skull, only to have it fall forward over his forehead in an act of defiance.

"I'm not sure. But there is definitely something unusual going on. I haven't seen anything yet."

Seconds after he spoke, Baier saw what looked like a Soviet T-54 or T-55 tank crawl down the street, its turret revolving as though it was searching for a target. A smattering of soldiers trotted behind the tank, rifles cradled in their arms at their waists. Leaning against the glass, Baier saw several more tanks in the street behind the first.

"Jesus Christ," Baier shouted. "Those fucking Soviets have invaded."

In a second, Sabine was at his side by the window.

"Oh, my God," Sabine hissed. Her voice was barely above a whisper, more like the sound of shock than anger. "Those bastards have really done it. I didn't think they'd have the courage or determination for something like this."

"I'd better get dressed." He turned from the window and headed for the closet. "Wake our guests. Have them get dressed. I'll have to see what information the Embassy has before deciding what to do next."

Baier drove slowly and cautiously. His biggest fear was that some overeager second lieutenant or corporal would mistake him for some sort of resistance figure or Czechoslovak official and therefore a legitimate target.

As it was, he was stopped twice by Soviet Army patrols. Each time, the routine was the same. An enlisted man motioned for him to stop, came to the driver's side window, and held out his hand. Baier handed over his American diplomatic passport, which lifted the eyebrows of the young man—presumably from somewhere on the Central Asian steppe—and caused some initial confusion. A quick shout and hand gesture brought an officer—Baier was uncertain of the rank—who asked Baier a question in incomprehensible Russian. Baier tried to explain that he was on his way to the American Embassy. The last two words seemed to bring a degree of understanding, and he was waved through. Sullen groups of Soviet infantry, rifles at the ready, watched his car lurk away.

The Embassy presented a scene of complete chaos. Baier passed through the cordon of Marines in full battle gear as he drove into the basement garage. Upstairs, staffers were running about, shouting orders, questions, and explanations in a swirling sea of words, gestures, curses, and just plain desperation.

Outside, the streets of Prague were already filling with the people of the city, who swarmed over the tanks and confronted the Soviets in their vehicles and on foot. The Czechs all seemed to be under the illusion that they could debate their way to freedom and end the invasion with words and logic, as well as occasional bursts of graffiti. A few brave souls were beginning to daub swastikas on the sides of tanks and lorries or draw them on the walls with an equation pointing to the Soviet red star. That all appeared to make little impression on the Soviet soldiers. They had probably been told they were being deployed to fight that very fascism. Baier had to admire the courage and earnestness of the Czechs and Slovaks swarming in the streets below.

"Dubček has pleaded for no violence in response to this."

Baier turned from the window at the building's front. The speaker was a young Foreign Service Officer, or FSO, whom Baier had met on occasion. He, too, was an earnest young man, here on his second tour after a stint in Bucharest. Baier blinked, then refocused. He was stunned to see tears in the diplomat's eyes. Baier couldn't blame him, especially when he realized he felt like crying himself.

"He said he has ordered the Army to stay in the barracks," the FSO continued. "He wants to avoid unnecessary bloodshed."

"It's just as well," Baier said. "It's not like they have any hope of repulsing the attack."

"Still, there have been some deaths." The FSO's lips tightened. "Those bastards. Maybe now the world will see what the Soviet Union is really all about."

"I think they already know," Baier replied.

Baier turned and ran to the stairs. Once upstairs, he made for his office, happy to see that the area was fully staffed, as best he could tell, with all the excitement. The first thing he did was to call down to Gruszauskas to see if there were any reports of US citizens harmed or arrested.

"Not so far," Gruszauskas said. "But we are still trying to account for everyone. It's hard to do at this point. The road in isn't exactly worry-free, if you know what I mean."

Baier thought back to his own traffic stops on the way in. "Yes, Ralph. I know exactly what you mean. Keep me posted, okay?"

When he looked up from the phone, Baier saw Garrity, Kehoe, and Krohn standing in the doorway to his office.

"I guess we couldn't get you out of here fast enough, Paul. Sorry about that."

"Oh, don't apologize. I can't think of any place I'd rather be right now," Krohn replied.

"Me, too," Kehoe interjected.

"Well, we'll have to see how long we all stay. Some of us, probably a lot of us, will be heading out of here soon. Families, too. In fact, I'm going to inform Headquarters as soon as we finish here that I am ordering an evacuation of all non-essential Station personnel. And, of course, that means all family members."

"Of course," Garrity responded. "Any word on that matter from the front office?"

Baier shook his head. "I haven't had a chance to speak with the Ambo. I'm sure he is swamped right now. In any case, I'm going to head down to see him as soon as all our people are accounted for. Have we started the call chain to make sure everyone is notified and has responded with their whereabouts?"

Garrity nodded. "You bet, Chief. All officers have arrived here, and their families are safe and accounted for. They're all hunkered down at home and have been told under no circumstances to go outside."

"Good. I'll let everyone know in an all-hands meeting what our next steps are as soon as I've spoken with Beam."

• • •

The Ambassador's secretary waved Baier into his office as soon as he walked through the door of the suite.

"He's waiting for you," was all she said.

The Ambassador stopped his pacing as soon as he saw Baier and walked over to shake his hand. He was wearing the same clothes he had on yesterday, but minus the usual regimental striped tie. The suit jacket lay in a heap on the floor beside his desk chair. Baier figured it must have fallen off the back of the chair. Appropriately, it was black, like the slacks.

"Well, I guess we know now who was right."

"It's a small consolation, Ambassador."

"True. Are all your people all right?" the Ambassador asked.

Baier nodded. "Yes, Sir. So far, so good."

"Excellent." The Ambassador turned to take in a woman seated just to the back on the plush, brown leather sofa near the door. "You will have to excuse me, Karl, but you have not had the chance to meet my guest. Let me introduce Shirley Temple Black."

The famous movie star rose, her right hand out. She was dressed casually in a pair of khaki slacks and a white cotton blouse. "I am truly sorry we had to meet under these circumstances. I had hoped to have more time to sit down and discuss the changes underway in Czechoslovakia, Mister Baier."

"I, too, am sorry we haven't had that chance. From the looks of things, we probably never will. How did you come to be in Prague, and at such an auspicious moment?"

She smiled and glanced toward the window. "I am here on a humanitarian call primarily. I represent the International Society of Multiple Sclerosis. I was supposed to meet with Mister Dubček this afternoon. Instead, I took refuge on the roof of my hotel." She motioned with a nod of her head toward Ambassador Beam. "This good gentleman was able to send a squad of his own diplomatic security team to rescue me and bring me here. I feel much safer now." She smiled. "To a point, of course."

"Well, welcome aboard. I think." Baier turned to the Ambassador. "Will there be an evacuation? And if so, how soon?"

The Ambassador walked back to his desk and shuffled through some papers. He looked up first at his guest, then at Baier.

"Yes, I believe so. These plans are only tentative and little more than a set of suggestions. Naturally, we need to organize a safe passage with the Soviet military now that they appear to be taking control of the entire country. I understand their army has surrounded the Czechoslovak military bases and seized the airports." The Ambassador frowned. "They have already closed the country's airspace."

Baier nodded, then studied the floor at his feet. Not finding an answer there, he looked up at the Chief of Mission.

"In that case, may I have a word with you, Ambassador? I have a request to make."

• • •

The East German had been right about Baier's wife. Baier knew he would be. Once back home, Baier could see that Sabine had accepted the news of the invasion and the likelihood of an evacuation with a calmness that Baier would have expected from few others. For Sabine, it was almost routine.

"We will be taking our guests as well, of course. I've made sure they've packed their bags," Sabine said.

"Yes, absolutely. How many suitcases are there?"

"Just the two. I only allowed them to have one each."

"The first step will be to get them out of here and to the Embassy. And we should not wait any longer. There is always a lot of confusion in the early stages of a military operation such as this one. We need to move before the new authorities have established their control. I am sure the new regime and their Soviet friends will be on the lookout for the Pillars."

"And the Russian *Frau*?"

"She will probably be the easiest one to move. My guess is that von Hoehn has arranged things so that no one will be looking for her. Not yet, anyway."

"How are we leaving? Do we need to drive to the airport?"

"I discussed that with the Ambassador this morning. The airports and Czechoslovak airspace are all closed. We're going to try to get all dependents and non-essential staff out in a convoy. That will also be the easier way to sneak our guests out."

"How so?"

"Well, we haven't had enough time to put together new documentation for the three of them. I'm hoping we can hide them in the crowd and avoid having every individual in the party checked."

"Do you really think the StB and KGB will let everyone out that easily? That would suggest a new level of cooperation far beyond the scope of anything those fucking Russians can imagine."

"I'm counting on our allies still working within the StB to help us out."

"I'll say a prayer."

"Lutheran or Catholic?"

"Both."

• • •

Baier had driven home more slowly than on his earlier trip to the Embassy—if that was even possible. He drove with the same, deliberate pace on the return to the Embassy, but this time it was not the Red Army that held him up. It was the swarm of enraged Czechs and Slovaks who now overwhelmed the streets. People were marching with placards that had signs in Russian, Czech, and even English, protesting the invasion and occupation. Groups broke off to surround Soviet tanks and patrols. It was a good thing that Baier knew the way, because many of the street signs had been removed or switched to create confusion among the Soviet forces. He had to laugh when he saw that many signs had the name of Dubček painted on them, a glaring rejection, an open challenge even, to the Soviet invaders.

On the way back to the Embassy, he had paused momentarily at Wenceslas Square to watch a solitary figure, a man in nothing more than slacks and shirtsleeves, carrying his briefcase as though on his daily hike to work, frozen in place at the edge of the Square. His muscles did not move. Even his face was still, wrinkled with confusion, as he took in the scene before him. Soviet tanks and groups of infantrymen stood sullenly with faces devoid of any expression. They were surrounded by Czechs gesturing, arguing, cursing, and weeping, as they tried in vain to ward off the inevitable occupation of their country and the end of their experiment in a more humane and open socialism. Faces of stone from the soldiers grouped around the tanks and trucks stared back at the solitary individual and his countrymen . Finally, the lonely man lowered his head and turned away. He was obviously not going to his office today. Baier fought back a tear and drove on.

The great majority, however, stayed in the square. Their crowd was even growing as more civilians rushed to the scene. Baier paused for a moment to gaze at the small sea of earnest and frustrated humanity spreading like a wave of protest from the foot of the statue of King Wenceslas to the broader city beyond.

"My God, these people are amazing," Sabine said. Her eyes were wide with wonder and admiration. She turned and spoke to Mrs. Pillar, who was spread lengthwise across the floor in the back seat with a blanket hiding her from prying eyes outside. Von Hoehn's wife was curled in the trunk, a blanket covering her as well. Baier had been mildly—and pleasantly—surprised at how easily and comfortably both women had responded to his suggestions for hiding them in the car.

"We just do not know what to expect," Baier had explained. "I have already been stopped several times by the Soviet Army earlier this morning."

Mrs. Pillar had smiled and taken his hand. "We will do whatever you ask. We are already deeply indebted to you."

Frau Hoehn had simply nodded. "*Ich danke Ihnen. Herzlich.*"

After about an hour, they reached the Embassy. It took another twenty minutes to navigate through the horde assembled along the street that fronted the compound. Fortunately, the Marine guards waved Baier's car through almost immediately. Once in the garage, Baier hurried to help both women from their hiding spaces. After a quick stretch to get their circulation running again and their joints realigned, they embraced Baier and Sabine.

Upstairs, Baier took his new guests to the conference room, where Pillar waited. The couple immediately fell into each other's arms. They held that hug for several minutes. When Pillar approached Baier there were tears in his eyes. The Czech diplomat held out both arms, and he grabbed Baier by the shoulders.

"You cannot believe how relieved I am."

Baier thought back to his own escape from Hungary in 1955 with Sabine at his side after freeing her from a Hungarian prison.

"I believe I can. I am happy for the both of you, all the same."

It was then that Baier noticed the tears in Frau Hoehn's eyes as well.

"I am sorry that you have been separated from your husband. But I am sure you two will be together again. Somehow, somewhere."

"Yes, thank you. I hope so."

Baier asked the party to be patient and to try to make themselves comfortable.

"I have no idea how long it will take to organize our convoy. The biggest challenge will be getting a safe passage agreement with the Soviet Army. I also have no idea how the Czechoslovak authorities will respond either. That is, if they even have anyone operating with authority over all or any of the ministries at this point."

As he made his way to the door, Sabine took Baier aside.

"Karl, will you be coming with us?"

Baier held his breath, frowning.

"No, Sabine. Not yet. I can't leave my colleagues at such a drastic and important period."

"So, we will be separated once more."

Baier took his wife in his arms.

"Only for a short time. Or so I hope. But you know that this is what we expect in the life we choose. My work is even more important now. At this moment. I have to stay to help sort out what is to come of this mess Moscow has created."

Sabine stroked her husband's face.

"Of course, I understand. But please be careful. I will wait for you. You know I will."

Baier knew that was true. He just wished he knew how long it would be before he saw her again.

• • •

In the end, it took just twenty-four hours to organize the convoy, assemble the necessary vehicles, and reach a safe passage agreement with the Soviets. The Embassy had become quite crowded with all the dependents and non-essential personnel gathered for the exodus, and the patience of some was wearing pretty thin. Baier was happy to see that his contingent was bearing up well.

All things considered," Pillar counseled, "the alternative is a lot less pleasant."

The Czechoslovak government, represented by an StB officer Baier did not recognize, watched in silence. The Soviets also had an officer—a major, Baier believed—and two infantrymen as guards to observe the departure.

As the group gathered to board the vehicles, Baier tried to reassure the Pillars and von Hoehn's wife. Sabine held Frau Hoehn's hand, while Pillar's wife had her arm interlocked with that of her husband.

"Everything will be all right," Baier said. "Try not to be nervous. That will only raise suspicions."

Easier said than done, Baier realized; his confidence fell as soon as the first vehicle left the garage. That car carried the famous and former movie star, Shirley Temple Black. It had been stopped by the StB official and his Soviet counterpart. Windows were lowered, documents passed, and words exchanged. Then, oddly, more documents were given to the two officers, who glanced through them, laughed, and waved the car on. For Chrissakes, Baier thought. Souvenir hounds. It's the same the world over.

When the buses with the bulk of the passengers emerged, the Soviet officer signaled for the first one to stop. He was intercepted by his StB companion, who shook his head and waved the bus through. The two men exchanged words, several of them apparently heated. The Soviet officer was not persuaded, however, until the Czech officer nodded in the direction of a lone figure standing off to the side in the shadow of St Nicholas Church. The Soviet's face changed expression then and there once he recognized the two men who seemed to blend in with the statues of the elegant baroque cathedral.

The Soviet officer shrugged and spoke a few words to his companion in Russian.

"Okay, Pavel, you win. This time."

Baier wheeled around to find Kehoe at his back.

"I thought you'd like a translation, Chief."

Baier hadn't realized he was holding his breath, and he let a breeze of stale, heated air escape. "Yeah, thank you, Frank."

The Soviet turned and continued to wave the other vehicles in the convoy through. It was then that Baier recognized von

Hoehn as one of the two figures in the darkened square. The other stepped back into the shadows, but not before Baier recognized Yuri Spekov, the local KGB boss. Von Hoehn's eyes concentrated on each vehicle as it drove past the entrance to the Embassy. Twice, Baier could have sworn that the Soviet and Czechoslovak officers looked in von Hoehn's direction and nodded. When the entire convoy had departed, von Hoehn looked over and caught Baier's attention. The East German's eyes showed no emotion, just a hard determination.

• • •

The trip to the West German border took about six hours. Baier followed in his own car. He hoped the diplomatic plates would prevent him from being stopped by each and every Soviet military detail and patrol. It did that, although the convoy was stopped four times by Soviet patrols, who were clearly exercising their control over the country's traffic and transportation. But each time, the group was waved on.

The Soviets did not even blink in Baier's direction, probably assuming he was part of the American parade. Luckily, someone must have signaled ahead that the group was coming and identified the American diplomatic plates so that there would be no interruptions. That made sense to Baier. He guessed that, given the international protests the Kremlin had to be expecting, they almost certainly wanted to avoid any additional diplomatic incidents.

It was just past Pilsen when Baier realized that another vehicle had been on his tail for about an hour. The driver wasn't even trying to avoid detection. He stayed no more than four or five car lengths behind. As soon as Baier identified the car as a familiar off-white Mercedes, he knew that the driver was none other than von Hoehn. Of course. The man was making sure that his own precious cargo was being delivered without any unexpected complications.

Once they reached the border, Baier pulled over in almost the same spot he had parked in when he watched Havlíček cross over twenty years ago. He was almost nostalgic. A chill started to run down his spine, but then Baier remembered all that had happened over the last seventy-two hours. There was no time for that kind of sentimentalism…or even a touch of nostalgia.

He was also shaken out of his skip down memory lane by a tap on his window.

"So, they made it," von Hoehn said. "I thank you, Herr Baier."

Baier climbed from the car. "And I you. It's good to see we can still cooperate on occasion."

"I think there may be more of those opportunities in the future."

"How so?"

"Let us discuss that further once we have returned to Prague. This is hardly the place."

Baier watched the Stasi officer walk away. He wondered if any place was right for what von Hoehn seemed to have in mind. That is, if Baier was guessing right.

"When and where?" Baier shouted.

The East German waved. He did not turn around. Baier had no way of seeing his face to gauge how serious the man was. All he saw was von Hoehn's back and shoulders.

"I will be in touch."

The words drifted over Baier's head, and he couldn't be sure he had heard them right.

CHAPTER TWENTY-SIX

"Those were some intriguing remarks you left me with," Baier said.

It was August 24, three days after the Soviet invasion. The city had settled into a somber calm. The streets were quiet, if still crowded. But there had been little violence. The Czechs and Slovaks in the capital—as elsewhere in the country—had adopted a form of neo-passive resistance. No guerrilla campaign had emerged, although the government appeared to be hanging on, refusing to acquiesce and justify the occupation. The chief ministers had been taken to Moscow, where they argued amongst themselves over how to react and move forward.

Still, it was clear where the country's future lay. The citizens of Prague and elsewhere in Czechoslovakia, however, had made it abundantly clear that the Soviet interlopers were not welcome. More street signs had disappeared, been renamed, or shifted to provide the wrong directions and addresses. Signs and graffiti continued to appear on a nightly basis throughout the city, protesting the invasion and occupation. They demanded the return of Czechoslovak freedom and sovereignty, and the end of the Moscow-imposed government that tried to rule an unforgiving and disbelieving populace. Occasionally, corpses appeared, shot by undisciplined or overly nervous Soviet troops. The victims were glorified as martyrs for the nation.

"My remarks? I thought they would be," von Hoehn replied.

They were seated at the same café around the corner from the Charles Bridge where Baier had met von Hoehn, his wife, and Mrs. Pillar on the eve of the Soviet invasion. It was almost deserted, and the two men had an isolated table for the exchange that looked out over the gently swirling pool of water outside the window to their front.

"So, what did you mean by those words? Where do you see this going from here? And what do you mean by 'this'? Czechoslovakia?"

"No. Surely, you know what I mean. Us."

"Come again?"

"Excuse me?"

"I'm afraid I do not understand what you mean by that either. Or what you intend. You still have a lot to explain. Especially after the other night. You were very mysterious at the border after our spouses crossed over into West Germany."

"I believe we can help each other, Herr Baier."

Baier laughed. "I have no intention of helping you. I got your wife out. That's as far as it goes." He paused to study the East German. "Unless you have something else to offer me."

Von Hoehn shifted in his seat. He glanced out the front window and studied a deserted sidewalk. Baier followed his gaze, wondering when the next surge of demonstrators would pass.

"You haven't forgotten the two people who helped you before the invasion, have you?" von Hoehn asked.

"No, I have not. And I have every intention of finding Hašek at least. I want to free him and get him into the West."

"Good," von Hoehn said. He nodded and pursed his lips. "I believe I can help. But you will have to get Havlíček out as well."

"Why?"

"Because he is in danger now. The West Germans have been sniffing around, and it is only a matter of time before they discover his dual role."

"Dual role? You mean he's been working for Bonn as well as for you?"

"Hmm, you could say that. But regardless of whom he has been working for, he was instrumental for your freedom and your cause on several occasions."

Baier smiled. "Yes, I know of one case in particular. He and several companions from the StB saved my ass when those GRU pricks tried to kidnap me. Was there anything else?"

Von Hoehn nodded. "Oh, yes. And there is more. He was the one who tried to deliver the infamous May letter from Brezhnev to you through his asset in the StB. The unfortunate young man who was killed."

Baier shot back against the cushions in the booth. "You mean Havlíček, the guy who I thought was your asset, works for Bonn? The BND?"

Von Hoehn smiled and leaned forward. He almost laughed. "That's right. Amazing, isn't it? The BND, or *Bundesnachrichtendienst*. West German intelligence. They actually had an operation here. And a relatively successful one."

"Well, until you corrupted it."

"Not entirely. I never had Havlíček feed disinformation to Bonn. I simply used him to keep tabs on what the Westerners—I mean primarily the West Germans, not all Westerners like yourself—were up to here." The infamous smile returned. "He was also a convenient messenger for me, especially when I wanted to reach out to someone like yourself."

"Now, I can make sense of how he was able to operate here in the absence of a West German diplomatic post. Normally, he would have invited all sorts of suspicion and attention. But you kept the Czechoslovaks away from him. And the Soviets as well?"

"Yes, I did my part. But apparently it was not quite enough."

"I see. So, if Mister Havlíček works for the BDN, and under German Foreign Ministry cover—not to mention whatever you've been doing for him—why not just return on his own?"

"Because it seems the Soviets are on to him as well, thanks to their Stalinist friends in the StB. That, I am sure you can see, poses a threat to me as well."

"And why is that?"

"Let's just say I have not always pursued the interests of the Communist International."

"Ah, I see. And I take it you are both under observation?"

'Yes, but that can prove advantageous for us. I can always divert their attention away from you."

It was Baier's turn to laugh again. "Yeah, good luck with that. You think they aren't all over me these days?" He sat forward again. "But what about Hašek? He's the guy I really care about."

"Oh, I haven't forgotten him. He will be a more difficult case. Havlíček is staying with his own family. They refuse to leave, by the way."

"And Hašek? I mean, you can have Havlíček. Hašek is the one I care about. Havlíček and I are even. So, you have to help with Hašek first."

"The Soviets have him stuck away somewhere. I believe they are getting ready to ship him back to Siberia. So, we do not have a lot of time." The East German stood. "We have work to do."

Baier reached out to grab von Hoehn's arm as the Prussian turned to leave.

"What about that fucking letter? Why didn't Havlíček just deliver it himself? Especially after the death of that young man?"

Von Hoehn shook his head. "He no longer had it. And by then it had simply become too dangerous."

• • •

It took von Hoehn only a day to locate Hašek. The Soviets did indeed have him squirreled away. However, the East German must have been able to use his StB and KGB contacts to find out exactly where.

It was in another KGB safehouse on the outskirts of Prague, presumably a location that would make it easier to transport Hašek back to the Soviet Union—not that the pricks had a lot to worry about. The Red Army was firmly in control of the country. But with the sullen, even though passive, resistance still strong, the KGB probably wanted to avoid any miscalculations or chance encounters that would disrupt their plans. The same went for the GRU, as they were probably involved as well—or at least Baier had to assume they were.

Baier did not doubt his ability to get the man free. The real challenge would be in getting him to safety in Prague and then out of the country. And this was where von Hoehn and Havlíček would have to come in.

The house, a freestanding, two-story structure with a yard that covered about half an acre, stood in a fairly isolated neighborhood. The street included only four other houses before it stretched into a set of fields covered in wheat, sunflowers, and hops. The other three houses appeared to be occupied by Czechs, but Baier guessed that at least one may also have been an observation post for the Soviet service, or services.

This was also where Baier realized he needed to rely on von Hoehn's connections, especially if he wanted to survey the house to establish the captors' routines and the layout of the property and home.

"Have you been able to spend much time in the neighborhood?" Havlíček asked.

Baier searched the road through the windshield of a car he had borrowed from the Embassy. He had parked underneath a row of linden trees about a mile from the safehouse. The old Skoda 445— it had to have at least a decade under its hood—looked normal and innocuous enough to blend into the local scenery. At least, Baier hoped so. The scratches and dented fender should help. Anything to give himself an advantage, however slight. The Czech plates also helped.

He glanced toward his new partner. Havlíček had shown up at Baier's house shortly after the initial meeting with von Hoehn. They quickly set about planning their surveillance of the property, agreeing to leave the bulk of the work to Havlíček. The former Czechoslovak diplomat not only had a web of contacts inside the StB, but he also had access to more than one vehicle. As it turned out, the house next door to the one that was serving as Hašek's temporary prison also housed an StB observation team.

"Not really," Baier said. "There's not a lot of cover in that block, such as it is. They'd pick up on me pretty quickly."

"Yes, they would. That is smart of you. Two members of the StB team are former contacts of mine. I have been able to get their cooperation on figuring out where they are holding Hašek inside, and the size of the KGB team there."

"Is that GRU squad a part of them?"

Havlíček shook his head. "No, thankfully. Apparently, sitting and holding someone who isn't bait is of little interest to them. They'd much rather be banging down doors or trying to poison someone. Besides, I have heard that most have been transferred elsewhere now that the Red Army is here in strength."

"And where is Hašek staying?"

"Upstairs in a bedroom at the back. But he appears to have the freedom to move about the house. He is not, however, allowed outside."

"Have you been helping to survey the house?" Baier asked.

"Oh, yes. And I have not driven the same car twice. Just to be safe." Havlíček paused to give his next words greater weight. "I will need some money to pay off my contacts on the StB team."

"You mean they are no longer helping out of a love of freedom?"

Havlíček smiled and shook his head. "No, not anymore. I am afraid those days may be gone for now. Not forever perhaps, but for now. By the way, the two inside were with the team that pulled you away from the GRU goons."

"Well, in that case, I should be able to scrape up some funds. Dollars okay?"

"Of course. They may decide to jump to the West themselves."

"Today?"

"No, no." Havlíček smiled while he shook his head. Baier thought he was about to laugh. "But someday. Soon, probably."

• • •

Baier decided they would move in the next day, August 28. More time would have been nice, but von Hoehn had gotten word that the Soviets wanted to move Hašek east on the 29th. Baier asked Garrity to come along to accompany him and Havlíček. Frank Kehoe also volunteered to join them. Looking to offset a Soviet advantage in numbers—surveillance had indicated a team of five KGB officers—Baier had reluctantly agreed.

"No heroics," Baier had warned. "And no revenge. Getting the guy freed will be revenge enough."

Given the openness of the surrounding area and the scarcity of other buildings, Baier decided that speed and surprise would be their only hope of a successful operation. He had not informed Headquarters of his plans, fearing that any delay in obtaining approval would result in a long and early trip to Siberia for Hašek. To avoid serious damage to his career, Baier had to be able to present Washington with a successful *fait accompli*, one that would hold the hounds at bay for taking such a considerable risk and putting himself and others in serious danger.

Baier drove one car, and Garrity the other. It was past seven o'clock in the morning, and, hopefully, the team would just be finishing or even beginning their breakfast and coffee. Whatever they were doing, Baier wanted them stuck in the middle of their early morning routine, when they would presumably be most vulnerable.

The American team drove toward the safehouse slowly at first to avoid setting off an early alarm. Then, once they came within about one hundred meters of the house, they shot into the driveway and front yard. All four men burst from the vehicles. Two men—Baier and Havlíček—rushed at the front door, while Garrity and Kehoe ran to the back.

Havlíček pushed himself in front of Baier and rammed his way inside. Two startled KGB officers jumped from the kitchen table, pistols leveled at the intruders. Havlíček fired twice. Both men dropped. Blood stains spread over their chests.

Baier made for the stairs. He took each step one at a time, his Browning extended from his shoulders, just as he had learned in the weapons training course at the Farm. The first door on his left led to what looked like a master bedroom. It was empty. The door on the right opened onto a full bath. That was also empty.

The next door on the right should have held Hašek, since it was the bedroom at the back. Baier kicked the door open. Hašek was there, standing next to the bed. Another man was there as well. He spoke to Baier in German.

"Greetings, Mister Baier. You have done well." He looked past Baier and over his shoulder. "And thank you as well, Jaroslav. You have played your part very well."

Baier lowered his pistol when he heard the others enter the room. He turned to find Havlíček at his side and two others behind him. They spoke to each other in Russian. Baier did not need to understand the language to guess that both men were agitated. Their arms jerked toward the ceiling and Baier, semi-automatic pistols clutched in their right hands. Shouts echoed from both men. One started toward Baier.

The German barked a command in Russian. The one nearest Baier halted and looked from Baier to the German, then back to Baier again. He nodded. But his face still wore a scowl that showed more anger than menace.

"Ah, they are understandably upset about their colleagues downstairs. I am assuming those shots hit them?'

Havlíček nodded. He pointed at Baier.

"It was the American cowboy, Friedrich. I think they say, shoot first and ask questions later."

CHAPTER TWENTY-SEVEN

Baier stared hard at Havlíček. He pressed his lips together and narrowed his focus to the Czech's eyes. Baier wanted to get as good a read of the man's intentions and his integrity as possible.

"You son of a bitch," Baier said. "And here I thought we were almost even."

"Almost?" Havlíček asked.

"We're not even close now. Not anymore."

The German officer smiled and shook his head. "Allow me to introduce myself, Mister Baier. "My name is Friedrich Herr of the German Democratic Republic's State Security Service, known more broadly as the Stasi." He bowed.

"What the hell..." Baier answered. "Are we on a stage?"

Herr smiled again and shrugged. "Why not?" He glanced over at the KGB officers who remained standing behind Baier. Herr spoke in Russian. Both men shook their heads. When Herr spoke again, they simply shrugged.

Havlíček smiled at Baier. "He is asking about the other two men who came with you."

"Now, who could that be?" Baier replied. "You and I are the only ones who came to pick up my friend, Mister Hašek."

Havlíček spoke to Herr, first in English, then with a few exclamations in German.

"Forget about them," the Czech said. "They probably fled when they heard the gunshots. Not everyone is a cowboy like this one."

Havlíček waved his pistol in the air as he spoke. His voice quivered as though he was nervous. Then he stepped closer to Herr, creating more distance between himself and Baier.

"Let's get moving," Herr said. "We can take this American with us and dump him at the border once we get Hašek inside the Soviet Union."

"Tell me, how is that a Stasi officer is running this operation?" Baier asked.

The East German rolled his eyes. "Consider it a display of Socialist brotherhood, Mister Baier. My Soviet colleagues are extremely busy, as you can no doubt understand. They were happy to take me up on my offer of cooperation."

The party made their way quickly down the stairs and out the back door. Baier searched desperately for his two colleagues but found nothing. The two Soviets pushed and shoved Baier toward the two cars. Then they threw him into the back seat of the one closest to the garage, making sure he bounced off the door first. Hašek was forced into the vehicle closest to the street.

Havlíček looked around the yard and walked onto the street. When he returned, Baier noticed that he still had his Makarov knock-off, the CZ52, out with his finger sliding toward the trigger guard. A rush of noise and movement behind him forced Baier to spin around. Garrity and Kehoe sprinted toward the convoy. Another shot rang out.

Out of the corner of his eye, Baier saw Herr fold in half and fall to the ground. Havlíček's gun was pointing at the East German. Herr held his stomach with both arms, as though he desperately hoped he could prevent his life from dribbling away.

Havlíček's face resembled a chiseled stone from a medieval mason. His eyes, though, were wide and white with desperation.

Baier leaped at the Soviet closest to him. Another shot echoed across the yard. The other KGB man rocked back against the car with Hašek inside. A stream of blood spurted from his shoulder and began to run down the front of his dirty white shirt. He screamed in pain and dropped his own Makarov. Baier slammed his prisoner to ground, pushing his face into the gravelled driveway. Garrity stood in the middle of the yard, his Browning at his side. Kehoe ran to the wounded KGB officer and took his gun.

"Nicely done. I wasn't sure you Americans had it in you." Von Hoehn ambled in from the street, the perennial smile spreading across his face. "I guess we can cancel the ambush I had planned."

"Why am I not surprised to see you?" Baier said. It was half in greeting and half in exasperation. "But it is good you're here."

Von Hoehn marched up to Baier, took his Browning, then walked over to the silent and unmoving Herr. He lowered Baier's pistol and put a shot in the younger East German's head.

"We will blame that one on you as well." He looked over at Baier, shrugged, then returned the Browning. "I expect you'll need this back. You know, you are accumulating quite a scorecard in the halls of the Lubyanka and *Normannenstrasse*." He shook his head. "Now get your man Hašek to your embassy as quickly as possible, and do not forget to take my man Havlíček with you." Von Hoehn waved his arm at the scene before him. "I will clean up here."

• • •

Baier rode in the car with Garrity in the front seat and Havlíček and Hašek in the back. He sent Kehoe back alone, figuring that a single American diplomat would encounter less trouble getting to safety than those with two fugitives in tow. Besides, Kehoe was too junior to have to accept the responsibility and risks when his two bosses were available.

Luckily, Baier encountered no Soviet or StB roadblocks on their trip back into town. The mechanics of the invasion must have been thrown together pretty quickly, since the Soviets and their Stalinist allies in the Czechoslovak government appeared to be incredibly slow in establishing their control. Baier chuckled to himself and shook his head. August 28. Seven days since the Red Army had crossed the border. It probably had something to do with the long stay the members of the Czechoslovak Politburo were spending in Moscow as prisoners of the Kremlin. From what Baier and the Ambassador had been hearing, the talks on the formation of a new government and over the communique that would be released to explain the invasion and occupation of the country as a fraternal exercise in assistance against a counter-revolution and Western imperialism had been slow and drawn out. Several Czechoslovak members refused to buckle to Soviet pressure and kept calling for an end to the Soviet presence in their country.

"What is so funny?" Havlíček asked.

"Oh, nothing," Baier answered. "Tell me, though, what was that charade about back there in the house?"

"You mean my seeming alliance with Friedrich Herr? You know he was one of Markus Wolf's protégés."

"Doesn't that make his demise all the more dangerous? Especially for von Hoehn."

"I have learned not to question that Prussian's motives and plans." Havlíček looked over at Hašek. "Wouldn't you say so, Josef?"

Hašek stared back at his Czech compatriot. The man had not said a word throughout the operation. He just sat there, his face ashen and his body wrapped in silence. Hašek shrugged and leaned toward the front seat.

"Thank you, Mister Baier. I will not forget this," Hašek finally said. Nothing followed. Hašek sat still and silent, his gaze alternating between the front seat and the world outside.

"We're not out of it yet," Baier said. "But tell me again, just what was the plan today? And why all the dramatics?"

Havlíček looked out the window. He sighed and studied Hašek again. Then he spoke.

"That bastard Friedrich Herr had sniffed out the rescue. I only came to suspect something when I tried to deliver your money to my contacts in the other safe house. Both men had been replaced by older men who had always remained loyal to the old Stalinist regime. I alerted von Hoehn and he warned me to play along. I was not aware of the ambush he had set up, so I decided to act when I realized your two men were still there, hiding." Havlíček blew out his breath and shook his head. "My days are definitely numbered if I stay here. There was no way I was going to travel into the USSR with those bastards."

"So, I guess we are still even," Baier said.

"Only if you get me out of here with Mister Hašek."

CHAPTER TWENTY-EIGHT

The German border was no longer an option. That was one area where the Soviets had set up extensive patrols, accompanied by some units of the Czechoslovak army and police that Moscow felt were trustworthy enough. It usually depended on the leadership in these contingents.

Baier and company also no longer had the advantage and safety that the larger numbers brought with the earlier convoy. This time, it was just Baier and his two fleeing spies. He did not want to jeopardize anyone else in the station by having them accompany his band of pilgrims. If anyone was going to end up in the bowels of Lubyanka, it would have to be the Chief of Station.

"I am sorry, but you guys are going to have to stay behind and see what we can do to help provide Washington with the information it needs on developments here in Prague and elsewhere in the country."

Baier held up his hand to stem the protests that started to erupt from Garrity, Kehoe, and Krohn back in the Station. Mikulski remained silent, his eyes not leaving Baier's. The chief focused on the younger officers. "And I especially do not want you involved, Paul. Frank either, come to think of it. You two have got to be on the premier shitlist of American targets in town." He laughed. "Except for me, of course. They must have me down as the most successful serial killer in the history of espionage. Aside from their own."

"But doesn't that make it incredibly risky for you to be the one driving the exfiltration route?" Kehoe asked.

"Maybe. But we've got some pretty good documentation for Hašek. Did you know his family settled in Chicago after their escape from the Nazis in 1939?"

"Say what?" Garrity exclaimed. "Since when?"

"Since we provided the new passport," Baier replied. "That will cover his accented English, should the police or border guards question him."

It had taken a week, but the forgery team Headquarters had sent right after the invasion on the 21st had done a remarkable job. They had arrived just days ago under cover of the need to replace diplomats who had allegedly left with their families.

"What about the other guy?"

"Oh, Havlíček? He still has his West German passport and ID. He should be okay. Besides, he might be able to count on von Hoehn's patronage if he gets grabbed. Hašek himself ain't got nothin' no more."

This car still had American diplomatic plates to explain Baier's presence in the car. He had told the Ambassador his plan was to claim that he was transporting some American leftovers from the earlier evacuations. He had chosen the Austrian border because of the rumors of fighting between the Soviets and isolated patches of resistance near the German border. There hadn't been any, of course, but Baier was good at feigning ignorance…or so Sabine always said.

The first part of the drive was uneventful. It wasn't until they had passed Bratislava, the capital of Slovakia, that their troubles began.

"Jesus,' Havlíček shouted, "we're only about an hour from the Austrian border."

"Well, I'm guessing it will take a little longer now," Baier said.

The police car pulled them over on the side of the road, blue lights flashing strobes of warning across the open fields and to the clouded ceiling above. Baier turned to see Hašek sitting in the back by himself, his face so pale he looked as though he had never seen the sun. Baier smiled and nodded, hoping to reassure the man as he tried to sink deeper into the upholstery.

"Your identification, please."

The officer stood by Baier's driver-side window, his right hand resting on the hood while his left hand was extended to receive whatever Baier passed through the window space he had opened. Baier did not say a word.

"And your purpose out here. You are a long way from Prague."

Baier gave him the explanation he had prepared. The officer looked back at his companion, who sat behind the steering wheel, speaking into the microphone of his radio.

"And you?" He motioned toward Havlíček. The officer took his passport and leafed through it. "It says you are West German. Why are you here?"

"I am just accompanying my friend on his way to Austria. I have some family in Linz who have been worried about my safety since the recent developments. My timing for a visit here was obviously horrible. My family needs some reassurance."

Havlíček spoke these words in German. After he finished, the officer shook his head and circled his finger in front of the window, a sign to repeat everything in Czeck or Slovak. Havlíček obliged him.

"I see. How convenient for you." He peered into the back seat. "And you?"

Hašek did not move for several seconds. Baier was about to reach back for his documents, but then Hašek seemed to come to life. He slid his passport forward.

"Ah, so you escaped earlier to America. In 1939 I see. How fortunate for you. Why the hell did you come back at this time?"

"I wanted to see how things had changed. There does not appear to be much point in staying now."

"No. Tell me about Chicago? Do you like it there?"

"Oh, yes. I live in a neighborhood called Pilsen. Ironic, isn't it?" No answer. "It not only has plenty of Czechs and Slovaks, but other East Europeans as well, Poles, Ukrainians, Balts. You name it. Almost like being home."

Baier was amazed. The man had actually been paying attention when Baier had delivered his lecture on Chicago's ethnic complexion.

"Okay then, have a safe trip home."

The officer returned the passports and then strolled back to his car. The driver had been on the radio the entire time.

"We are going to have to pick up our pace," Baier said. "I am willing to bet a pile of koruna that the other guy was reporting back and asking for instructions. Let's just hope we get to the border before anything reaches them."

They were not to be so lucky. With the border post in sight about half an hour later, Baier started to speed up. As he closed the distance, he realized that the lights on the Slovak side of the crossing had been turned off. Two patrol cars sat across the road leading to the crossing. Baier smiled when he saw that the bad guys had left him an opening. The car on the left had its trunk on the road, nosed up against the front of the other one.

"Hold on. I'm not stopping for these assholes." He looked at his passengers. "You know why they're here, right?"

Both men nodded. Havlíček was smiling. Hašek's eyes were wide, perhaps with fear, perhaps with excitement. Probably both, Baier thought.

Baier rammed the gas pedal to the ground. He wanted to build up enough speed to carry them through. He aimed for the trunk of the car on the left, usually the lightest part of the vehicle with the engine block in the front.

His Mercedes battered its way through the roadblock. Czechoslovak border guards and police leaped free of the road to avoid the collision. Baier did not stop. He rammed through the guard rail that was supposed to stop anyone from carrying on before they had been released. That, too, shattered into a burst of splinters. Baier heard glass breaking in his own car's front end. A tire popped.

Then the rear window burst under a hail of gunfire from the Czechoslovak side. Baier fought to control the car along the football field-long stretch to the Austrian border. With both rear tires gone, the car swerved and threatened to run off the road. He fought the steering wheel, turning into the skids—like he had been taught at the crash-and-bang course at the Farm.

When they made it to the Austrian side, the firing stopped. Baier braked in the middle of the road, right in front of the Austrian barrier. He hopped out, along with Havlíček. Both men jerked the door to the back seat open and began to pull Hašek free of the car.

Only then did Baier see the blood pooling on the back seat. He turned Hašek over and found the holes in his back and neck. Blood spurted from both, then slowed to a trickle. Hašek moved his lips. No words came. Then his lifeless eyes stared up at Baier.

He set Hašek gently on the road, his back resting against the side of the vehicle. Baier stared at the man who had suffered through and endured so much in his life. The man had stayed true to his principles, his love of his country, and all of it despite the unrelenting pressure from the Nazi occupation, a Stalinist regime, the Soviet gulag, and the threat of a return to the USSR as a prisoner once again.

A rage overwhelmed Baier. He stood and grabbed a rock at the side of the road. He hurled it and a string of curses at the murderous jerks on the other side of the border.

"You fucking assholes! Goddamn you and all the people over there like you. You are the real traitors." He grabbed another rock and threw it after the first. "I swear that your day will come. I just hope I'm there when it does." Havlichek followed with a couple stones of his own.

A single rock whistled past in return and bounced off the trunk of the car. Baier flipped the other side the bird and shook his finger in the air.

Baier lifted Hašek and held him in his arms. He turned and walked toward the Austrian guards. Havlíček followed him, his head hanging. Only then did Baier realize he had tears streaming down his cheek.

EPILOGUE

It raised more questions than it answered, at least in Baier's mind. The church, at first glance, looked to be a modest place, well hidden from the bustle of tourists and official traffic along the *Ringstrasse* and the human waves that flowed around the *Stephansdom* in the heart of Vienna. But then, when you walked inside, past the small, even narrow entrance, the wealth and splendor of the church were overwhelming. Just why had von Hoehn chosen this location for the meeting he had requested with Baier? Was the Prussian getting religious as he aged? Even Roman Catholic?

"I am so glad you found this place."

The words from von Hoehn's heavily-accented English seemed to echo off the marble monuments that covered the walls and aisles of the half-dozen or so chapels lining the church's interior. His footsteps announced his approach to the front pew Baier had chosen for his seat.

"First of all, you can and should speak German with me, as you well know. But before we begin, can you tell me why you chose this place? Does it have some special meaning for you? Or do you just like lots of glitter?"

"Only a Catholic could be so cavalier about all this decoration. Are you sure you are so distant from the religion of your upbringing?" von Hoehn asked, continuing in English.

"Are you sure you are such a committed Communist? At least as much as working for the Stasi would seem to require?" Baier responded.

Von Hoehn laughed. His seemingly ubiquitous smile greeted Baier as the East German seated himself next to Baier on the polished wooden pew.

"I doubt either of us has the time to resolve such weighty questions this morning, Mister Baier. Perhaps we should get to the matter at hand, as it were."

"And just what might that be?" Baier asked. "I have to say your call came as a real surprise to me. And why meet here instead of Berlin or even Prague? You know, friendlier turf, for you at least."

Von Hoehn relaxed enough to settle against the hard back of the pew. He started to draw a cigarette from the pocket of his gray suit jacket, then thought better of it. Too much of a blasphemy in the presence of so much religion?

"Well, given your recent adventure at the Slovak border and the demands for your arrest and repatriation to Czechoslovakia, I doubted we would be able to accomplish much in Prague." He prodded Baier's shoulder with a long, thin forefinger. "And since you are currently cooling your heels, as you Americans say, in Vienna, this was the most convenient place for both of us." Von Hoehn studied Baier. The smile transformed itself into an expression of curiosity. "Just what have you been doing to keep busy here? I doubt the *Hofburg* would require more than one visit. The *Stephansdom* the same."

"No, I am already familiar with the history of this city. I have been preparing my report to Washington on those final experiences in Prague."

"I hope your report will put your time there in a positive light."

"That remains to be seen. There are detractors in our Headquarters, as well as supporters, as you can no doubt imagine."

"How so?" von Hoehn asked.

"I don't know how your organization would view something like the escape I engineered and how it ended, but there are those in Washington who are criticizing me for acting like a cowboy and before I had authorization to proceed with that particular operation. Hell, I didn't even have approval to rescue Hašek."

"That sounds a bit short-sighted on their part. I mean, the man was an asset of yours who had proven to be helpful. Didn't you owe it to him?"

Baier bounced his head up and down, glancing from his guest to the altar and back. He let out a breath of exasperation.

"Absolutely. And that is what others are arguing. I suspect the review panel will eventually let me off with a warning at worst. I'll have to cool my heels in Langley for a year or two before heading out again."

"Was it worth it?" von Hoehn pressed. "In your own view, I mean. Not what some desk-sitters think."

"Absolutely." Baier pressed his fist into his leg before pushing it against the pew.

"Even though your man died?"

"Well, I did get your boy out." Baier stared at the altar for nearly a minute. It felt longer. "But it's true, my man did not make it. I do regret that. Deeply. But I don't think I could have done anything more. We did not have the time for something more elaborate."

"So, would you do it again?"

"In a heartbeat. It was the right thing to do. Hašek deserved his shot at freedom. I'll live with the consequences. My career will survive. I'm pretty sure of that."

"And your wife?" von Hoehn added. "Where is she while you spend your days in Vienna?"

"She is with her parents near Hannover. I will join her as soon as I finish up here."

For the first time since he had known von Hoehn Baier's smile matched or even exceeded that of the East German.

"Well, then, let me add this to your collection."

Von Hoehn reached inside his jacket and extracted a three-page letter from the inside pocket. He passed it to Baier.

"What is this?"

"It is the infamous May letter. Or rather a summary of the discussions and decisions taken at the meeting in May between the Soviet leadership and select Warsaw Pact leaders. It was signed by Brezhnev himself."

"The original? How did you get this thing?"

"No, no. It is a copy. But I keep thinking of what a pity it was that you were not able to acquire it earlier. When it might have made a difference. Of course, we were both confused by the reference to a 'letter.' But I doubt that made all that much of a difference in the end."

Baier read through the passage, marveling at what it foretold of the events that transpired on August 21 and immediately afterward.

"So, the Prague Spring really never had a chance? Certainly, not as much as Dubček and so many other Czechoslovaks had believed. Or hoped."

Von Hoehn shrugged. "Perhaps. But perhaps not. You know well that nothing is inevitable. If you read that carefully, you can discern that Brezhnev had yet to make up his mind. Military intervention certainly looks possible, even probable. But he appears to have been keeping his options open. He appears to have been under conflicting pressures."

"Do you think the invasion could have been avoided?" Baier asked.

Again, von Hoehn shrugged. "Who is to say? All we know is that it happened. But I believe it would have been very difficult for Mister Dubček and his cohort to continue with their reforms. Not after the upheavals in the 1950s in East Berlin, Budapest, and Warsaw. The other leaders in the Eastern Bloc were too worried about their own survival. And Brezhnev was under tremendous pressure in Moscow, to which he was sympathetic in any case. Do you think your government would have been able to prevent it?"

It was Baier's turn to shrug. He reread the letter.

"I doubt it. We saw in 1956 how limited our options were. Still, it would have been nice to have a forewarning. Perhaps we could have come up with some alternatives."

He offered the letter back to von Hoehn.

"No, no, you keep it, Karl. If I may use your first name again. That is for you to share with your superiors in Langley. It may help your case back home."

"Thank you, Alexander."

Baier sighed as he surveyed the ornate altar and the long railing separating the altar from the congregation, a hallmark of traditional Catholicism. He turned back to his visitor.

"Have you noticed," von Hoehn continued, his eyes roaming the church's interior, "how the designers left no space vacant. It was almost as though they wanted to leave no room for doubt as to the Church's theology and future."

"Like the Communists in your country and elsewhere?"

Von Hoehn laughed. "Perhaps. Except our planners and designers seem to leave all kinds of space vacant." He laughed once more.

"So, what does the future hold for you now?" Baier asked.

Von Hoehn smiled and pulled the cigarette from his pocket. Again, he decided not to light it. He studied the cigarette. "A difficult habit." He looked up at Baier. "We shall see. I have been recalled to Berlin."

"Oh? Why?"

"That is hard to say. My own superiors probably want an explanation on my wife's defection—"

"She is with her brother, by the way. Safe and sound."

"Thank you for that. I shall not forget your assistance."

"Just why did she want to leave? And why did you help her?"

Von Hoehn twirled the cigarette in his fingers, stuck it in his mouth, and then removed it. He studied the thin tobacco cylinder. He still smoked Winstons.

"I helped her because that was what she wanted. And I love her. She said she saw no future for either of us if we stayed behind."

"So, what are your plans? What is your story going to be?"

"I will tell them that she took advantage of the chaos surrounding the Soviet invasion to sneak to the American Embassy while I was engaged in assisting our Communist brethren."

"I can help you if you want to join her. You know that."

The smile returned. "Yes, I am aware of that. Of course, I would be much more confident if your wife were involved."

"That can be arranged as well."

Von Hoehn stood. "Then perhaps we should wait and see what develops for me in *Normannenstrasse*. I know I will be able to find you."

"You always have in the past."

Von Hoehn stood and walked to the end of the pew.

"You might want to light a candle at one of the altars on your way out, Alexander."

Von Hoehn shook his head. "I haven't come that far, Karl. Not yet anyway."

The Prussian's smile returned and widened as he waved goodbye on his way to the back of the church. Baier watched him walk out into the sunny, early fall day in Vienna. Then he stood and walked to the first chapel to the right of the altar. He stopped and lit a candle.

ABOUTH THE AUTHOR

The Prague Spring is the seventh book in Bill Rapp's Cold War Thriller series, which draws on his forty-year career with the Central Intelligence Agency, as well his previous time as an academic historian on Modern Europe (B.A. from the University of Notre Dame, M.A. from the University of Toronto, and Ph.D. from Vanderbilt University). He taught for a year at Iowa State before moving to Washington for an eventful four decades spent primarily in Washington but with tours in Europe, the Middle East, and the White House. Upon his retirement in 2017, Bill was awarded the Distinguished Career Intelligence Medal. Bill also has a stand-alone thriller about the fall of the Berlin Wall, *Berlin Breakdown*, and a three-book P.I. series set outside Chicago, where he lives with his wife, their older daughter, and two dogs.

www.ingramcontent.com/pod-product-compliance
Lightning Source LLC
LaVergne TN
LVHW031539060526
838200LV00056B/4565